MORE THAN A DOZEN SUMMERS

The Margaret Trilogy

Bonnie Rokke Tinnes

Beautiful Thoughts

*This book is lovingly dedicated to my family: my parents,
my husband, my children, and my grandchildren.*

CONTENTS

MORE THAN A DOZEN SUMMERS

More than a Dozen Summers is fiction, and all characters and places are formed and created from the writer's imagination. It is written to depict the people and culture of the 1950s and 1960s, and the characters are not based on anyone specific.

Published by Beautiful Thoughts
Bemidji, Minnesota 56601
United States of America

bonnietinnes@gmail.com

ISBN: 979-8-9904561-1-2

Cover and book design
by Bonnie Rokke Tinnes

ABOUT THE AUTHOR

Bonnie Rokke Tinnes was born and raised in Minnesota where she has lived most of her life. A graduate of both Bemidji State University in Minnesota and the University of North Dakota, she is a teacher and a registered nurse with a love for writing and for the days she grew up on a farm in the 1950s.

GROWING UP MARGARET

Bonnie Rokke Tinnes

Copyright 2011

BEST FRIENDS

For me the first day of sixth grade couldn't come fast enough. "This is the year I will find my best friend," I told Grandma I needed a best friend more than ever after Mother died. Besides, spending so much time with Grandma Olson wasn't cool anymore.

We were sitting in her newly painted white kitchen with its high ceilings passing time on an August morning. On her table was a red and white checkered oilcloth, and right in the middle of the table was a Mason jar holding a bouquet of golden black-eyed Susans.

"Your house is lady-like, Grandma. Frilly, white dotted Swiss curtains and all," I said to make conversation.

I thought, "I'd rather be talking about boys with a girl-friend instead of white frilly curtains."

Grandma smiled, making me feel good. Coming from a big city to Norden made her seem uppity, but not today. "Thank you, Margaret," she said. "I also hope you find your best friend this year."

The first day of sixth grade arrived as if I hadn't even waited for it. Up early and wearing a new red plaid, pleated skirt, white blouse, red sweater, white anklets, and shiny black, patent leather shoes, I raced down the stairs of our old farmhouse for breakfast stumbling on the rag rug by the kitchen door.

"Ouch," I screeched as I picked myself up and brushed off my clothes.

"Be careful," Grandma shouted back. "No broken bones the first day of school." I was happy she had spent the night with Dad and me on the farm and had made breakfast.

Brushed off with no injuries, I entered the kitchen. "Morning, Grandma," I cheerfully greeted her. "How do I look?"

"You look nice."

"Do I look beautiful?" I asked.

"Beautiful."

"What's for breakfast? Sure smells good," I added.

"Made your favorite. French toast with maple syrup and bacon."

"Love you, Grandma."

"Love you, too."

"Grandma, well...how do I really look?" I strutted around the kitchen swirling now and then. "Do I really look beautiful?"

"You look nice and beautiful."

"Thanks."

Grandma always used the word nice before beautiful. I wondered, "What does nice mean anyway?" I had always believed nice meant pleasant and kind and fun to be around. Many people were nice. Not everyone was beautiful. Today I felt I looked beautiful in my new clothes, thanks to Grandma.

Two weeks before school started, Grandma and I went through the new fall *Sears Roebuck* catalog and ordered my school clothes that arrived just in time. "Wonder if Mrs. Berg will like them," I thought. To impress my new sixth grade teacher was part of getting a new outfit. Mrs. Berg was beautiful herself and liked beautiful clothes.

Mrs. Berg, petite, neat, and fresh-looking all the time and usually dressed in a brown suit and starched white blouse with brown pumps. Her soft brown hair gently fell in waves around her heart-shaped face with its glowing skin and deep brown eyes. "Can see why Harry Berg married that one," the people in town said.

Harry Berg owned Berg's Garage, a business he had opened just before he fell in love and married Mrs. Berg. With a new business and a beautiful young wife, he was the envy of all the young bachelors in town. "Maybe I'll become a teacher, move to a place, and marry the most eligible and best-looking man in town to become the envy of everyone," I mused.

The noise on the bus, now full of children, brought me back

to my surroundings. For almost thirty miles we had wound around the back gravel or dirt roads picking up students. I had day- dreamed the whole ride away.

The old school building smelled clean over the smell of old books and chalk that all schools and libraries had. I could tell the janitors had scrubbed it down during summer vacation. As I looked up, my eyes caught the huge familiar portrait of George Washington hanging above the blackboard. I said, "Hi, George." and bowed slightly to giggles and snickers coming from the back of the room.

Mrs. Berg was not in the classroom, so I sat down in the desk by Yanni Tollefson.

"How was your summer?" he asked.

"Just great," I answered as my heart fluttered. I still had a crush on him.

"And yours?"

"I had a great summer, too."

"You're blushing, Pumpkin," Willie Smith hollered from the back of the room.

I felt my face get hotter and redder by the minute. It always did when I talked to Yanni, but Willie Smith just made it worse.

Chatter continued about the county fair, summer trips, and swimming lessons. A paper airplane, made from someone's tablet, landed on my desk. I grabbed it and crunched it together just in time.

Mrs. Berg entered the room, followed by a new girl with her mom and dad. She was a small, brown-eyed girl with dark brown curly hair and caramel-colored skin. Quietly, with her head hanging down, she stood waiting to be introduced.

Looking around the class, I noticed that everyone was staring, eyes wide open and mouths gaping, with surprise, almost to the point of awe, at her. I felt uneasy and squirmed, embarrassed for everyone, and I turned around giving everyone a dirty look. It was a look that said, "What's the matter with you? Haven't you seen a sixth- grade girl before?"

As much as I loved our town, Norden, I sometimes hated it. This was a hating day.

I believed I understood how she felt in front of our whole class. Later I knew that there was no way I could understand. "I could almost hear them gasp," I told Grandma.

The staring continued and didn't stop until Mrs. Berg began to speak, and everyone finally turned to look at her. "Thank goodness," I almost said out loud.

"Good morning, Class. I want you to meet Mary Elizabeth Anderson. You all know her parents, Mr. and Mrs. Anderson." Kindly and gently, she added, "Mary Elizabeth, why don't you sit here by Margaret," as she put her hand on the desk in front of me.

As Mary Elizabeth sat down, she lifted her head and faintly smiled at me. Mrs. Berg explained to her that my name was Margaret but I was called Pumpkin sometimes. Next, she nodded at me with a look that implied, "You will be in charge of helping Mary Elizabeth and be her friend."

Just like that. She was an answer to a wish and a prayer. Just like that I was given a new friend. Maybe she'd become my best friend.

I couldn't wait to tell Grandma. The next day Grandma stopped by our house for a visit, and I had my chance.

"Grandma, I met a new friend in school yesterday. Her name is Mary Elizabeth, You'll like her."

"What is she like, Pumpkin?"

"She's tiny and has curly dark brown hair and skin the color of caramel. Everyone says she's from the South. And you know what?"

"What?"

"I think she will be the best friend I have ever had."

As time went on, Mary Elizabeth and I not only became friends, but we did everything together. Grandma often said, "You girls are so much alike you are like identical twins." Then Grandma would smile.

BLUE PATCHWORK

Grandma often told others that I fit my name, Pumpkin, with my reddish-blonde hair, bangs, and freckles across my nose. Often she'd remark exaggerating and embarrassing me, "That girl! If she isn't a spitting image of a perfect little Norwegian girl, I don't know who is. If I took Pumpkin to Norway, she would fit right in." Although it sometimes embarrassed me, she was Grandma, and I adored her.

It was1920 when Grandma Olson first came to Norden, Minnesota. Born and raised in Southern California, she met Grandpa when he was stationed in the Navy there. "It was love at first sight. I just knew she was for me the first time I set eyes on her," he said and smiled.

"Your grandpa was a tall, muscular, blonde and blue-eyed farm boy who won my young heart one night at a community dance for soldiers," Grandma often said star struck, love and adoration in her eyes and voice. "When his time in the Navy was done, we eloped, came to Minnesota, and built the house on the farm. He was the handsomest young man I'd ever seen."

"Did he look like Yanni Tollefson?"

"I never thought of it like that, but you know what? He did." She smiled.

When Grandpa died, my parents and I moved to the farm, and Grandma moved to town. Since Mom died, I went back and forth from the farm to town as Grandma helped Dad raise me.

I had spent the night at Grandma's house, and Mary Elizabeth came over to play. Golden leaves covered the ground, and we could see our breath in the crisp, cool air as we played tag through piles of leaves.

It was mitten and stocking cap weather, and a warm jacket was needed to block the icy, fall wind. Mary Elizabeth was wearing a brand- new red wool jacket with a white stocking cap and mitts her mom just knit for her. The Andersons didn't spare anything to give her the best.

"Love your new coat," I smiled at her. "Red's your color."

"Thanks, Pumpkin."

"The red and white. They go good with your hair and skin color. Make you stand out."

"I love it, too. Imagine that. I have a brand- new coat with mitts that match."

"Mary Elizabeth, I am so glad you moved here. Are you glad you are here?"

"For now I am," she said quietly with a faraway look in her eyes.

"You're missing home, huh?" I asked.

"Yes," she answered. "I just hope I fit in here."

"Someone treating you bad?"

"Nope, not yet."

"What do you mean, not yet?"

I felt bad for Mary Elizabeth. Underneath everything, she was worried. This change was big for her, and there was always the fear of rejection that could happen anytime.

At supper time Mary Elizabeth headed home. Her parents were waiting for her to come and wouldn't eat without her. I went back in the house.

Grandma had spent the day finding a place to store the fruit and vegetables she had gathered before the colder weather arrived. There were baskets of potatoes, carrots, tomatoes, both red and green apples, plums, cabbage, and red beets in Grandma's cellar. She had taken great care to preserve her gar- den produce, especially this year's abundant crop.

"I wouldn't believe it, if I hadn't seen it," people from town often said. It surprised them that someone from a rich Califor- nia family, who, they felt, never had to work or sacrifice, made a good member of a small Minnesota town and fit in.

"I love my husband," she told them. "That love and abso- lute devotion drives me to become the farm wife that I feel he deserves."

That is why she learned to cook, sew, garden and can its produce, keep a spotless home, and help in the church and the community right beside the best of women. Besides being a good wife to Grandpa, she was a wonderful mother to my dad, and a perfect, loving grandmother. It was what Norden expected.

No matter how hard she tried to fit in, Grandma's high society past showed in the way she walked and talked. She carried her medium height and size with confidence, always outgoing, never hesitating in anything she did. The way she curled her dark brown hair, now gray around her temples, just made her more sophisticated. After Grandpa died, Grandma taught herself to drive and never stopped driving or going places. Not many local women had enough confidence or drive to do that.

"Your Grandma's a snob from California," Willie Smith told me once in fifth grade.

"I hate you, too, Willie!" I answered back even though I felt like crying. I couldn't help it. I wondered how many other people in Norden felt that way. My imagination told me there were many.

Not long after Mary Elizabeth went home, Grandma and I sat down for supper. "It's time for me to go see Pavel," she said. "This year I want you to go with me."

There was one thing that Grandma especially looked forward to. Each year before the snow, Grandma went to see Pavel Ivanovich, her childhood friend, now living in Minnesota. "Pavel is Russian for Paul, and his family called him Pavel as a more endearing name." Grandma explained to others. Eventually everyone called him Pavel.

"For the life of me, Katherine, I can't see what on earth you see in that derelict of a nobody who moved here from California," some old ladies in the community regularly said, sometimes just to hurt Grandma.

Grandma felt they needed to get a life of their own and ignored them but told me, "He came from a wealthy family. They were our good neighbors, and we spent hours playing together when we were children. I know him well."

"Why do you want me to go this year? You've never taken me with before."

"I want you to personally meet him. There's a lesson in his life."

The truth is I didn't know the man. I'd seen him from a distance only, and despite their close friendship, Grandma never encouraged any association for Pavel and me. From a distance I'd seen him staggering down the streets of town before dark heading back toward his house on the other side of the railroad tracks.

"Shut up!" I once hollered at some kids from my class who were teasing him. "Just shut up!"

"He's just an odd, old drunk," they hollered back. "Why do you care?"

first-class snot. But I was angry, frustrated having to defend him and also Grandma more than I wanted to.

For the most part, Pavel never bothered or hurt anybody. "So? So he's different! What else is new?" I answered like a, so people left him alone and let him live his life the way he wanted. I felt sorry for him because he had a cloud of rejection over him that followed him wherever he went. Today for the first time I was going with Grandma to visit Pavel and it would not be from a distance.

I watched as Grandma carefully and lovingly prepared to visit him. She packed a beautiful, over-sized patchwork quilt, made with her own hands and stuffed with the softest down filling. It was made with multi-colored patterns of navy blue and tied with navy blue yarn. "Blue is Pavel's favorite color," she said.

Next she packed a bag full of new, soft socks and a bag full of mittens made from our own sheep's wool, which Grandma's friend, Hannah Peterson, had spun into yarn. Last she packed a picnic basket full of thick roast beef sandwiches on homemade whole wheat bread, thermoses of hot steaming coffee, and paper cups. Only when these jobs were completed were we ready to go.

"The food is for him to share with his friends," she informed me. She must have read my mind. I was thinking that was a lot of food for one man.

Today, as she drove toward town, Grandma was unusually serious. She had a mission that she did not take lightly. Seeing Pavel always troubled her, and she tried to find a way to help him come back to those who loved him. "Pumpkin," she said. "Never judge others. We never know the plan for another's life, nor their personal journey." Then she added, "We don't know exactly what life has in store for us either."

Was Grandma preparing me for what I was going to see today or what I would see the rest of my life? Probably both. She hated judging of any kind, and I knew that is why she didn't let me get by with my comments about Willie Smith sometimes.

I listened as she spoke and tried to understand what she said while trying to watch where we were going. I saw we were close to town, and when we crossed Sky Bridge, Grandma turned, drove a few blocks, and then crossed the railroad tracks. She stopped the car right in front of a run-down, one-room building with weathered paint and smoke rising from the chimney. Every few feet around the building, someone pounded nails into lathes over tarpaper to cover any holes. "We're here," she said.

"Is this where he lives, Grandma?" I asked taking in as much of the run-down place as I could. I guess I knew where he lived but hadn't gotten this close before.

Grandma replied, "Follow me."

When we reached the door, Grandma knocked several times, but no one answered. Slowly she opened the door until we saw an old stove surrounded by several scruffy –looking people. There were others in the room. I noticed a wrinkled, skinny old man in dirty, torn and worn bib overalls warming his hands by the fire. Another old man was sitting on a wooden fruit box and staring into space talking to himself. He didn't notice we were there. Others were just sitting by the stove, talking to each other trying to keep warm and pass the time.

Seeing Pavel's friends all together in one place for the first time frightened me. I moved in closer to Grandma as we walked further into the room. I know Grandma knew my thoughts and let me hang on tight. "Let's go home, Grandma," I pleaded, the sound of my voice quivering. "Let's go home! **Please!**"

"We're safe, Pumpkin. We're all right," she assured me.

I felt safe with Grandma, and I knew she would not put me in danger. I also believed that she knew what she was doing. Grandma had done it herself several times in the past, and she walked with confidence past everyone toward the stove to Pavel.

Pavel, a thin, tall balding man wearing an old, brown, wool topcoat, tattered around the sleeves, stood closest to the stove. His trembling hands were bare, his fingernails jagged and dirty, and he had at least a week's worth of whiskers.

As Grandma approached him, he looked up. His face lit up when he recognized her, and he stopped warming his hands to extend his hand for a handshake.

Grandma smiled as she greeted him and asked, "How are you, Pavel?"

"Not too bad," he replied.

Grandma had told me that Pavel said that no matter how he felt.

"This is my granddaughter Margaret, Pavel. She's Halbert's daughter."

"Pleased to meet you," he put out his hand and smiled at me with his yellow, broken teeth.

Pretending I didn't see him, I quickly put my hands behind my back and looked up at Grandma, who nodded for me to shake his hand. I brought my hands back and gave him my right hand putting it right into his dirty, cold hand. It only took a moment, and it was over.

"I have something for you, Pavel," she said as she hugged him. "And I brought enough food to share with your friends. Please ask them to join us."

Pavel went with us to the car to help carry the packages. Once back inside, Grandma and Pavel passed out the sandwiches and coffee to everyone. Many quickly gulped their food and wanted more. Others, whose appetites were small, shared what they could not eat.

When they finished eating, Grandma gave each of them a pair of woolen mittens and soft socks to keep their hands and feet warm. Then she kindly turned to Pavel and softly said, "I have something special for you, something to keep you warm."

Pavel's eyes lit up as Grandma pulled the beautiful patchwork quilt from the box. When Grandma gave it to him, they filled with tears.

"Pavel," Grandma asked," Is there anything else you need or anything else I can do for you?" She hesitated and then in a concerned tone continued, "Would you like to come with us? I'll take you home to your family."

"No thank you, my little *Katya*. You have done too much for me already."

Grandma replied, "Well, you know where I am if you need anything."

He nodded as he said in Russian, "*Da, Katya. Ya znayu.*"

He had said, "Yes, I know, Katya." in Russian. It sounded like he wanted to change the subject.

Grandma meant what she said to Pavel. She had kept in touch with him all these years, and she made a special effort to know where he was and what he was doing.

As we left, Pavel thanked Grandma for her visit, the delicious food, and the gifts, especially the quilt. "I will be warm this year," he gratefully added. "*Spasiba*, Katya. *Bolshoe spasiba.*"

He watched as we drove away until our car was out of his sight as he waved good-bye to us repeating, "*Do svidaniya! Do svidaniya!*"

I was full of questions and thoughts of all kinds on our ride home and could not keep them to myself. "Grandma," I asked, "Why is Pavel living like that?"

"Some people live like that because they are sick and feel they have nowhere else to go. Some live like that because they have no job or home. Others choose to live like that. When he was young, Pavel became hooked on alcohol."

"What do you mean hooked?"

"He craves it. He needs it. Some people are like that. It's an addiction that's hard to overcome."

"But, Grandma, he seems lost and so alone. The only one he has is you."

"I know, Pumpkin, I know. One year he came here to visit your grandpa and me and never went home. He said there was nothing to go home for. I often thought he came here because it was a quieter and safer place to live."

"But, Grandma, you said he came from a wealthy family, once in the fur trading business."

"Money isn't everything and does not buy happiness. We all live with our personal choices, you know. In the meantime, we somehow need to help people like Pavel have a better life. I wish I could figure out a way to help him."

"Grandma, why do you care so much?"

"When we were children, Pavel always watched out for me. We were best friends, and because of him, no one was allowed to bully me without answering to him."

Back at Grandma's, I thought about my day with Pavel and her. I learned two important things. One was that true friends were friends forever no matter what happened in their lives. The other was that friends were gifts to each other, and some days it was our turn to return the gift.

Still, I could not help but think about Pavel, once wealthy, now living dirty, ragged, and homeless in a one room shack facing a cold, Minnesota winter. I also thought about Grandma, who cherished her old friend despite his choices in life. I knew it hurt her deeply to leave him there that day knowing there was so little that she could do.

Despite everything, Grandma faithfully visited her friend, who was shaky and fragile like the baby robin whose wing we tried so hard to fix last summer. He was dressed in rags and old tattered clothing, and probably a disgrace to his rich family. If he were my brother, he'd be a disgrace to me.

It did not seem to make a smitch of difference to Grandma what anyone thought. She loved Pavel. And Pavel loved her, calling her "My Little *Katya*" to show how much he cared.

"What does he live on, Grandma?" It was obvious that he didn't have a job or anything.

"His family sends him money now and then because he's too proud to ask for welfare."

This bothered me a lot. How could they leave him here all alone with only a few dollars now and then? This was something I would think about for a long time. Didn't he need family more than money?

Despite everything I learned and felt about Pavel's life, the first thing I did when we got home was wash my hands. I didn't like the handshake one bit.

A THANKSGIVING GIFT

Grandma asked me a few days before her trip to the Jenne-weins to go with her. "This year I want you to go with me when I visit the Jenneweins," she said.

"But, Grandma, I can't," I answered. "I just can't."

"And why is that?"

"Nobody likes them, Grandma. Nobody in my class likes Bridget. They'll give me a bad time about it."

"You don't know that for sure. Maybe it will be way different than you think. I really want you to go and meet my friends." Then she added, "Besides, they shouldn't be treating Bridget that way."

We dropped the topic for a while, but as Thanksgiving got closer, I knew that it would come up again. Knowing Grandma, I would be going to visit the Jenneweins.

Grandma had a unique way of making others feel special. It didn't matter how rich or poor, how popular or unpopular, or how old or young, or what one had done or not done. Grandma respected everyone and was especially a champion of the less fortunate, the needy, and the underdog. It seemed like she knew everyone, and everyone knew her. She reminded me, "Don't judge anyone. You never know who God has sent to help you or who you have been sent to help."

Thanksgiving gave Grandma another chance to be gener-ous. Every Friday before the week of Thanksgiving, she met with members of the community to put together baskets of food for people who could not afford the makings of a Thanksgiving dinner. The baskets included a large frozen turkey, fresh pota-toes, canned corn, canned cranberry sauce, stuffing mix made from scratch consisting of dried white and dark bread, home-grown squash from Grandma's garden, and canned pumpkin for pie. Before they met, they knew exactly who would receive the baskets, and when they were done preparing the baskets, each was delivered until they were gone.

Grandma always saved one Thanksgiving basket that she delivered the next day, Saturday, in person. "You will enjoy the visit, I'm sure," is all she said.

That is how Grandma told me I was definitely going with her. There would be no more talk about it.

Eva and Charles Jennewein lived in a log cabin in the woods, and there was only a narrow road to get there. Grandma always worried that once we were there, it would snow, making it difficult to get back to the main road. Early Saturday morning, we turned on the radio for the weather forecast. It was going to be a cold but sunny day and no heavy snow. Plans were made to spend the night with the Jennewein family.

The Jenneweins had come from New York during the Great Depression. They brought their family to Minnesota to live in a log cabin in the woods so that they would have enough water to drink, a place to raise a garden, and wood to keep warm. They never returned to New York.

They stayed by themselves most of the time because they felt everyone knew they were poor and looked down on them. People laughed at their large family saying, "They have too many children they can't t support."

Classmates did not want to be with them, and as the children became older, they quit school and moved away from home. People also laughed at how they dressed in worn-out hand-me downs and how they smelled of wood smoke from the stove that heated their house. It didn't matter to Grandma that from this day on they'd also laugh at me.

I was quiet and in a bad mood. I didn't want people to think I was a friend of the Jenneweins, but I didn't want to hurt Grandma's feelings either. "I'm just here for the ride and to please Grandma," I told myself.

Bridget Jennewein was the youngest child and the only one still living at home. Tiny and pale, she looked sick all the time. Her mousy brown hair in pigtails didn't add to a picture of health either. Although she was in my class at school, we didn't know each other. She always stayed by herself and always looked lonely and very sad.

I finally broke the silence. "I haven't seen Bridget all fall. Wonder if she's even home today."

Secretly I hoped she wasn't home. Then I wouldn't have to explain to everyone what I was doing at her house.

The day was cold and windy. Light snow already powdered the frozen ground from the night before last, and only a few dried-up leaves remained on the trees. It seemed that life had completely stopped or shut down in the woods. Only the evergreens showed signs of life, and we occasionally saw a deer wandering through the trees probably looking for something to eat.

Our car was full of groceries and gifts for the Jenneweins, including the turkey Grandma thawed the night before so it would be ready for Mrs. Jennewein's oven. "If we are going to eat turkey with them tomorrow, it can't be frozen," Grandma said as she left to get it from the town's locker plant.

She also made a pumpkin pie and whipped cream topping to go with it and packed the car full of milk, butter, coffee, apples, oranges, carrots, celery, squash, tomatoes, corn, fresh homemade buns, and anything else she thought they needed.

"The Jenneweins will never starve to death for sure with Grandma around," I thought.

Beautifully wrapped gifts were brought for all of them. Mr. Jennewein's gift was a red, plaid flannel shirt with long sleeves. Mrs. Jennewein would be pleased, I felt, with a new fall tablecloth of colored leaves and pumpkins.

"How about a new Scrabble game for Bridget?" I asked Grandma. "She's smart in school when she comes."

I could see by the things in our packed car, including a new Scrabble game, this was a Thanksgiving-Christmas-Holiday party all in one weekend and not just a visit. In fact, Grandma's car was packed full of things she was bringing to the Jenneweins.

As we came closer to the Jennewein cabin, we smelled wood burning. "The smell of the wood smoke outside is so good, Grandma. It's not like the smell of stale wood smoke on clothing."

Grandma didn't even bother to answer. Instead, she said, "We're almost there."

I was relieved because we had driven far into the woods already. Now I knew how difficult it was for Bridget to attend school. Grandma said, "It is this long, narrow road Mr. Jennewein uses to take her to the school bus. If he doesn't feel well or if there is bad weather, Bridget doesn't go to school that day."

Mr. Jennewein answered the door. He was kind and serious-looking, small in stature, medium height and extremely thin, with graying hair and deep set, brown eyes surrounded by dark circles. "Hello and Happy Thanksgiving," he greeted us cheerfully as he shook our hands and offered to help us carry in our food and gifts.

Although his greeting was cheerful, his eyes were dull and sad. People said he had lost everything during the Great Depression days, and he never recovered from the loss. Was this the reason he looked so sad? I would ask Grandma on our way home.

Short and chunky, Mrs. Jennewein had a kind, round-shaped face and a big smile. She hugged Grandma and me and said, "Welcome, my dear friends. I am so happy you made it. Please come in."

She looked like Mrs. Santa Claus with her curly short hair, wire-rimmed glasses, a green plaid house dress and a dark green apron. Grandma and Mrs. Jennewein embraced, delighted to see each other.

Bridget was tiny and small-boned, like her father. She wore old-fashioned clothing, probably ten years outdated. Today she was wearing a brown straight skirt, too long for someone as little as she was, with a dingy-white, short-sleeved button-up blouse. Shyly she acknowledged me only as someone she knew from school. "Hi, Pumpkin," she barely got out without looking up at me.

"Hi, Bridget," I said. I was ashamed I had not defended her more and been her friend. I felt guilty for not wanting to drive out to her house for a visit.

Grandma and Mrs. Jennewein immediately began to prepare dinner. I looked around the room to check out their house, and it didn't take long.

Their house was made of logs and had one large room that included the kitchen and living room with a master bedroom off to the right. A step ladder led to the loft where Bridget slept. All the furniture was old and worn and a mixture of different styles in blues, and browns, and greens. In the corner of the living room was a huge rock fireplace that was blazing, keeping the cabin toasty warm and cozy. On the other side of the room, was an old wood burning range used for cooking and for heating. There was no indoor bathroom or running water. When it was inconvenient or below zero and too cold to run to the outhouse, they used chamber pots. I wondered how they had been able to raise a large family in this tiny house.

It did not take long until the room filled with the smell of roasting turkey and sage dressing. While the food was cooking, Mrs. Jennewein spread her new fall tablecloth of pumpkins and leaves on the table. She carefully set the table as if she was serving President Eisenhower or Queen Elizabeth. Everything was set in perfect order according to Emily Post. Even if none of her dishes or silverware matched, it was obvious that somewhere she had learned how to be a proper hostess.

We sat down for dinner, and Mr. Jennewein asked us to bow our heads for the blessing. Asking God to bless the food and everyone present, he also thanked for the blessings of the past year, our friends, our families, our healthy lives and good times together. Then he carved the turkey, and we ate our dinner prepared on an old, wood burning stove.

After dinner, Mr. Jennewein appeared with a shiny violin. There was excitement and pleasure on everyone's face as he began to play perfectly "Turkey in the Straw." It was magical, as if it was the spark bringing the glow to our evening. Next, he played "Orange Blossom Special" with his long, slender fingers flying over the strings faster and faster.

Bridget came and took my hands, "Wanna dance?" she asked.

"Sure," I replied.

We began to promenade, dance, and swing around until we were dizzy from spinning and almost fell down. When the song was over, we sat down exhausted and out of breath and giggled.

"That was so much fun, Bridget," I said almost gasping for breath.

Once the dancing began, the rest of the evening was easy. Dancing somehow put both of us at ease. We laughed and talked about how much fun we were having. And we talked about school.

"We should do this more often," we both said.

As bedtime came closer, Mr. Jennewein played "The Vienna Waltz" and finally "The Blue Danube." It was magnificent. I felt sleepy as Bridget and I swung back and forth to the waltz tempo.

"Did anyone else know Mr. Jennewein was a talented violinist? If not, why?" I wondered. I didn't know myself until tonight.

"It's time to go to bed, Girls," Grandma said. "We need to get up early to go home."

Bridget and I slept well that night under her warm patchwork quilt falling asleep, listening to Grandma and Mr. and Mrs. Jennewein discuss art, current events, and, Mr. Jennewein's favorite, music. Of course, there was the rest of their family. Grandma needed to know where every one of their children was and what they did.

The loft was warm and cozy with all the warmth rising from the fires, Grandma, and Mr. and Mrs. Jennewein. Their conversation continued way into the night before they went to bed. Grandma made a bed on their old couch. They became quiet long after Bridget and I fell asleep.

The next morning, we awoke to talking, laughter, and the

wonderful smell of bacon and eggs frying. Grandma and Mr. and Mrs. Jennewein had awakened early to fix breakfast.

Right after eating, we left for home. In our good-byes, Bridget and I hugged each other and vowed, "Let's be friends and keep in touch. See you in school."

On the way home I turned to Grandma and said, "I really enjoyed myself, Grandma."

"I know you did."

"They're nice! I liked them."

"I knew you would."

"This is the best Thanksgiving I have ever had."

Grandma just smiled. She wasn't much for "*I-told-you-so's.*"

"Oh, and Grandma. Is it true that Mr. Jennewein lost everything in the Great Depression?"

"Yes."

"People around town say that is why they are so poor and he is so sad. Is that the reason, Grandma?"

"I really think so. Some people just aren't strong enough to start over from nothing. As time passed, so did his chances."

"Grandma, maybe Bridget will be the concert violinist. She told me her dad is giving her violin lessons."

"Maybe. Let's hope." Grandma seemed pleased.

CAVIAR, ANCHOVIES, AND CULTURE

It was a cool and crisp early December day. Grandma had planned a trip to the cities for months and announced, "Pumpkin, put on your best dress and long stockings. We are going to Minneapolis tomorrow. Ask your dad's permission to pack a bag to stay overnight. Oh, by the way, we are leaving early so we get there by midafternoon. Okay?"

When she picked me up, she was wearing her brown fur jacket, blue dress and blue high heels. She had rouge on her cheeks, red lipstick, and a bounce in her step. Her smile made her face light up and her eyes twinkle.

"You sure are in a good mood, Grandma," I said.

"You know me. I miss my old city life. Today is my chance to have some of it back again."

It was at least an eight-hour drive to Minneapolis, and it would take us all day. Grandma had packed enough food to last till we arrived at the hotel downtown where we planned to spend the night.

As we drove to Minneapolis, Grandma said, "Pumpkin, I've always felt you need culture in your life. You live in the country where you aren't exposed to it."

"What do you mean?" I was puzzled. "What's culture, Grandma?"

"You'll see. Today I will show you some culture"

After hours of driving to the city, we finally arrived. Grandma maneuvered her car into a huge parking lot that belonged to the hotel. We settled in and walked to Dayton's, the tallest and biggest department store on the huge city block. On the way, Grandma pointed out the festive lights hanging everywhere on lamp posts and stores to help put everyone in a holiday mood. "Look at all these lights, Pumpkin. Aren't they out of this world?"

I hadn't seen anything like it. Huge stores with all kinds of colored lights were everywhere. Everything was decorated.

As choirs along the street sang Christmas carols, we window shopped and watched all the early Christmas shoppers. Grandma and I thought, "Everyone has the same idea--to shop early and avoid a last-minute rush."

Each time we passed a Santa bell ringer, Grandma took change out of her purse and put it in the kettle. It would ring and clang as the coins hit all the others. "Pumpkin," she leaned down and whispered, "I never pass the bell ringers without giving them a gift. They do a lot of good in this world." Then she added, "You always get back what you give a hundred-fold."

In a special gift shop Grandma helped me buy a holiday souvenir for my father. "Don't you think he'll like this?" I asked.

It was exquisite! Snuggled in a display of unique gifts was a special little snow globe with a winter scene and falling snow that played, "White Christmas." I loved it.

"I think it is the most charming snow globe I'd ever seen, Grandma said."

Then Grandma turned to me and asked, "Are you hungry?"

"Sure am," I quickly answered. I'd been hungry since noon hour.

"Come with me."

We entered Dayton's Department Store, leisurely walking and window shopping. There was a Snowman Village Display right in the middle of the store where little children went, one by one, to sit in Santa's lap. Excitement lit up their faces, exploding with enthusiasm, as they whispered to Santa what they wanted for Christmas. Watching them made me giggle.

As I looked around, it seemed there wasn't much that wasn't festive. "Oh, Grandma, it does look just like Christmas," I whispered because it had taken my breath away.

"Be careful not to trip," Grandma cautioned as we both stepped on the escalator.

Once we reached the top floor, we stepped off the escalator and walked to The Sky Room. "Here we are, Pumpkin. Do you like it?" Grandma asked.

"I love it!" I exclaimed.

The tables had white tablecloths with red and white flowers and candles. The places were set with green napkins, white china and silverware. The waiter showed us to our specially set table and gave each of us a menu.

"What do you want to order, Pumpkin?" Grandma asked.

"A hamburger and French fries," I enthusiastically answered.

Grandma looked at me for a moment and then at the menu. "This is what I want you to order today," she said and pointed to a green salad with anchovies and caviar. "You should at least try this once."

And that is exactly what she ordered for me. One bite of the caviar was enough for me. It reminded me of the cod liver oil my father gave me so I wouldn't get rickets. "You need that Vitamin D in the winter because of lack of sunshine," he reminded me as I gagged when I swallowed it.

Grandma enjoyed her food. I left most of mine, but our time together was delightful. We had sat in a restaurant enjoying the holidays in a place of culture where I tasted anchovies and caviar for the first time.

After dinner, Grandma and I went to "The Nutcracker." Grandma leaned down toward me and whispered, "This is truly culture, Pumpkin. This is the ballet."

Filled with the magic of Christmas with its joyful sights and sounds and beauty, I quietly watched the ballet dancers, listened to the music, and sat close to Grandma. I felt wonderful, special, and loved all at the same time.

"I love today, Grandma, and I love you."

She smiled. I felt Grandma had given me one of the best days of my life. It was the day she introduced me to culture, and it made her happy.

"I love you to pieces, Margaret Louise Olson," Grandma hugged me and said.

CHRISTMAS EVE

It was the week before Christmas. We were busy buying and wrapping gifts for friends and family. Some of them were coming home just for the holidays.

Dad and I always celebrated Christmas Eve at Grandma's house. I begged Grandma for weeks to invite the Andersons. One day she said, "Well, I guess since we all are good friends, it makes sense to celebrate together."

That same day, Grandma phoned her friend, Marion Anderson. "What are you folks doing Christmas Eve?" she asked.

"We have no plans so far," Mrs. Anderson answered.

"How would you like to have dinner with us at my house?"

"I am so glad you asked. We'd love to come. And I'll bring dessert."

Christmas Eve came, and Grandma prepared roast goose, a gift from the Tollefsons, giblet dressing, mashed potatoes and gravy, peas and carrots, mashed rutabagas smothered in butter, all kinds of pickles, and fresh cranberry salad, Mrs. Anderson brought two steaming apple pies and vanilla ice cream from their restaurant that would be closed Christmas Day anyway.

"That was some meal, Katherine," Mr. Anderson said rubbing his stomach.

"Yes," we all echoed. "It was some meal."

"Thank you, Peter, and all of you. It was my pleasure. And thank you, Marion for the delicious pie and ice cream."

It was all arranged that Mary Elizabeth would go with us to Grandma's church in the country. After Mr. and Mrs. Anderson left for home, Dad, Grandma, Mary Elizabeth, and I left for church. On the way, we picked up Thea, who wanted to go with us.

Thea, my tall, athletic cousin on my mother's side of the

family from Southern Minnesota, was friendly, outgoing, and fit anywhere. Mary Elizabeth was tiny and ladylike. I was somewhere in the middle. We were definitely individuals, but we got along.

The night was crisp and clear with little wind when we headed out of town. Dad drove leisurely. "We have lots of time," he said. "It's only ten miles."

Stars filled the clear sky. Dad suggested, "Why don't you girls try finding The Big Dipper?"

"I see it!" Thea exclaimed right away.

Then Mary Elizabeth thought she had found it. "I see it, too!" she added.

Finally, I thought I saw what they saw and chimed in, "Me, too!"

It seemed as though we'd just left town when we saw the white church with its high steeple, standing proud and tall on a corner of the intersection. Warm lights in its windows invited us to come inside, telling us that this was a good place to be tonight. Because the church area was already crowded with cars, Grandma feared we had waited too long and there would be nowhere to sit. Disappointed, she said, "I guess we should have left town earlier."

Inside, there were garlands of pine trees on the banisters, wreaths on the doors, and a gorgeous, lit Christmas tree with a star on top that reached to the ceiling. There was the smell of freshly cut pine boughs and burning wood from an old wood stove. There were people, old and young, greeting each other with warm Christmas wishes. The whole evening's atmosphere tugged at my heart and made me feel warm all over. "I never want to forget this," I thought as I tried forming a permanent picture in my mind to keep the moment alive forever.

Just in time, before the procession began, we all found seating together. Thea and Mary Elizabeth went in first. I followed them. Then Dad and Grandma followed me. Here I was on a wonderful night sitting with my wonderful dad.

Just before the overhead lights dimmed, I looked to our

right where the whole Tollefson family sat, and I caught Yanni's attention. He smiled at me, and I thought he winked. Then he mouthed the words, "Hi" and "Merry Christmas."

I felt my face start to get warm and red as I smiled and waved back. He was so handsome that Yanni Tollefson. Who could help but like him?

My thoughts of Yanni were interrupted. The program had begun.

Children in white robes sang, "Joy to the World," as they walked down the aisle to the front of the church. The taller children came in first, then the middle- sized ones, and last the little ones, and they all lined up in position in front of the church and finished singing with, "And heaven and he-a-ven and nature sing."

We heard how Jesus was born in a stable and how the shepherds and wise men came. We sang "Hark the Herald Angels Sing," "O Little Town of Bethlehem," and "Oh Come All Ye Faithful." Yanni's visiting cousin sang, "Star of the East," about the star that led the wise men to Bethlehem, and when he was done, everyone clapped. The minister spoke about the greatest Christmas gift of all. We, Thea, Mary Elizabeth, and I, listened to every word thinking how lucky we were to have such a wonderful gift, a baby.

It did not take long before the service was over with all of us singing "Silent Night." To close the minister prayed thanking the Lord for everything and asking the Lord to give everyone in the whole wide world a blessed, merry Christmas.

Then at midnight the church bell rang. DONG. DONG. DONG. DONG. DONG. DONG. DONG. It was repeated over and over again to celebrate Jesus' birth. At the door, church members passed out brown paper bags with Christmas candy, a delicious red apple and unshelled peanuts. It was a gift to all who came to celebrate. "Merry Christmas! Merry Christmas! Merry Christmas!" could be heard coming from everywhere as people left to go home.

Outside it was snowing soft, light fluffy flakes that shone

like diamonds under the lights. Dad drove slowly on the snowy roads. "It must be an Alberta Clipper," he said. "It moved in fast."

"I am so happy tonight," Grandma said and began to hum "Silent Night."

We three girls were still in awe of all we had seen and heard and did not say a word all the way home. It was unusual for us to be so quiet.

Before Dad parked Grandma's car, he let all of us out in front of Grandma's house. Standing on the sidewalk, Grandma looked up at the heavens as the soft white snow fell gently around her. Softly and reverently, she said, "I wonder if the Heavenly Hosts in all their glory are much whiter than this."

As we walked from the street to her house, Grandma added, "Come with me. It's too beautiful out here to go inside right now."

She took us to her back yard, still untouched by footprints in the snow. Streetlights gave us enough light to see sparkling snowflakes covering everything, including the white picket fence enclosing her back yard, with diamonds.

After we had stood quietly in awe for a while, Grandma said, "Watch this," and she threw herself backward in the snow high heels, fur coat, and all, and made a snow angel. Soon we were all lying on our backs in a circle making snow angels, looking up into the beautiful white heavens, celebrating Christmas Eve as never before.

"I never knew snow could be this lovely," Mary Elizabeth told us. "Hardly ever saw it down south."

"It is lovely," I agreed. Then I added, "To tell you the truth, Mary E. I didn't know snow was this lovely either."

"To be honest, You Two, I didn't either," Thea said.

The whole evening was perfect, almost magical. It was like I always believed Christmas Eve should be. "Merry Christmas, Grandma," I said meaning it more than I ever had in my life.

"Merry Christmas, Pumpkin," Grandma answered.

"Merry Christmas, Thea," I added. "And Merry Christmas, Mary Elizabeth."

"We wish you a Merry Christmas, World," Thea almost sang.

"And a Happy New Year," we all chimed in together.

Looking up into the snow falling softly down us in Grandma's back yard, I whispered, "Merry Christmas, Mom. I miss you so much."

JANUARY SNOW

There were weather forecasts that January morning for a severe snowstorm that would dump a huge amount of snow on us. Beginning Christmas Eve, we had already had our share of snow. Major snowstorms and piling snow made it difficult to go anywhere or do anything outdoors. Deep snow covered all the ponds, making skating impossible. When it wasn't snowing, it was too cold much of the time for outdoor activities like tobogganing or skiing.

Giant snowbanks, some created by the snowplows, were higher than our house and were great for sliding down on cardboard when we had warmer days. Today I climbed to the top of the highest bank and looked as far as I could see, where it looked like earth met sky, where I could almost see the nearest town. I promised myself, "Someday I am going way beyond where I no longer can see today."

Someday I would be somebody special like Yanni Tollefson and make people proud. Maybe I would be a famous writer, a movie star, or a musician. Of course, I would have lots of money to help the less fortunate and the needy. I would dress in elegant, fancy gowns and furs and wear diamonds for jewelry. I would drive a big Cadillac and people would acknowledge me wherever I went. I, Pumpkin, would be special.

My daydreaming was interrupted when Grandma called me in for hot chocolate and fresh chocolate chip cookies. As I took off my warm snowsuit and snow boots, I noticed the grim look on Grandma's face. She was concerned about something and was quiet as we sat drinking hot chocolate. She had driven out to the farm that morning to be with Dad and me.

Interrupting the quiet, she finally said, "The way the weather feels, I think we have a bad snowstorm coming. It's so still outside, you know. It's the calm before the storm," she solemnly predicted. "I think you should stay inside for the rest of the day."

"Are you going home before it hits?"

"No, I plan to spend the night. Just heard on the radio that those right west of us got several feet of snow. It's dangerous out there. Just dangerous! I'm glad that you are home and we are all safe and sound."

"Where's my dad, Grandma?"

"Your father will be in as soon as he finishes the chores."

"I'm glad we're safe, Grandma. I hope everyone else is," I sighed.

Grandma usually knew what she was talking about when it came to weather. I sat on her couch to read a magazine and to listen to "Hit Parade" on KTIG Radio just in time to hear Elvis Presley sing "Love Me Tender." "His singing is so groovy," I decided.

It was not long before Grandma announced, "Well, it's here. The storm is here," and she called me to the kitchen to look out the window with her just as Dad came in the side door.

Dad looked at Grandma and me and said, "Sure had that timed right. It's bad out there."

I could not believe my eyes. The snow was coming down so fast and forcefully that we could not see the yard light at the next farm. It was a total whiteout of everything past our steps. Stunned at what I had just seen, I looked at both of them. "I've never seen a storm like this," I said. "Ever."

Grandma hurried to turn on the porch light while she instructed me, "We have to have the lights on in case someone needs to find his way in the storm." Our house was along the highway going into town and had been a refuge for many travelers over the years. Tonight, all the lights in our house would be burning to show the way to those stranded in the snow.

It snowed all evening and all night. I went to bed early, but Grandma and Dad stayed up in case someone needed their help. When I awakened in the morning, it was still snowing but not as hard. You could see the road from our yard, but you couldn't see any traffic moving. There was snow everywhere, with banks higher than the rooftops. Neighbors and friends probably were shoveling themselves out of the huge drifts that had piled against their homes. Streets and roads were deep in snow, making driving almost impossible.

"There's a family with a little baby stranded in their car a couple miles down the road," Grandma said. "Your father and Peter Anderson left a half hour ago to rescue them. Peter said he had a terrible time getting here from town. I sure hope that they are all right. It's too bad that someone didn't get to them sooner."

Like Grandma, my father was caring and compassionate. But I was worried and afraid for him out in the storm looking for stranded people. "I hope Dad gets here soon," I replied. I couldn't lose him, too.

My thoughts of Dad immediately went to thoughts of my mother. She had beautiful auburn-red hair, green eyes, and freckles. Gracious, she made my father proud that she was his wife. She could flash a smile with her straight, white teeth that stole the hearts of everyone. Besides being beautiful, she could keep a tidy, clean house, cook, sew and garden with the best. The best thing about her was she was my mother and best friend.

Dad was considered the best catch by all the available girls in the county before he chose Mother for his wife. Tall, athletic, and handsome with dark brown hair, like Grandma's, he was ambitious and was already known as one of the up and coming farmers in the area. His deep blue eyes twinkled when he talked and especially when he smiled. Not only was he handsome and ambitious, but he also had a heart of gold and often found himself in life and death situations like today.

Grandma and I waited and waited and worried. Then we waited and worried some more. It seemed it took Father and Mr. Anderson a lifetime to rescue the Larsons, Susan, Daniel, and their baby Emily. At noon Grandma sighed with relief as she saw the rescuers and the Larsons in the driveway.

"We're cold but thankfully still alive," Mr. Larson told Grandma. "Spending the night out there wasn't fun."

Mrs. Larson jumped into the conversation, "But we huddled together to keep warm. We're cold to the bone but not frost bitten." She added, "I kept Baby Emily wrapped in several blankets close to my body all night."

Thankful that there was no frostbite, Grandma took steps to warm them inside and out. She brought her dining room chairs and set them around her kitchen stove with its oven door open. She gave each of them a basin of warm water for their feet, a cup of hot chocolate to drink, and a warm blanket to wrap around their shivering bodies. It was not long before their shivering stopped, and pinkish color returned to their cheeks and hands.

"Thank you, Mrs. Olson. We are so happy and grateful to be in this warm, cozy home," Mr. Larson said with such sincerity he wiped tears and almost cried out loud. Everyone settled in for the rest of the day. Although the snow was not coming down as heavy and hard, the wind began to blow it around, and the storm lasted three days. The Larsons were our guests the whole time.

Protected from the storm, everyone made themselves at home. "Maybe we should enjoy ourselves and make the best of it," Grandma suggested.

I helped with Baby Emily when I was not reading a book, playing games like Monopoly, Scrabble, or cards, talking with our guests, or listening to the radio. Grandma was always providing food, making sure none of us was hungry.

"May I help with something, Mrs. Olson?" Mrs. Larson asked.

"Oh, please call me Katherine. Whatever you want to do, you are welcome to help, Susan."

Grandma helped her find all the makings, and Mrs. Larson baked us delicious gingerbread. "It's my grandmother's recipe," she proudly informed us.

After it quit snowing and blowing and the roads were drivable, a grateful Larson family thanked us again for our hospitality and left for home. Grandma went to her home in town. I stayed with dad on the farm. Once it was over, I knew I would not forget this storm and how lucky we were. During the storm, I was safe with my loving family, who went out of their way to help someone else. I felt so lucky to have them, my father and my grandma.

We knew we had just lived through one of the worst snowstorms in our community's history. It was a storm that would be discussed for years to come. There would always be talk about the big snow that created drifts higher than our two-story house. Emily Larson was always remembered as the baby who spent the night in a car on a blocked road in the big storm with her parents, while people in the community spent the night trying to find a way to rescue her.

A VALENTINE SURPRISE

Since Thanksgiving with the Jennewein family, Bridget and I had become good friends. Mary Elizabeth willingly accepted her into our group, and we became a threesome. Having good friends, Bridget wasn't as shy anymore. Still fragile and pale, she managed to keep up with the rest of us.

It was February, and we all looked forward to Valentine's Day. In art class we began creating our personal Valentine boxes from shoe boxes, cereal boxes, or oatmeal boxes by using red and white construction paper and lace doilies. The challenge was to make the prettiest Valentine box of all.

As Bridget created hers, she recalled the pain of rejection in past years when she received only a few valentines. "I hope I get more valentines this year," she said.

"You will," both of us said to make her feel better.

Busy talking and working, we didn't notice Willie Smith come over to our table. He was big for his age and towered over everyone in the class hunching over to hide his height. His feet were also growing faster than everyone else's, and he often stumbled over them. He was obnoxious and mean, and he teased Bridget.

Sneaking up behind us, he looked at Bridget and began to taunt her in a singsong, sarcastic tone. "Wood Smoke! Wood Smoke! You won't get no valentines," until Bridget hung her head and began to cry.

I jumped up first. Mary Elizabeth followed. We probably looked comical as we stood up to Willie, towering over us both. I stood with my hands on my hips, and Mary Elizabeth stood behind me with her hands on her hips.

"Willie Smith, You Big Bully! Leave her alone or you'll be in big trouble!" I screamed at him.

"Yeah," Mary Elizabeth echoed. "Big trouble!"

"Whatcha gonna do, Pumpkin?" he asked and took Bridget's Valentine box, designed as a bowl of flowers, and smashed it into the floor flat as a pancake. Then he smashed Mary Elizabeth's and then mine, leaving all of our beautiful creations in a heap on the floor.

"Thank you, God," I thought to myself. "I'm glad he took all of our boxes."

I turned to Bridget, "Don't you dare cry because of him. He's not worth it."

The next day everyone showed up for a meeting with the principal. Since my father was out of town, Grandma came with me. She was miffed. Grandma wanted everyone to be treated equally and well, and she did not like those who mistreated the underdog. She wasn't in any mood to face the Smith family after what happened. Olaf and Ingrid Smith and their son Willie had just challenged her belief in the goodness in everybody.

On the way I asked, "Grandma, why did Willie do such a mean thing to Bridget?"

"He probably likes her—or you maybe, and this is his only way to show it. He wants your attention."

I didn't dare tell Grandma that I thought Willie Smith liking Bridget or me was the most ridiculous thing I had ever heard. We arrived at the principal's office, so the conversation ended with me puzzled by Grandma's words.

Principal Albert Overby was tall, lanky, long legged, and thin. It was easy to know when he was coming down the hall because he had long strides especially when he was in a hurry. He had just arrived from another meeting in the school and was somewhat short of breath. A man of few words when he spoke, he had a deep, strong voice of authority.

Mr. Overby wore glasses that he desperately needed to read and hardly ever smiled. He did not smile today either. As he entered his office, he nodded to everyone and did not say a word. He was bald, and the ceiling light reflected on his head.

Mr. and Mrs. Jennewein also came to the meeting, hurt

and sad as if their hearts were broken by another rejection from the community that targeted their family. Mrs. Jennewein had dismay and anguish written all over her face and was wringing her hands in despair, as if to say, "Why us?" It was almost as if she felt Bridget would be blamed for the incident over the valentines.

"Oh dear, what is going to happen?" she said to Grandma while wringing her hands.

"Don't worry, it will work out. Always does," Grandma answered.

Mary Elizabeth's parents came, and they asked, "What can we do to help solve this problem?"

Relaxed and easy going, they never seemed to be bothered by anything and walked into a storm and came out the same as when they entered. From owning the restaurant in town, they were used to dealing with all kinds of people.

Willie Smith's parents came of course, embarrassed to be there under the circumstances. Mrs. Smith didn't look at anyone and said nothing. She quickly sat down waiting for what was coming. Mr. Smith shook hands with Grandma and the Andersons.

Willie had often caused them problems with others. They never had adjusted to their misbehaving son, and here they were again in the principal's office.

Willie Smith was given a choice, suspension from school or a sincere apology to everyone, especially Bridget, and a promise never to do something like this again. He chose the apology and the promise.

On the way home Grandma said, "Pumpkin, maybe this bad day will turn itself around. Maybe some good will come out of it."

Grandma was right as usual. By Valentine's Day, the whole school had learned what had happened to us. Bridget, Mary Elizabeth, and I rebuilt our Valentine boxes out of shoe boxes. As far as Willie Smith was concerned, he had not been in trouble since the meeting.

That afternoon was a day to remember when it was time to open our valentines. Bridget's Valentine Box was overflowing, not just from her classmates but from students in every class in school. They were nice valentines saying things like, "You are Special." Or, "Will you be my valentine?"

Bridget was overwhelmed—and happy. She whispered excitedly to Mary Elizabeth and me, "I finally belong! I finally belong!"

After school that day, I told Grandma, "Guess what!"

"What, Pumpkin?"

"Bridget received more valentines than I did this year."

"That's wonderful!"

"I am so happy for Bridget."

That day I learned that it made me happy to see someone else happy. I was grateful that the students in our school finally realized how badly Bridget had been treated and tried to make it up to her. But, I still was puzzled over the possibility that Willie Smith actually liked us. He had a strange way of showing it. Someday I planned to tell Grandma I didn't like him.

Willie Smith in my opinion was nothing but a puke fossil! Definitely a puke fossil.

PET LAMBS

It was late March.   All the snow from the winter had thawed leaving everything looking black and drab. In addition to the blackness of early spring, most of the days were cloudy and bleak with raw, cold winds that went right through our snow pants and jackets.

"I can't wait for sunshine, green grass, and flowers," I said to Grandma. I hated this time of year and its drabness.

Potholes, low spots in the fields that were still filled with water from thawed snow, froze during the night. The thick ice, smooth as glass, made perfect skating rinks in the morning.

Mary Elizabeth spent the night with me on the farm so we could go skating. It wasn't hard to convince her to try things she hadn't tried before. "It'll be fun," she said.

When we left our warm, cozy house that morning, we dressed for winter. Snow jackets, snow pants, stocking caps, woolen mittens, and long scarves wrapped around our necks and faces, exposed only our noses and eyes.

"I feel like a mummy all wrapped up like this," I said as I tried limbering up my arms and legs from all the clothes."

"Me, too," Mary Elizabeth echoed.

We threw our tied together skates over our shoulders and started walking through the pasture to the field with the largest pothole for skating. It was the one that was clear and smooth, and the water wasn't deep.

Mary Elizabeth had been introduced to Minnesota winters, snow, and cold already and had adjusted well. As we walked, sometimes stumbled, across frozen clumps of dirt from fall plowing, she quickly learned walking in a frozen, plowed field was not easy or pleasant. But both of us knew that this was the best skating we would have so far away from the town rink, a lake, or a river.

"Skating in all these clothes sure is hard," I said falling down for about the tenth time that morning. "The good part is that with all this padding, it doesn't hurt."

We both giggled. Despite everything, we were having fun.

It was almost noon before we decided to stop skating and return home. "Wanna stop by the willow trees?" I asked.

Mary Elizabeth agreed, "Why not? We can pick stems of pussy willows for my mother and your Grandma."

They were ready to pick and their season was short. "We need to pick these before they're gone anyway," I said.

The willow branches were stiff and still frozen and snapped as we broke them off for bouquets large enough Grandma and Mrs. Anderson. "They'll remind all of us that spring is near and give us hope of better days ahead," Mary Elizabeth said.

Our house smelled heavenly as we walked in the front door. Grandma had homemade vegetable soup simmering on the stove. She was happy to hear that we had a good time and said, "Thank you for the beautiful pussy willows."

Grandma had just finished talking on our party-line phone with Yanni Tollefson's mother, Mrs. Emma Tollefson. We both nodded and said, "Yes," when asked us if we wanted to hear what happened to Yanni.

"He went through the ice on the ditch when he tried skating by their house. The minute he set both of his feet on the ice, he sank up to his waist in icy, cold water."

Grandma continued telling us how Yanni was so cold he was shivering with his teeth chattering. "Only his pride was hurt," she added. "I guess the rest of the morning Yanni sat wrapped in a wool blanket by their stove feeling sorry for himself.

"I'm glad he isn't hurt," I interrupted.

"Ya, me, too," Grandma smiled and added. "Guess that's what they call skating on thin ice."

Suddenly our bleak and dreary cloudy day had become bright and cheerful with the laughter, great stories, homemade vegetable soup with rutabagas and cabbage. The white kitchen, with its table and red and white checkered tablecloth, was warm and cozy, and we felt happy at home on a Saturday afternoon.

After lunch, Mary Elizabeth and I played Scrabble.

"That is not a word you can use, Mary Elizabeth," I told her.

"It is!"

"It's not! You can't use Ha*rry* as a word in this game. It's a proper noun."

"Can to!"

Grandma walked into the living room to see what was going on. "I think you girls should call this game Squabble instead of Scrabble."

I gave in and we used *Harry* as a word, and our game continued. "Who's Harry, Mary Elizabeth, anyway?"

"He's one of my friends down south. He lived in the orphanage with me."

"What about him?" I asked. "Was he special to you?"

"I'd rather not talk about that place."

"Okay," I answered and changed the subject, and we continued our Scrabble game into the afternoon.

It was the middle of the afternoon when Dad came home and announced, "The snow came down pretty hard on the way home from town. I hope it quits. We have several ewes at the old Nelson place ready to give birth. I don't want to lose any of them." Then he continued, "We have to keep a close eye on the weather. If the snow continues, we have to go before it gets dark. And, Ma, prepare to take in a lamb or two just in case."

It was five o'clock in the afternoon, and the wet snow continued. We all knew that it would soon be dark. We also knew that late in March, the snow would not last forever. Tomorrow might be warmer, but today it was a matter of life and death for the sheep.

"You girls come with me. I might need your help," Dad said.

While it was still daylight, Dad, Mary Elizabeth, and I took our blue, 1950 Chevrolet half- ton pickup truck and headed for the old Nelson place to check on our sheep. In a corner of Nelsons' yard under the trees was a newborn lamb, already standing, walking around, and nudging his mother, who had died giving birth.

Dad said, "We need to wrap him in blankets and take him home with us."

Mary Elizabeth and I held the shivering, little lamb close to our bodies as we rode home from the Nelsons hoping to keep him warm. "He'll be all right, won't he, Dad?" I begged for his assurance.

"I don't know for sure, but I am hoping that we found him in time," Dad answered not promising anything.

"We lost the ewe but brought home her lamb," Dad said to Grandma as we brought him right into our kitchen.

Once there, we put our lamb in another blanket and laid him on the door of our warm, open oven. All four of us watched him closely.

"I think we should name him Pee Wee," I suggested. They all agreed.

"Grandma!" I exclaimed. "I don't feel well."

"What's wrong, Pumpkin?"

"I have a stomachache, and my heart hurts," I cried. "Pee Wee lost his mama."

My crying turned into sobbing, tears flooding my eyes and running down my cheeks, and I couldn't stop no matter how hard I tried. My sobbing made Mary Elizabeth cry, and we let out our heartaches with tears as we snorted and blew our noses.

"I know it hurts but try to be glad for every minute you have on this earth, and never take anything, especially life, for granted," Grandma gently spoke while she put her arms around both of us and stroked our hair.

We all sat on the sofa where Grandma held us both in her arms for what seemed like a very long time until we quit crying. It was as though we had run out of tears.

I thought I understood what she meant. Mary Elizabeth and I felt the loss of our own mothers, and it hurt. It hurt so much.

Pee Wee was good that came out of a bad thing. As days passed, he was bottle fed, and he followed us around the yard wherever we went. Pee Wee grew, as did other lambs, and eventually joined the rest of the sheep. Life didn't stop but continued that spring day on the farm.

HANNAH PETERSON

The telephone rang two shorts and one long, and it was Grandma. "Pumpkin," she said. "Today is a good day to drive to the farm and visit my good friend, Hannah Peterson. She needs company. I'll be there soon."

Dad didn't care where I went as long as I was with Grandma and told him I was going. Besides, my life would never be boring with her around to take me places. I usually was willing to go with her at a moment's notice.

When Grandma drove into our yard, it was easy to see that she had come from the beauty shop. Her hair was freshly done. Her face was made up with rouge and lipstick. And she wore her best blue church dress, high heels, and a gold necklace.

"You look really nice, Grandma," I complimented her. "You look spiffy today."

"Thanks. I feel like I look good, too."

Why Grandma needed to dress up to visit Miss Peterson, I'll never figure out. There was nothing spiffy about Miss Peterson. She was just an old maid living by herself on her farm without running water.

As we drove to Miss Peterson's farm, Grandma pointed out the beautiful trees in the woods, the wildflowers in the ditches, the new green crops just coming out of the ground, and cows with new calves grazing in the pastures. She said, "Isn't this beautiful, Pumpkin? Isn't this beautiful?" Grandma had a way of seeing things I did not see.

Suddenly Grandma stopped the car. She quickly opened her car door, and said, "Come with me."

I followed Grandma to the side of the road and into the ditch of long grass and water that almost covered our shoes. She bent down and cupped a beautiful pink wild rose in her hands so she could enjoy its perfume as she inhaled deeply and smiled.

"Pumpkin," she said, "Smell these luscious wild roses, but be careful. Their stems have thorns. Wild roses are like life."

"What do you mean?" I asked. Grandma always had a different way of getting on a topic of conversation.

"Life is good at times, and other times it is quite difficult," she replied as she watched me gently hold the rose and smell its perfume. "If you are careful in life, you don't have to be stuck by the thorns."

I didn't understand anything that Grandma was trying to tell me. "May I pick one?" I asked.

"Let's leave them right here so others can enjoy them. They don't last long once they are picked."

Grandma and I walked back to her car and continued to Miss Peterson's. We rode quietly with the perfume of wild roses still in our noses.

The first thing we saw was Miss Peterson's red, well-kept barn and yard. The farmer who rented her land left his sheep there to graze in the barnyard. It was June, and there were dozens of little lambs playing in the pasture, running in circles after each other. It would be fun to quietly watch them play when Grandma and Miss Peterson visited.

Miss Peterson met us at the door, where she had stood and watched us drive her whole driveway into her yard and was happy to see us. One hundred percent Swedish, she greeted us in the strong accent she had never lost after years of living in America.

Immediately I felt the coolness of her house and felt good. It sat under the trees and had a second story that kept the rooms on the first floor comfortable. In her kitchen was an old wood stove that she used for cooking. By the sink was a red pump that stood out from everything else in the kitchen and caught my eye right away.

Miss Peterson's hair was gray and in a pug. Her face showed the wrinkles of aging. She was thin with small bones and slightly stooped over from what Grandma said was years of hard work on the farm. A large Roman nose stood out taking over her face, making her look like a perfect Halloween witch. Wearing thick, wire-rimmed glasses, she squinted over them whenever she looked at us, and she always cleared her throat before and after she spoke. "That's a habit she's had for years,' Grandma once told me.

Miss Peterson had dressed up for our visit in a blue and white, flowered house dress with a white apron, and she looked prim and proper and clean.

"Hannah usually uses a cane," Grandma also had told me.

Today there was not a cane anywhere in sight. Miss Peterson seemed to walk just fine.

"I made a little lunch for you and some Swedish coffee," she said.

"That's wonderful, Hannah," Grandma replied.

Miss Peterson always had *Kringla,* Swedish sweet bread made in the shape of the number eight, freshly made for visitors. With *Kringla*, she served butter and wild raspberry jam from raspberries she picked in her woods, and, of course, her strong, Swedish coffee. Grandma said nothing as I drank a cup of coffee with them while they caught up on the latest family and community news.

"You're looking well, Hannah," Grandma said. "Things must be pretty good for you now."

"I'm good. But it gets lonely sometimes out here by myself."

"I'll try to come more often," Grandma assured her before taking a sip of her coffee.

Miss Peterson turned to me and said, "Margaret, when you are old enough to get married, don't wait too long. You find a nice young man. Otherwise, you might end up like me." She continued as she squinted and looked at me and then at Grandma.

"Don't think I couldn't have married, though. I had many a young man ask me to dances." Then she readjusted her gray hair in her pug with an air of importance.

Horrified at the thought of getting married, I decided it was a strange thing to tell me. I almost choked on my *kringla*. "Why in the world is she telling me this? I'm only twelve years old," I thought but kept quiet.

I imagined Miss Peterson having fun at dances. Perhaps she danced the schottische, the polka, or a waltz or two. I could see young men asking her on dates, and it puzzled me that she never married and still lived alone.

Time passed quickly, and our visit seemed short. When it was over, Grandma thanked Miss Peterson for a wonderful day. In return she thanked us for coming.

We rode in silence for a while. Then I finally asked, "Grandma?"

"Yes? "

"Why didn't she ever get married?"

"She stayed at home to care for her parents," Grandma answered.

"Oh."

"In Hannah's day it was common for one of the children in the family to stay home and care for their parents. There was no other way. There are sacrifices we all make in life. This was Hannah's sacrifice."

I gained a ton of respect for Miss Peterson that day. She wasn't just an old maid living by herself that no one wanted.

I wondered if she was chosen to have this life by someone else or if she chose it herself. I somehow felt that
with the slight tone of regret in her voice, it was not her choice.

FOURTH OF JULY

It was a special Fourth of July. Grandma had organized a picnic for the whole family at Winding River State Park. "I want this picnic to be a regular old-fashioned picnic like the ones we used to have," she told everyone she invited, making suggestions for what they could bring for potluck.

Grandma and I left early in the morning to set up the picnic site. "We want to get there as soon as possible to find a barbeque pit near the swimming pool. You know how you kids love to swim," she said.

Once there, we walked down into the valley where the river flowed into the pool and out the other side. There were only a few people milling around so we found a good spot.

"Here's a shady spot under the trees. "This should work. Looks big enough for everyone," she said. Grandma expected a good turnout.

As we began putting several picnic tables together, an occasional firecracker went off. Several people walked by waving small American flags.

Family began to arrive. There were uncles, aunts, cousins, and more cousins. There were relatives we had not seen for years. "I'm so happy you came," Grandma said as she hugged and greeted everyone.

The women made lemonade and coffee and set up the food while they caught up on all the family news. Children quickly disappeared to change into swimming suits and jump into the pool. The men discussed everything from politics to sports to local and national news and President Eisenhower.

As I passed by them once, I overheard Uncle Bob tell Uncle Arnie, "Ike is a popular president."

"I think he is more popular than President Truman,"

Uncle Arnie replied.

"You just wait and see. I think Harry Truman will be one of our best," Uncle Bob answered.

I didn't stop to enter their conversation.   It was just like them to get into politics at family gatherings.

When my cousin, Joe, arrived, we headed straight for the diving board. We dived right to the muddy bottom, touching it with our hands and springing back to the surface of the water. When we came to the surface, we saw our old friend, a large turtle, resting on the nearby rocks. Sometimes he swam right beside us.

"Race you to the other side!" Joe challenged.

"Okay," I answered swimming as fast as I could.

"I'll never beat you, Joe. You have those long arms and legs. It's impossible."

"Guess why I want to race you all the time," he laughed.

We swam until we were called to eat. Time had flown by, and it was already noon.

The park was now full of people. Aunt Ruthie said, "Glad you came early so we have such a nice spot for our picnic, Katherine."

The sounds of "America the Beautiful" filled the air from the hill, covered with people as a church service began. At the shallow end of the pool, children screamed gleefully as they splashed in the water. There were celebrations everywhere as we lined up to eat.

After lunch, we waited an hour before our parents allowed us to swim. They said our food had to settle so we wouldn't get a cramp and drown. One hour seemed like a year when we sat only a few feet from the water. We kept asking, "How much longer, Grandma?"

The day was nearly over when Grandma announced, "There is one more thing we need to do to have an old-fashioned picnic. We need a softball game. When I was young, we never got together without a ball game."

Looking around the group and sizing everyone up,

Grandma said, "Joe and Pumpkin, you be captains and choose sides. We'll flip a coin to see which side is up first."

Cousins, aunts, and uncles were divided into sides and the game began. No one remembered who won, and no one cared. We were a family, bound together by blood as relatives, at an old-fashioned picnic, and it was wonderful. When our ball game was over, we gathered our belongings and shut down the picnic site, leaving it as neat and clean as we found it. The picnic was over, but our warm feelings would last.

On our way home I said, "I had fun."

"That is good, Pumpkin. I don't want you to ever forget your family."

"I won't, Grandma. I won't ever forget my family."

AFTERNOON WITH YANNI

Johnny Tollefson had to be the best-looking boy in our little community. He was tall for his age, slender, with the biggest, most beautiful blue eyes you have ever seen and a crown of curly blonde hair. I fell in love the minute I set eyes on him and so did all the other girls in our town. "He is so cute," the girls said as he walked by.

Grandma loved Yanni's parents, Ole and Emma Tollefson, second generation immigrants from Norway. They held on to old, Norwegian customs and a Norwegian brogue. For example, they never pronounced the letter **j** correctly. Instead of saying Johnny's name correctly in English, they called him "Yanni." Because of this, we also called him "Yanni," and to us he was Yanni Tollefson.

Classmates snickered when Yanni said **"*shickens*"** for **"*chickens*,"** but he quickly learned the correct way of saying his words. Someone would tell Yanni, "No, Yanni. It's *chickens*, not **shickens*.*"

His parents were like Grandma and felt the only way to improve one's status in life was to have a good education. Their goal for Yanni, since the day he was born, was graduation from the university, becoming someone important. Everyone in the community felt it would happen. It wasn't unusual to hear, "That Tollefson boy. You wait and see. He'll be important someday."

Yanni himself told me one day, "Pumpkin, I'm going to be a doctor. And a good one."

"I believe you, Yanni. I believe you'll be a doctor," I agreed.

Spending a day at the Tollefson farm with Yanni was an exciting experience. They had all kinds of animals. They had cattle, sheep, pigs, chickens, ducks and geese, a collie dog named

Pal, and, at least, a dozen kittens.

There was a huge, red barn with a hayloft where we played basketball when it was empty. Several yards away from the barn yard stood their huge three-story farmhouse with a first floor that was always cool when it was hot outside.

There was a path with hundreds of bluebells growing beside it, grain fields, and a woods, full of chokecherry and Juneberry trees. At the edge of the woods was Mrs. Tollefson's huge vegetable garden. Their farm had everything.

It was after lunch when Grandma and I arrived at the Tollefsons. Mrs. Tollefson met us at the kitchen door and greeted us, "*Gud dag*. How are you today then?"

Grandma hugged Mrs. Tollefson, "Just fine, Emma. Just fine. And how are you?"

"We're good," she answered.

"Thank you for the invitation. Pumpkin has been asking to visit Yanni before school starts."

She handed Mrs. Tollefson a bag of groceries. Grandma never went empty-handed to anyone's house.

The light-yellow kitchen was bright and smelled of bread baking. Mrs. Tollefson offered us a piece of fresh bread with butter and strawberry jam. It was still warm.

"Thank you, Emma. This is very good." Grandma smiled as she complimented her.

I felt good. Here I was eating in Yanni Tollefson's house. I wondered what my friends would think.

Yanni was riding his bicycle in the pasture when we arrived, but quickly rode back to their house when he saw Grandma's car. He entered the kitchen and asked, "Hi! Do you want to go for a walk?"

"We'll be back," he said to Mrs. Tollefson and Grandma as we went out the door.

We walked through the trees to the pasture and past his mother's huge, vegetable garden. We walked past the Juneberry and chokecherry trees. We picked wildflowers, bluebells and wild daisies. We smelled the wild roses, saw a garter snake slither across our path, and sidestepped an army of ants carrying food back to their hill.

"That's interesting," Yanni said. "The line of ants is so long, and each ant is carrying something. It's almost like they are getting ready for winter already."

We climbed the barbed wire fence into the pasture where cattle were grazing and walked until we reached the end of the farm, where we took a drink from the old flowing well. Then we headed back to Yanni's house.

"Are you ready for seventh grade?" I asked.

"Sure. Why not."

"I think I am ready. It'll be different."

"Sure will."

"Well, thanks for asking me to go for a walk."

"You're welcome. Thanks for coming."

"We're back!" Yanni announced as we presented his mother with a bouquet of wildflowers. "They're a little limp and wilted now but should freshen up in water."

"Thank you both," his mother said.

Grandma and Mrs. Tollefson were putting bread dough on a cookie sheet. They both said, "We have a surprise for you."

As we waited in the living room for supper, we talked about our walk and what we had seen along the way. I didn't mind that supper wasn't ready.

"I love your farm, Yanni. Wish our lives could always be as good as today."

"I love it, too, and I really did have fun on our walk."

Mrs. Tollefson finally called us for supper. We washed our hands and sat down at the table. When Grandma set our food on the table, she said, "This is pizza, made from a Chef Boyardee Pizza Mix in a box. It's spicy tomato sauce and cheese on bread dough. I hope you like it."

Pizza mix had just arrived in our world, and Grandma was one of the first to try it out. Mrs. Tollefson liked it, Grandma liked it, Yanni liked it, and I liked it. "This is different from anything else we had ever eaten," we decided.

"It is like something you'd get in the Big Apple," Yanni said.

"Big Apple?" I asked.

"The Big Apple is another name for New York City."

"Oh, I think you're right. It does taste like something you'd get in New York City," I agreed.

Pizza was almost better than the twenty-five cent hamburgers with ketchup and French Fries at Anderson's Café or the French fries that everyone made at home from their homegrown potatoes. We all wanted more.

That day the outside world quietly crept into our small community and into all of our lives. We not only wanted more pizza but more of the outside world. We didn't realize at that time that communication and transportation would continue to advance, and our world would become much larger. We didn't realize that our idealistic and innocent lives would continue to change. We didn't know that one day we'd wonder if the loss of innocence was worth it.

AUGUST

It seemed like just yesterday that the buses delivered everyone home on the last day of sixth grade. Summer had disappeared like a magician's magic rabbit, leaving us wondering where it had gone.

I felt it was too soon to go back to school even if the summer activities had slowed down and I needed something to do. Swimming lessons at Winding River Park were done. The county fair, where we represented our Valley Giants 4H Club, had been over for a month. And the Fourth of July sped by with our grand, family picnic. Summer Fest Day, with its long and unique parade, was over until next July. The school's band director, Mr. Wynd, was on vacation so there was no longer band practice. Mary Elizabeth had gone to visit her relatives down south. Thea had returned to the cities to prepare for her school year after visiting us for two weeks. Yanni was busy helping his father harvest their crops. Bridget's brothers and sisters were all home at different times during summer vacation, so I could not see her often either.

I told Grandma, "It's no fun preparing for seventh grade, junior high, without my friends. We need to go shopping together or something."

"Pumpkin, why don't you just enjoy these days instead of fretting them away?"

Grandma was right. August had its own pictures, sounds and smells. The hay fields had their own infinite smell of freshly mown alfalfa. Farmers were raking and stacking hay in 90-degree heat, sweat running down their brows, and their clothing soaking it all up. It was not hard to recognize the odor of hard work.

Golden wheat, swathed in perfect rows ready for the combine, was something to see. It was beautiful when wheat fields added a rich golden color to the greens of trees and grasses. The dust behind combines on sunny dry days filled the atmosphere, adding a misty-looking haze to everything.

After Summer Fest, farmers had no time for anything but work, work, and more work. Bringing in the harvest meant they would be able to farm another year and maybe buy something special for their families if there was anything left after all the bills were paid.

Yanni was invisible during harvest, but we had spent a lot of time together during the summer. We worked together at the county fair in the 4H booth for the Valley Giants. Yanni exhibited his pet lamb as a 4H project and won Grand Champion. Later in the fall, he and his pet lamb would take a trip to the State Fair in St. Paul hoping to win the state championship. It amazed me that Yanni had trained Stet so well that he behaved long enough to win anything. Pet lambs were known for being difficult and spoiled and not listening to direction.

"I'm so proud of Stet," Yanni often said.

Yanni and I also saw each other on Summer Fest Days and watched the parade together. Parades always began with the American Legion members marching with the United States, the Minnesota State, and American Legion flags. Then came Grandma, who was chosen Grand Marshall of the parade. She rode in a new, yellow and black, Chevrolet convertible, smiling and waving at the crowd as she passed. When she passed Yanni and me, she smiled and waved. "Hi to both of you," she said

Businesses, churches and other organizations were represented by floats in the parade. The little country church, where we attended Christmas Eve service, had a float with signs on both sides saying, "GOD LOVES YOU." Joe's Hardware Store had employees, dressed up as mechanics and carpenters, riding their float and throwing penny candy to the children along the street.

My second cousin, Madeline, Dairy Princess Candidate, rode on the Milk Producers float. It was covered with pastel yellow and blue crepe paper and had a sign in large black letters that identified her as our Dairy Princess. The crowd cheered and clapped with approval as she passed. The back of her float had another huge sign with large black lettering that said, "DRINK MILK, THE PERFECT FOOD."

Madeline was gorgeous in her strapless blue gown of satin and tulle over several crinoline petticoats making her skirt stand out full and wide emphasizing her tiny waistline. Recognizing us, Madeline waved and smiled at Yanni and me. "Hi, You Two," she said when she passed by us.

Turning to Yanni I sighed, "I hope I'm that beautiful someday. She looks like a movie star."

Yanni smiled and replied, "You will be. You know that don't you?"

The Summer Fest Parade was long gone, and all that was left was waiting for school to start. Sometimes this made August the longest month of the year.

It wasn't just the outside activities that identified the time of the year. Women were gathering produce from their gardens, picking berries in the woods, or buying lugs of fruit at the store to can for the long winter ahead of them. Kitchens everywhere smelled of sauce and pickles as pantries began to fill up with food.

Grandma and I went into the woods one day and picked chokecherries for jelly. There was a big crop, and when we returned, we cleaned the berries and cooked quart jars full of juice. Some juice we used to make jelly. The rest we left in jars in case there were no chokecherries next year.

"There is nothing tastier than fresh chokecherry jelly," Grandma said. "The reddish, purple jelly has a sweet and sour taste and makes me want to smile and pucker at the same time."

One day Mrs. Tollefson gave Grandma a chicken she'd butchered that morning. "We'll have a feast tonight," Grandma announced.

And we did. For supper, Grandma made fried chicken, creamed fresh peas from her garden, and boiled new potatoes. We also had pickled beets, bread and butter pickles, and fresh lettuce from the garden. We spread the fresh creamed peas like gravy on the new boiled potatoes. Dessert was vanilla ice cream with chokecherry syrup.

"Oh, yum, Grandma. That was absolutely yummy," I repeated as we did the dishes. "That was yummy!"

It was like Grandma's and my celebration meal before school began. "I don't know if I want be in seventh grade," I shared with Grandma while we were eating dinner.

"Why?"

"It's like. Like I have to be on my own."

"But, isn't that good, Pumpkin?"

"I guess so. But it's not that long until I will graduate from high school and leave home."

"You'll be ready by then. I know."

Knowing that the next six years would fly by just as fast as elementary school, I paid close attention to what was around me. It helped me love my family more and learn as much as I could from them. "I want to hang on to this life forever, Grandma. I never want to forget it."

"Am I ever glad of that! I'm glad you will have good memories."

MARGARET OLSON/ AKA PUMPKIN

Two weeks before the end of August, Norden High School scheduled class registration. In our community, junior high was part of the high school.

Up bright and early that day after spending the night in town at Grandma's, I was ready to go at 9AM to see my friends and register for seventh grade. There were no dress requirements for registering, so all of us were casual. I wore light green pedal pushers and a white short-sleeved blouse with white fabric tennis shoes that I had just polished. I thought they looked almost brand new.

"I'm on my way," I hollered to Grandma as I walked out the door.

"Good luck!" she answered.

It didn't take me long to walk to the schoolhouse where Bridget and Mary Elizabeth were waiting for me. "Ready for seventh grade?" I asked.

"Sure am," they both answered almost together.

We walked together to the lunchroom where we registered. There were a few students scattered throughout the room at different tables.

The classmates I'd already seen had grown during the summer and looked older. Most of them had tans like me. I guess we had made the best of summer sunshine.

Mr. Wynd was lining up people to be in the school band. All of us had fun talking about how appropriate the name Wynd was for a band teacher. He was just like the big bassoon he played, way over six feet tall and straight as a stick, "a tall drink of water," we thought. He was a hometown farm boy, who returned from the nearest teacher's college to teach in his old high school. He was talented, so they said.

Coach Jorgenson sat at a table eyeing every boy that walked through the door, looking for football players, and he ignored us. A hometown farmer's son, he went to the same nearby teacher's college as Mr. Wynd and returned to be coach of his old school. Round faced with a ruddy complexion, he was short and stocky with a potbelly. Coach was gruff, loud and commanding, often demanding, but managed to talk people into joining his teams.

Everyone watched as Yanni Tollefson entered. He was taller, blonder, filled out, and had a golden tan that made him look like a Norwegian god. Coach took giant strides over to Yanni to speak with him about joining the football team. We could hear him ask Yanni, "Are you trying out for the team this year? We sure could use someone like you."

It would have surprised me if Yanni said yes. He'd often told me, "I don't plan on playing football. It's too rough."

But with a sales pitch like Coach's, anything was possible. I couldn't wait to talk to Yanni.

Slowly, the registration line moved forward until I reached Mr. Wynd's table. Standing up and stooping way down to talk to me, he asked, "Margaret, do you plan to play flute in the junior high band this year?"

His saying my name Margaret took me by surprise, and I almost looked around to see if he was talking to someone else. Louise was my mother's first name. Margaret Louise Olson was my full name, but all my life everyone called me Pumpkin most of the time. Seldom did anyone call me Margaret.

The name "Margaret" smacked me in the face with the truth of entering a new part of life. It smacked of stepping out, growing up, and leaving secure places. I felt uncomfortable for a moment.

Jarred from my thoughts by his repeating Margaret, I looked up at him and softly said, "Yeah, sure. I will be in band with my flute." Then I walked to the next table.

Seventh grade Math, English, History, Music, Science,

Band, and Physical Education were the classes for which I registered. In addition we girls were also required to take a half year
of Home Economics to learn things like cooking, sewing, decorating a home, budgeting time and money, taking care of children, and becoming a good woman and housekeeper.

By the end of registration, my seventh-grade year was
planned except for one thing. I needed to speak with Mary Elizabeth and Bridget to see if they would try out for cheerleading
with me.

"Being popular is every girl's dream. Being popular and
cheerleader kind of go together," I had just told Grandma.

"Well, are we gonna do it?" I asked Mary Elizabeth and
Bridget. "Are we gonna try out for cheerleader this year?"

"Let's do it," they both said. "Let's get together and practice
today."

"It's all set then," I said. "Promise?"

"Promise," we said together.

With two weeks left before school began, there was still
time to buy a few new outfits for school and school supplies.
Grandma planned a day for us to go shopping. To my horror she
said, "We also need to get you a new brassiere. That old training
bra just doesn't work anymore. You're growing up, Margaret."

I was growing up. My body was changing fast along with
my feelings. I also noticed my friends were growing up. It was
just life, I guess, but discussing training bras, those ugly white
things, and buying brassieres with Grandma was embarrassing.
I cringed and thought, "Do you have to say brassiere so loud and
clear?"

Would I get used to being called Margaret all the time and
not Pumpkin --a name first given to me by Grandma and then
picked up by everyone else? To tell you the truth, being called
Pumpkin had begun to embarrass me. Not that the name Pumpkin was bad, but I was getting tired of it. And Margaret Louise
had a nice ring to it, a grown- up ring. Besides I loved the name
Louise, my mother's name.

Maybe my friends would call me Maggie. Yes, Maggie.

Going into seventh grade I would be known as Margaret Louise Olson, also known as Maggie. Yes, Maggie was a good name for seventh grade. When I told them, Bridget and Mary Elizabeth thought so, too.

I would look back fondly on 6th grade when I made my best friends. My trips with Grandma. My time with Yanni. It had been a wonderful year.

Most of all I vowed never to forget all the good people, whom I had just really met for the first time, from our small farm community who were part of my life. How could I? All of them, good and bad, had grown on me as I grew up there. They were part of me forever.

Forever.

"Agree to meet regularly until school starts so we know what we are doing?" I asked.

"Yes," we said.

We spent the next to the last day of summer vacation on our farm in the shade of our oak trees and made plans for our first day of seventh grade.

THE PROMISE

"We'll stick together as friends, won't we?" Bridget asked with a squeaky, worried tone to her voice.

"Of course, we'll all be friends," Mary Elizabeth reassured her.

"You bet we'll be friends," I confidently and adamantly promised.

"Cross our heart and hope to die friends?" Bridget asked.

"I cross my heart and hope to die," Mary Elizabeth answered.

"Me, too! I cross my heart and hope to die," I added.

"I cross my heart and hope to die, too," Bridget finished the whole thing.

"We are friends forever and ever," I said.

"Best friends forever," they both said at the same time.

"We'll stick by each other, defend each other, and help each other," I suggested as rules for our friendship. "We'll try out for the cheerleading squad together," I added.

Bridget and Mary Elizabeth nodded in agreement. It was all set.

All three of us knew in our heart that with each other this year would be better. For sure.

MARGARET INC

ALLISON BERG

"Your grandma's crazy, Margaret," Maynard Swenson informed me, as he cocked his head to the side with a nasty smirk on his face, "Everyone says so. The truth is that she's so loony she belongs in the loony bin." As if he hadn't said enough, he added, "And she runs with all the nobodies around here."

First, his words took me by surprise, even if he was one of my least favorite boys in Norden, and then they stung, stung like fire in my heart and gut. Anger welled up in my whole body, and I wanted to reach out and strangle the pipsqueak of an eighth-grade boy for interrupting our leisurely walk with his nasty, mean words.

"Is not true," I snapped back, stepping closer, feeling like smacking him squarely across his smart mouth. "It's a lie! Say it's a lie and not true," I demanded.

His next few words stung worse than stepping barefoot on a bumblebee. "Is *too* true! She's nuttier than a hundred Christmas fruitcakes. And you also run around with all the nobodies in town."

I took one step towards Maynard, but suddenly felt someone grab my arm and hang on to me until I winced from fingernails that cut deep into my skin. "Let's go!" Mary Elizabeth ordered. "Let's get out of here before something worse happens." And she dragged me right off the street into her parents' restaurant with its shiny chrome tables and chairs with their red tops that shone under the cheerful, bright light of sunshine streaming through the windows.

During supper that night I studied Grandma's face. It was obvious that she was getting older. There was more gray hair surrounding her temples, and there were more crow's feet around her eyes and more lines around her mouth, getting deep as furrows it seemed. "Life hasn't been easy for you, has it Grandma," I said.

"Why do you say that?" she asked.

"Just thinking," I answered trying to change the subject.

For days, Mary Elizabeth and I spent hours going over the incident with Maynard in our minds and in conversations. I started the questioning with, "Who? Who makes up these lies? And who spreads them? Don't they know that it doesn't only hurt Grandma but us, too?"

"They don't care. That's all I can say."

I continued, "Why? Why are they saying such horrible things about you, about Grandma, about me?"

"Don't know," she answered deep in thought. "Don't know. You know your grandma isn't crazy. They could be jealous of her, that's all. You're not used to it, but I am," she added as an afterthought. "They don't look down on you. I know I'm different, Maggie. I'm not one of them. I'm used to hate."

Hearing her say that made me shiver. "But they don't know you," I said.

Mary Elizabeth replied, "It doesn't matter."

"You think too old for your age," I said. "Is this why you know so much?"

Mary Elizabeth looked at me and quietly said, "Been there already."

I wanted to vomit and get rid of the thought. I felt the same way that day in front of Andersons' Café where we had just been insulted.

Mary Elizabeth, seeing the anguished look on my face, knew what she just said hurt me. My beautiful friend with her caramel-colored skin and dark curls had seen and experienced more already than I probably would in a whole lifetime.

By the time school started, I was happy we had gotten over discussing Maynard Swenson. As planned, Bridget, Mary Elizabeth and I met on the front steps of the school. It was a sunny and beautiful, perfect day to begin seventh grade at Norden Junior High, and we all were in a good mood.

"Aren't we cute dressed alike?" I said, proudly swirling my skirt as I smiled and winked at my two best friends.

"Yeah," Bridget chimed in. "We look great."

To dress alike was our plan. We would wear our short-sleeved white blouses, plain-colored circle skirts, and white bobby socks with black and white saddle shoes. My skirt was red, Bridget's was blue, and Mary Elizabeth's was green, and our ponytails would be held together by ribbons that matched our skirts.

I turned to Mary Elizabeth commenting, "You have the curliest, bushiest ponytail I have ever seen in my life."

"These tight curls of mine aren't easy to tame," she replied. "But I tried."

Bridget, whose mousey brown hair was as straight as Mary Elizabeth's was curly, chimed in, "I think your ponytail is cute. You know, really cute!"

My reddish blonde hair wasn't curly or straight. Grandma once suggested, "Why don't you wear bangs? I bet you'd look good in them." Now, I wore them all the time. Today I had a ponytail with bangs.

Side by side, arm in arm, we walked all the way to math class; taller, more grown up, somewhat clumsy and awkward, but ready for anything. At least that's what I thought until Bridget blurted out, "Geez, Margaret, I'm scared. I have butter-flies. Never been with high schoolers before."

Then Mary Elizabeth said, "It'll be different, that's for sure. Different." She even sounded uneasy.

"Seems like yesterday we began sixth grade. Now look where we are," I said, changing the subject and trying to be more positive.

We mingled with students from seventh to twelfth grade as we headed to our lockers, trying to look inconspicuous. Despite our effort, it was easy to spot us. Our lack of self-assurance and confidence showed.

I said, "We must look silly and naïve to upperclassmen."

I'd seen them cover their mouths and snicker. "Well, I

guess they let anyone in here," a ninth grader shouted from across the hall.

I lost even more confidence. "I hate sticking out like a sore thumb, looking lost and dumb," I said under my breath.

Grandma had warned me, "Everyone else before you has gone through the same thing. Maybe you'll be kinder to the seventh graders next year."

Despite everything, I felt a new freedom that made the moment somewhat bearable. All I had to do was accept and enjoy everything that was new, but it was easier said than done. I wanted to be in eighth grade and skip today.

Math was in our home room. We chose desks beside each other, but Mr. White, our teacher and class advisor, had his own ideas and assigned us seats in alphabetical order. I sat close to Bridget, but Mary Elizabeth was way up in front.

Mr. White was assigning books when a tall, slender girl with long shiny blonde hair and bright blue eyes walked in the room, hips swaying like Marilyn Monroe, right up to Mr. White. "I'm sorry I'm late," she apologized and then smiled at him. "My name is Allison Berg, and I am attending school here this year."

I turned to Bridget and whispered, "She sounds like Marilyn Monroe with that raspy, breathy voice."

Bridget nodded.

"Where'd she come from?" Whispers were heard coming from all around the room.

I wasn't the only one who looked at Allison Berg over head to toe. She was wearing a red sweater with a straight gray skirt that had a kick pleat. Her smile showed white, straight, and shiny teeth, and she had a golden tan as if she had spent the summer on a beach.

Mr. White introduced her almost immediately as if he wanted to head off all the misleading thoughts flying around the room. "This is your new classmate, Allison," he said.

"She is Mr. and Mrs. Berg's niece and is spending this year with them."

Allison said "Hi" to us as everyone glanced at each other

with stunned, surprised looks. I nudged Bridget and whispered, "She looks way too old to be in seventh grade, don't you think?"

Bridget agreed. She always agreed with me.

Mr. White showed Allison her seat close to Mary Elizabeth at the front of the room. It was obvious that he knew she was coming because he had left a place for her, where she sat down, placing her pencils and notebooks on top of the desk, and prepared for class to begin.

That is how Allison Berg came to our class in Norden, Minnesota. No one knew why she came or where she came from. All we knew was that we had never seen such a sexy person ever walk the halls of our school or the streets of our town. And we had a whole year to get to know her as a person.

"I think that we should go around the room and tell everyone what we did over summer vacation," Mr. White suggested.

Bridget told the class, "I spent most of the summer in our cabin in the woods. Also visited with some of my brothers and sisters, who took turns coming home. Oh, and I practiced violin every day. My dad was my teacher." She smiled and added, "Sometimes I got to town and saw Mary Elizabeth and Maggie. And sometimes went swimming with them at Winding River Park."

Mary Elizabeth said, "I mostly spent the summer helping my parents in our restaurant. Sometimes I went swimming, played softball or basketball, and visited Maggie at the farm. Maggie, Bridget, and I went to the county fair. It was fun."

I know that once during the summer the Andersons went to Alabama, but she didn't mention their trip. I wondered why.

Yanni Tollefson shared, "I won Grand Champion with my pet lamb at the county and state fairs. I worked in the fields for my dad. Did some exercising for football and basketball and practiced shooting baskets in our barn loft before haying time. Maggie, Mary Elizabeth, and I were on the 4-H softball team, but we didn't win many games. I also went swimming."

"Sounds important, that Yanni," I thought. I was ready to whisper that to Bridget when Allison Berg caught my eye again.

With a face full of confidence and poise, with her eyes sparkling and a smile on her face, she watched closely as Yanni spoke. It was easy to see that she already liked him.

It was Allison's turn to introduce herself and tell about her summer. We all sat wide-eyed, attentive, and waiting.

"I spent the summer taking singing lessons," she said. Then she added, "I can't wait to get to know all of you. I always wanted to attend a small school like this. That is why I came to stay with my aunt and uncle."

By the time everyone in our class was done with introductions, including mine, which I totally have forgotten, the bell rang, and it was time for science class with Miss Helgeson. As we walked down the hall, we were quieter than before school started. Bridget, Mary Elizabeth and I barely said one word to each other until I bent down and whispered to them, "Well, what do you think of her?"

Both replied, "Don't know."

"I think she already has a crush on Yanni," I said and turned to Mary Elizabeth adding, "It's not like last year when you first walked into our classroom. We were best friends, like sisters, right away. I wonder how she's going to change things. I don't like her."

"You sound worried, Maggie," Mary Elizabeth said. "Don't think you have to worry about Yanni, do you? He really likes you."

Bridget added, "Ya, Maggie, he likes you a lot."

Between classes the school halls were bouncing with sounds of students talking, locker doors slamming, books slapping, and hundreds of feet shuffling to another room for the next hour and a different teacher. Seventh grade was systematic and regular with each day scheduled in the same order as the previous day. A never-changing schedule set to a clock.

After school, Grandma came out to the farm to visit Dad and me. I told her about Allison. "I don't like the new girl in our class. You know, the one staying with the Bergs? She's their niece."

"Why?" she asked.

"I don't know," I answered, not wanting to admit that maybe one reason was that she was gorgeous, and I didn't want Yanni to have any ideas about her. I didn't want to admit that I had never met anyone my age with so much maturity, confidence, and exposure to culture. She stood out from everyone else. I didn't want to let Grandma, who always stressed not judging others, know that I wished Allison Berg had never come to our town and that I was so insecure and small.

"Give it some time," Grandma added. "By the end of the year, you'll probably be good friends."

I doubted that would ever happen. It was as though I had just met my archrival. Besides, other girls had reasons of their own for not liking Allison Berg. They didn't want her looking at their boyfriends either. I doubted there was a boy in our town or for miles around that wouldn't some time have a crush on Allison. When she walked down the hall or the street after school, there was a loud wolf whistle coming from somewhere.

"Did you see that, Mary Elizabeth and Bridget? I asked. "Yanni turned his head when she passed."

Yes, even Yanni couldn't help but turn his head. She walked as if she were deliberately wiggling her hips for attention. And as the days passed, Allison became a force that all of us girls had to reckon with. She was the competition. *The most unwanted, number one, enemy.*

Grandma went back home that night. Dad and I had a good time together as we sat reading in our living room until bedtime. He liked to have me home on special nights such as the first day of school, birthdays, and holidays. Otherwise, he didn't mind if I stayed at Grandma's.

"It's nine o'clock, Margaret, and time for bed. The bus comes early," Dad gently reminded me and kissed me on the forehead.

Getting dressed for bed, I stopped for a minute to look out the window at the sky with its millions of shining stars and its huge, bright moon. I said, "I wish you were here, Mom. If you were here, you'd know exactly how to deal with the likes of Allison Berg."

My beautiful mother was gracious and had younger ideas. "Grandma just wants people to get along and accept each other, no matter what, so that there will always be peace," I continued out loud.

Mother had died when I was nine years old, and I missed her. I hoped and prayed that she was watching over me every day as I went through my life, especially now, today, this seventh-grade year.

She would have never embarrassed me like Grandma when we went to the clothing store in Winding River. Grandma just walked into the women's section and announced to the clerk in what I thought was the loudest, matter-of-fact voice I'd ever heard, "This young lady needs a fitting for a new brassiere."

I hate the word brassiere, Mom, and I could have died right then and there. I could hardly wait to leave the store," I said as if my mother was in the room with me.

The rest of the time Grandma and the clerk picked out what they thought I should have without asking my opinion. I thought everything they chose looked too childish. After meeting Allison Berg, I knew they were too childish. They were not at all like the clothes she wore.

"I'll never go back to that store, Mom," I vowed as I pulled down the covers, crawled into my soft bed and shut off the bed lamp. As I lay my head on my down pillow and closed my eyes, I continued my thoughts of Mother, Grandma, the first day of seventh grade and, of course, Allison Berg until I fell asleep.

"God, is it possible to grow up without a mother?" I asked. "I hope so cause if it isn't, I'm doomed and will never speak to you again."

HOMECOMING DAY

September! Wonderful, beautiful September! It remained sunny and around seventy degrees all month, perfect for harvesting as farmers steadily worked in the fields without rain to stop them or ruin their crops. Gradually all the landscape became black, as the tractors and plows turned over the stubble and straw left in the fields from grain harvest into straight furrows. Only potato harvest would be left when the weather cooled around the first of October.

It wasn't only the farmers who enjoyed the sunny days and warm weather. Getting up early and waiting for the school bus was much nicer than standing and freezing in the rain. Football fans loved nice afternoons that made the Norden Warriors' football games more enjoyable to watch.

Cheerleading tryouts were at the end of the first week of school since Homecoming Day was the Friday of the second week leaving only four days to practice. "Aren't you glad we practiced all summer?" I asked Bridget and Mary Elizabeth.

Didn't know it would come this fast," answered Bridget.

"Hope we're good enough to make it this year," added Mary Elizabeth.

Most of sixth grade, we talked about trying out for Junior Varsity Cheerleader. I don't know if any of us thought we would actually win against eighth and ninth graders, but the first day of school we signed up for tryouts. The night before we had our parents give us permission.

After school the next day, we all met at Grandma's house to make plans and practice. Bridget and I would spend the night there so Grandma wouldn't have to drive through the woods in the dark to the Jennewein cabin.

For tryouts we planned to dress in the same outfits we wore

on the first day of school. "That way we'll look like a team," I told them.

"Maggie," Mary Elizabeth asked. "Do you know who else is trying out from our class?"

"No, who?" I replied to the question.

"Allison Berg," she replied. "I heard some eighth graders talking in our restaurant yesterday."

Bridget and I gasped at the same time. No one said anything right away, but I think we all wondered how any of us could compete against slim, graceful, Allison. If anyone from our class made the cheerleading squad, it would be her.

"We're in trouble," Bridget finally said.

"Yeah, big trouble for sure," Mary Elizabeth agreed.

"We've signed up already," I said. "So we have to go through with it."

Friday afternoon came, and I was happy the anticipation and worry would soon be over. Bridget, Mary Elizabeth, and I were first. With me in the middle, since I was the tallest, we ran out to the middle of the gymnasium facing the whole junior high student body and began to cheer.

Bridget to my right began, **"GIVE ME AN N! GIVE ME AN O!"** and went down on one knee.

Then Mary Elizabeth to my left followed, **"GIVE ME AN R! GIVE ME A D!"** and went down on one knee.

Then it was my turn. **"GIVE ME AN *E*! GIVE ME AN N!"** and I went down on one knee.

Jumping up together, we cheered, **"NORDEN! NORDEN! NORDEN!"** Our cheerleading tryout was over.

We watched Allison Berg, the eighth graders, and ninth graders try out, hoping we were good enough to make it. "Allison Berg was good," I said to Mary Elizabeth and Bridget. "In fact, she was really good."

When the results came in, none of us had made cheerleading squad... none of us except Allison Berg, the only seventh grader chosen. Quiet and dejected, we left the gymnasium that day to go home. We wondered if the whole thing was worth it.

The student body of junior high had voted, and we had lost.

Bridget said, "I'm never doing this again."

"Me either," added Mary Elizabeth.

"I'm going to have to wait and see," I said.

Since there were other pressing things to do for homecoming festivities, we couldn't dwell on cheerleading. By the weekend, each class would begin planning and decorating a float to enter in the parade on Friday before the big game. We also would elect a homecoming queen from two candidates chosen by and from the senior class.

Mr. White told us that he expected help over the weekend and every day next week to "plan and create our float entry." Mr. Wynd, our band director, had us marching during band practice so that we would impress the community when we marched in the parade.

"Make sure your white shoes are polished and shiny, your white gloves are spotless, and your uniforms aren't wrinkled," he instructed us preparing for the first big band performance of the year.

All our spare time for the next week was spent on Homecoming. We built a float on Yanni's father's hayrack using purple and gold steamers and an old, decorated barrel. We stuffed a homemade cloth tiger and made it look bruised and beaten and placed it in the barrel labeled *"TRASH"* in the center of the hayrack. We nailed signs on the side of the float that said in huge purple and gold letters, *"TRASH THE TIGERS!"* Seventh grade football players, including Yanni, would ride the float. His dad volunteered to pull it with his John Deere tractor. When we were finished, we thought we had created the most impressive float in the whole school.

Mr. White complimented us, "You seventh graders have done a superb job. I won't be surprised if you take first place. I am proud of you and your hard work."

Homecoming Day came, and we were glad it was warm and sunny. All morning our thoughts weren't on class, and the time dragged by slowly as all of us wished to be somewhere else. Finally the bell rang for lunch, and some of us had to run and dress in band uniforms to march behind the queen's float, that was mostly white with purple and gold crepe paper flowers.

Queen Janna Erickson, chosen from the two senior class contestants, sat a few feet higher on the float than her princesses, one senior, two juniors, and two sophomores. It was easy to see why she won because she looked like a queen with her bright red hair, green eyes, and beautiful smile. She wore a white strapless taffeta gown covered with white tulle, decorated with tiny red ribbon roses, and long white gloves. In her arms was a bouquet of red roses, and on her head was the queen's rhinestone tiara that shone above her long, shiny hair. There were nods of approval by spectators along the way as she waved and smiled at them. Everyone knew Janna was not only beautiful, talented, and smart, but she was a gracious person. The school had chosen well when they voted her for homecoming queen.

Behind the queen's float was our band keeping in step to John Phillip Sousa marches and songs like "Hold That Tiger." While I played my flute and marched, I tried to sometimes look sideways to see what the people on the sidewalks thought of us. We marched and played from the school, all the way down Main Street, until we reached the football field.

It was there Mr. Wynd complimented us on our performance saying he was sure that we were received well. "Great job, band members. Great job! The community liked you."

We trashed the Tigers that day. The final score was 31-0. Our team did nothing wrong. They did nothing right. They were skunked and went home a few inches shorter in pride and confidence than when they came.

There would be other homecoming games and other parades, but this homecoming day was special. It was the first in which we took part as seventh graders, the first in which we were made to feel a part of our school. The best part of all was that our seventh-grade float won first prize, making homecoming for us even more special. We were involved from beginning to end and would not forget it in a million years.

After the game I stopped at Grandma's house. Dad was working in the fields, and Grandma planned to take me home.

"I really like Junior High, Grandma," I said and meant it.

"I'm glad, Maggie."

"Janna was a beautiful queen. She's nice, too."

"She sure was. And she sure is. Now you know where you get some of your looks," Grandma added.

"Thanks," I answered. Janna was my mother's cousin's daughter.

"I just wish we had made cheerleader. Don't know if I'll ever try again."

"Just wait and see. You might."

"Maybe." I kept the option open but doubted that I would ever try again.

We were so busy all homecoming week that none of us had time to think. Now that the big game was over, I had time to think about not making cheerleader. It hurt especially that Allison Berg was chosen. When you are thirteen, it is hard to understand that there is something in life that each one of us can do. Cheerleader probably was not something for me.

And I worried. I worried that I just wasn't as pretty as Allison Berg and never would be.

OCTOBER GOLD

Beautiful September was gone. Indian summer had come and gone with it. An early, overnight October frost had moved in making the air cool and crisp. Soon the trees turned gold and red before they fell and left everything barren for winter.

"This is my favorite time of the year," I told Grandma. "Days are beautiful, and nights are cool."

The fall rains hadn't begun yet. It was almost perfect, and deep inside of me I always felt a promise and anticipation of winter's quieter times.

There still were things to do. There was potato harvest, for example, since potatoes couldn't be dug when days were hot.

Dad always had a potato crew, including high school students, who were let out of school for six weeks to help with the harvest each year. The potato crew dug, picked, and hauled his potatoes.

For me, it was fun running up and down the rows that were already dug and talking to the women who were picking and putting potatoes into wire bushel baskets. When their baskets were full, they dumped the potatoes into gunny sacks. Behind them was a row of filled sacks six feet apart for the haulers to come and lift onto the truck as it slowly made its way along the rows.

Dad knew the crop was good before harvest, but when he saw how close together the filled sacks were, he smiled and said, "The potato crop is exceptionally good."

Most of the women pickers were working for Christmas money. They tied their hair up with a kerchief like Aunt Jemima on the syrup bottle and wore warm clothing that included long pants of some kind, usually blue jeans, a good pair of canvas gloves, and a gunny sack, ends attached by a metal hook, around their waists. On their backs, over this gunny sack, they layered several other sacks so that they had them to fill as they picked.

"That looks heavy," I thought as I watched them bent over picking potatoes as fast as they could.

Not running out of sacks was especially important this year with the bountiful crop. If they ran out, they'd either have to wait until the trucks came to drop some off or run to the end of the row. Either way it would take too much precious time because they were paid by the number of sacks they filled.

The soil was sandy and easy on my bare feet as I moved down the rows making conversation. Mrs. Eva Jennewein, Bridget's mother, and her friend from town, Mrs. Anna Gunderson, picked together. I wished, as I approached them, that Bridget had taken the bus home with me. She could have ridden home with her mother.

"Bridget should have come home with me today," was the first thing I said to Mrs. Jennewein. "May she can come with you and spend Saturday with me?"

"Of course, Maggie. I'll tell her when I get home."

I felt bad that Mrs. Jennewein was out in our potato field working so hard. Yet, I knew why she was there. Her husband, Charles Jennewein, had been ill the past few months, and they especially needed extra money this year if they wanted to have any Christmas at all. "This job gets easier every day, especially when the muscle stiffness wears off," she turned to me and said as if she read my mind. "Only thing is by the time that happens, we are done. By the way, did Bridget tell you that David is coming home for a visit next week?"

"No," I answered. I had never met David Jennewein, their oldest son. He quit school and left home at age sixteen before Bridget and I were born and must be way over thirty years old by now or close to it. Bridget once told me that he worked in potato harvest the fall he left and bought a one-way ticket to New York.

"We got a letter from him two days ago. He says that he has some business to take care of here. Have no idea what it is." There was definitely a puzzled look on her face. "He rarely comes back here. Says he's flying to Minneapolis and driving up here from there."

Saturday came, and Bridget spent the day with me in the potato field running up and down the rows visiting with all the workers and stopping to help fill potato baskets. This would be the last day of harvest, giving winter permission to come if it chose.

All Bridget talked about was David. It had been a long time since she had seen him. "It seems that he has made a name for himself producing rock and roll records in New York. My parents say he always liked music and was musical."

Listening to Bridget, I could hardly wait to meet David. "I wonder what unfinished business he has in Norden," I thought.

"I can't wait to meet him, Bridget," I said really meaning it. The thought of David Jennewein intrigued me. He had left Norden because of the difficulty and rejection living in a small community that looked down on his family and him. Now he would impress everyone if they knew he had become successful.

We were in school when David drove into town. He was a sight to behold when he stopped at the grocery store for a package of gum. Standing over six feet tall, he was handsome, tan and muscular with curly black hair and deep brown eyes.

He wore the latest style, a gray, single- breasted Ivy League suit with cuffed pants, a starched white shirt, a striped black and gray tie, and shiny black penny loafers. To complete his Wall Street look, he wore a gray felt hat.

As he exited his brand-new blue and white Chevrolet sedan with white wall tires and walked down Main Street, everyone turned to look at him. "Who's that?" they asked each other. No one knew who he was.

"I'm David Jennewein," he told Mr. Johnson, who owned the General Store. I'm here to visit my parents and little sister."

Mr. Johnson was speechless at first but managed to reach out his hand and introduce himself. "I'm Thomas Johnson. Glad to meet you."

The two of them made small talk for a while. They talked

about the good harvest, the beautiful weather, and the good potato crop. They talked about the school with its exceptional football team. They talked about David's father, who had been ill, one of the reasons he had come back to town. Then David politely said, "Excuse me, Sir, but I have to go now and pick up my sister Bridget, so she won't have to take the long bus ride home."

David left the store and drove to the school, where he waited on the front steps for Bridget and watched the students, especially the girls, look at him and pass him in awe. "Who's that gorgeous creature?" senior high girls were saying and not watching where they walked so they almost stumbled off the edge of the sidewalk.

David was standing by the front steps when Bridget, Mary Elizabeth, and I came out together. "Hi," he said. "How'd you like a ride home?" Then Bridget and David hugged as we stood looking at them, especially the tall, dark, and handsome man, who was our best friend's brother.

"David, these are my two best friends, Maggie Olson and Mary Elizabeth Anderson. Maggie and Mary Elizabeth, this is my brother David," Bridget gracefully said as she introduced us.

Speechless, I finally got out, "Pleased to meet you."

"Are you ready?" he asked Bridget. "I'm anxious to see the folks."

"Yes, let's go," she answered. They said goodbye and something about seeing us later as they turned and walked toward his car.

Mary Elizabeth and I, wishing we could have gone with them, decided that in our lifetime we had never met anyone as charming and good-looking as David Jennewein. I hated to get on the bus and leave amidst all the questions coming from everywhere and everyone around us. News and gossip travel fast in a small town. By the next morning everyone was talking about him.

David had come back to look for a lot on which he could build his parents a big, beautiful new house with a basement. It would be one-story with two bathrooms and a brand-new furnace, four bedrooms, and a music room where Mr. Jennewein and Bridget could play their violins. He would leave the new car, which he bought in the cities with them, take the train to Minneapolis, and fly back to New York. His unfinished business was to begin the building project before he left, if the weather cooperated, and come back when it was all finished to help them move into town. Everyone said that the Jenneweins probably wouldn't be able to move into their new house until spring because it was already October, even if David Jennewein had hired the largest building crew in the area to get the job done quickly.

I stayed overnight with Grandma the day David left. After supper, we sat on the couch discussing the Jenneweins and the good fortune that had come to their family. Grandma said, "There is justice in this world, Maggie. David left Norden and found a life in New York. He's a good boy, too. Willing to share and help his parents. They must be very proud of him."

Even if I was only in seventh grade, I knew, and so did all my classmates, what a struggle it was for Bridget to be accepted. She was looked down upon by others just because she was poor. It didn't seem to impress anyone that she had brains and talent. "I'm so proud of him, too, Grandma, and happy for all of them. Can't wait until they live in town."

Grandma looked at me and added, "It shouldn't be this way, but you will learn in life that money talks. You will see the Jenneweins will be treated differently from this day on."

Each day in home economics class we were updated by Bridget on the progress of their new house. They had the house on its basement foundation and enclosed before the cold weather set in and they were working inside now. "We'll have to paint the outside in the spring," she said. "We're planning to paint it gold with white trim."

It was easy to converse in class when we were sewing. Each of us was sewing a straight, lined, wool skirt with a kick pleat and a zipper. It was when we laid our patterns, pinned, cut, and sewed that we talked to each other. It was an ideal place to share and catch up on news and the latest gossip.

All of our skirts were the same color and the same material. Miss Wilson had found bolts of surplus Army green wool, and each of us was given enough to make a skirt. When we were done, every girl in junior and senior high had a lined straight, Army green, wool skirt with a kick pleat. And each of the skirts ended up in a pile in the girls' locker room, only used if someone came to school in slacks and was told by her teacher to leave class and find a skirt. Even if those Army green skirts were never used, every girl in our school knew how to use a pattern and sew one.

"Someday I'm running for school board in this town," Grandma almost threatened. "I think not allowing girls to wear slacks to school is a very stupid rule." I knew she meant it, too. She did not like to be told what to do. "It's too cold in this neck of the woods for a rule like that." It was rare to see a woman in pants, but lately Grandma was wearing them more often. Sometimes she'd even be seen wearing blue jeans, the Levi brand bought at Johnsons' store.

As October passed, the golden and red leaves dried up and fell. Harvest was complete for the year. Football season was over. Halloween would soon be here, along with the town talent show, which Bridget and her dad Mr. Charles Jennewein planned to enter as a violin duet. Mary Elizabeth and I were asked by Mr. Wynd if we would enter with a flute duet, but we didn't want to compete with Bridget, as if we could have competed with her anyway.

The night of the talent show, Dad, Grandma, and I were anxiously waiting to hear them play before the townspeople, who would be stunned by the talent that they were unaware of in their midst. The Jenneweins were good, but Grandma and I were the only ones who knew how good. Sad to say, we were the only ones who had ever heard them play in all the years they had lived in Norden.

"We've practiced for weeks now. We'll be ready for the talent show," Bridget told Mary Elizabeth and me. "It'll be our debut into Norden society," she laughed.

I loved her subtle sense of humor. "I can hardly wait," I replied.

"Oh," she added. "We're playing the same songs Dad played for you and your grandma last Thanksgiving at our house."

Allison was also practicing her vocal solo for the competition. It was well known that she felt she would win the talent contest hands down, which irritated everyone. Her bragging made her more unpopular as time passed.

For the rest of us, this truly was a golden October. Because of the potato crop, "we'll make money this year." At least that's what my dad said.

When David Jennewein showed up and began building a new house for his parents, everyone seemed impressed by this extraordinary young man and his consideration for his family. His good fortune took priority in town conversation, not the good harvest.

For the Jenneweins, however, it was the talent contest that would leave the greatest impression on the town. The night before Halloween, the high school auditorium was filled with people who came to see the show, one of the best-attended events in town every year. Decorated with orange and black crepe paper streamers and jack-o-lantern décor, the auditorium and the huge, enthusiastic crowd, who felt this was a much better way to observe Halloween than playing pranks on friends and neighbors, created a feeling of festivity in everyone.

Grandma, Dad, Mrs. Jennewein, and I arrived early and sat together. Mr. Jennewein and Bridget were in the music room tuning their violins.

It was easy to tell that Mrs. Jennewein was nervous and fidgety waiting for their performance. Grandma patted her shoulder and said, "You know they are good, Eva. Just relax and let them show the community how good."

It finally was Mr. Jennewein and Bridget's turn, and their duet was introduced. Mr. Jennewein looked so small on stage. It seemed that Charles Jennewein had shrunk more in size the past year and looked paler and older. His months of sickness showed.

It was just the opposite for Bridget. She had grown several inches, had color in her cheeks, and dressed much nicer than last year. When he was home, David had taken her to the best store in Winding River and bought her several new outfits. Tonight she wore a black jumper and a long-sleeved white blouse. She also had her hair in a ponytail. I turned to Grandma and said, "Wow! Doesn't she look beautiful?"

"Sure does."

Mr. Jennewein introduced their number by saying, "Tonight Bridget and I are going to perform "The Orange Blossom Special" for you."

They began perfectly in tune, each taking turns to play it faster and faster and faster until it was impossible for them to play any faster. People sat stunned in awe of their performance and how much fun the two of them had playing. When they finished, the audience stood up and cheered and clapped and cheered and clapped some more. Finally, the applause ended when they agreed to do an encore, "The Vienna Waltz" while all the stoic Scandinavians in the room, probably one hundred percent of the people, swayed to the music.

They won first place, beating Allison Berg's mediocre vocal solo. The gold ribbon and a fifty-dollar prize belonged to Mr. Jennewein and Bridget along with more admiration and respect from the community than they had in a lifetime.

"Our friend Bridget made us all proud tonight," Grandma said. "She has grown miles in poise and self-confidence over the past year." Then she added, "Partly because of you, Maggie,"

"Do you think so?"

"A good friend never hurt anyone. You know that there is more strength in two standing together than in one standing alone. Do you believe that, Maggie?" she asked.

"I have begun to believe it. A year ago, Bridget was a mousey, little shy person and part of the woodwork. Nobody noticed her in a positive way," I replied.

It was true. The Jenneweins were finally known as a family of worth. Soon they would be living in a brand-new home in town and would be able to adorn their fireplace with their gold ribbon. October was a golden month for them, too.

BLACK AND WHITE AND GRAY

The day after Halloween, Dad left for the School of Agriculture at the University of Minnesota's St. Paul Campus to take a two-week farming course, and I would stay with Grandma until he returned. Of course, Grandma was more than willing to let me spend time with her, and she also said I could have Mary Elizabeth over at her house whenever we chose.

It did not take long for us to ask Mary Elizabeth's parents for permission. My first day at Grandma's house Mary Elizabeth came with me after school to watch "American Bandstand" with Dick Clark on Grandma's new black and white television set in her living room.

For the first time we saw our music stars perform as if we were actually there. We danced, rocking and rolling, on an oval brown and tan braided rug as we listened to songs like "All I Have To Do Is Dream," by the Everly Brothers or "That'll Be the Day" by Buddy Holly. There was Elvis Presley's "Don't" and Laurie London's "He's Got the Whole World in His Hands." We watched closely to every move made by the dancers until we danced exactly like they did.

With the television antenna standing high on Grandma's rooftop, reception was good, and we watched "The Mickey Mouse Club" starring a darling little Mouseketeer, Annette Funicello, and wished that we were she. Sometimes we watched "The Howdy Doody Show" and Buffalo Bob, although we wouldn't admit it, thinking it too juvenile for us.

After supper, we watched programs such as "Wagon Train," "Leave it to Beaver," and "The Adventures of Ozzie and Harriet," and we swooned over Ricky Nelson. In Grandma's living room we were entertained by the best of the best and learned more than we had ever known. The world was big and interesting and entertaining.

In September we watched when President Dwight Eisenhower sent troops to help the nine black students in Arkansas as they integrated a high school for the first time. Mary Elizabeth sat glued to the television set and blurted out, "That's why I need to go back home, Maggie! It's so important!"

We watched when the Soviet Union sent Sputnik 2 with the first animal, a dog named Laika, into space. I'd heard people around town talking about how we had to "keep up our space program and catch up with those Russians."

After Grandma turned the television set off and sent us to bed, Mary Elizabeth and I would talk before we fell asleep. One evening she was still thinking about the Arkansas integration and said sadly, "You know, Margaret, down south I couldn't eat in a restaurant with white people, but here in Norden my parents own a restaurant."

"It's really sad you were treated like that."

"Rosa Parks is my heroine. She didn't give up her seat for that young white man," she added. "Until I came here, I rode the back of the bus all my life."

"Are you glad you came here?" I asked.

"It's better and safer than an orphanage somewhere, but I get lonesome," she answered. "I do stick out here, you know."

I nodded and then asked, "Where's your family, Mary Elizabeth?"

"Don't know where my dad is. My mother is somewhere down south. Her name is Mary, also. Easy to figure out who I was named after. Lived with my Grandma Leona till she passed on."

"Where did you go after your grandma died?" I asked concerned about my friend.

"To an orphanage for colored kids. Lived there till the Andersons came and got me."

The truth was that Mary Elizabeth was the first colored person I had ever seen in Norden, and she was still the only one living here now. It didn't surprise me that she felt lonely or out of place.

Over the years, there were stories of transient individuals of all nationalities traveling from town to town, many during the depression days. Often they rode the train in box cars looking for work or food.

I am sure everyone in town had heard at one time about two elderly women standing on the board sidewalk conversing in front of the general store when a young colored man walked by. One of the women turned to the other and said in Norwegian, "That is the blackest man I have ever seen in my life!"

To their surprise, he stopped, turned to look at them, and answered in Norwegian, "I might be black, but God is Father to us all."

The women probably thought, "How and where did he learn to speak Norwegian?" and probably were more careful from that day on.

Before we fell asleep that night, Mary Elizabeth turned to me and shared her future plans. "I'm going back to Alabama after I graduate and fight for civil rights for all people." Then she added, "And to find my mother."

I'll miss you lots." I became suddenly sad as I thought of my friend with such high expectations of herself and high goals leaving me in less than six years.

When Grandma woke us up the next morning, she had a hot breakfast ready for us. She always said, "To be able to learn in school, you need to eat a good breakfast."

Sometimes we had bacon, eggs, toast, and juice. Sometimes we had oatmeal or cream of wheat. Other mornings we had pancakes or waffles. Today we had waffles with melted butter and hot syrup. We never went to school hungry and were ready to take on the day.

Days were busy at school before Thanksgiving and Christmas. Not only did we have our regular schoolwork, but in band and in chorus we prepared for holiday concerts. We had sung "Carol of the Bells" so many times it was perfect. We played "Sleigh Ride" in band class so often it was flawless. There were other songs we had to learn, but we'd also perfect them before we were done. The only thing left to do for Christmas season was to decorate the school the day we returned from Thanksgiving vacation.

It was already the middle of November. It was early in the basketball season, and our basketball teams, A and B, were already doing well. In fact, the A team had won every game with Buddy Nelson as its star player, and the B team, with Yanni as its star player, had lost just one game. Everyone thought we were in great shape to win the district tournaments. "Ya, we've got powerhouses for teams," you'd often hear around town.

One Saturday evening in November, a free-throw contest was held in the high school gymnasium. Our school didn't have girls' sports, but this year Mary Elizabeth decided to enter the free-throw contest anyway. Since there were no rules excluding girls, no one contested her participation. And no one took her seriously enough to win.

No one knew, except me, that when Mary Elizabeth was in a children's home in Alabama, one of their pastimes was shooting baskets. She had played H.O.R.S.E. with the best, many of them older than she, and had learned to keep up with them with grace and precision.

Intrigued spectators watched as Mary Elizabeth, the little seventh grader, revealed her skill and agility at the free-throw line. In a modest, unaffected manner she handled the basketball with expertise moving and jumping as gracefully as a deer jumps over a fence, sending every shot she made right through the hoop.

"*Oohs and Aahs*" were heard throughout the gymnasium as the crowd grew around her. "Come, see this! Come watch this!"

There were only three players left until Buddy, the star of the varsity basketball team, missed and was out.

The contest was now between Yanni and Mary Elizabeth, two seventh graders vying for the trophy. Finally, Yanni missed, leaving Mary Elizabeth, who made her final basket and became the school's new free-throw champion.

People said they heard Buddy Nelson mumble under his breath, "She can go back down south any time," when the trophy was awarded. If that was true, I decided I no longer liked him no matter how important he was to our school. Everyone else seemed to wish Mary Elizabeth could play on our basketball team.

Dad smiled when he heard about Mary Elizabeth's victory after he returned home the next day and came to Grandma's for supper. Grandma had fixed us delicious roast beef, mashed potatoes, and gravy. When we were eating our dessert-- apple pie with vanilla ice cream-- Dad stopped, looked at us and said, "I have a lady friend in Minneapolis, and I've asked her to spend Christmas with us. Her name is Ava Franzen." Grandma was busy getting all the details she could, but numerous questions were racing through my head. "My dad has a lady friend? And he likes her enough to bring her here for Christmas? Who was this Ava Franzen from Minneapolis taking my mother's place? What was she like? Was she pretty? Smart? Nice? Kind? Would I like her?"

Because none of my belongings were packed and it was late, I stayed with Grandma another night. The last thing I remembered before I fell asleep was, "Would she like me, this Ava Franzen, whoever she is?"

I was learning that things are not always just black and white. Sometimes they were gray, and sometimes they weren't any color. I was learning that nothing stayed the same in our world for long. It changed constantly, sometimes for better and sometimes for worse. Maybe Grandma was right. It was how we reacted to change and what we learned that really counted.

NOVEMBER FAREWELL

November came quickly leaving all of us surprised that a year had already passed since I went with Grandma to Bridget's house. Only this November was not as mild. Snow and cold already had blanketed the countryside giving us a "white" Thanksgiving.

The weekend before Thanksgiving we did make it with our basket to the Jenneweins for our annual holiday celebration, but this time we did not stay overnight. Grandma was taken up with her Russian friend, Pavel, and his health.

"He doesn't look well," she said. "And I'm concerned about his sallow and gray complexion and the dark circles under his eyes."

His sad eyes that hinted of loneliness and rejection were enough, but with the dark circles under them, he must look ten times more ill. "Poor man sounds almost half dead already," I thought. But then how would I know at my age.

Grandma feared for the worst. In fact, she had been in contact with Pavel's California family several times during the fall to inform them that his condition had gotten worse.

Pavel also lost his appetite and lost weight. He was shakier than ever, lacking the energy to "pick himself up by his bootstraps," according to Grandma.

She was beside herself with what to do next, but on the way home, she glanced at me and in a concerned tone of voice informed me that this Thanksgiving she was going to have Pavel over for dinner. "He needs the nourishment," she said. She paused for a moment and then added, "And friendship."

Grandma continued to drive home, deep in thought, saying little. I also was quiet, thinking things must be very serious if Grandma was asking Pavel into her home.

"I wish I could have done more for him…and sooner," she continued when we had almost reached her driveway. "If you and your dad want to join us, you are welcome. I'll explain everything to your dad."

Grandma planned to integrate her son, granddaughter, and Pavel at the same Thanksgiving dinner table. Her regrets for not doing this sooner showed as she meticulously planned a feast. She was busy with only four days left and feeling the weight of making up for years of not including her childhood friend at dinner with her family. Her sad realization was this was an impossible task.

Grandma had cooked so many savory turkeys and stuffed them with homemade dressing that it was almost mechanical for her. She had cleaned the house and set the table for entertaining guests so many times she could do it in her sleep. It wouldn't be difficult for her to have anyone from any society in her house and make them feel welcome and at home. Not only that, but her guests, no matter how important, always left feeling that they had been guests of someone special. Grandma was born with the gift of being a perfect hostess.

It was already dark when we returned to Grandma's house after visiting the Jenneweins. It was the Saturday before Thanksgiving. I planned to spend the night with her and then go back home with Dad after church the next day.

As soon as we were in Grandma's house she suggested I go right to bed because I had said earlier I was tired from getting up early. It was evident that she would be up for a while, working on Thanksgiving plans.

When Dad and I left Grandma's that Sunday afternoon for the farm, she reminded us to come early on Thursday and help her cook. "And you, my son Halbert, you will have to pick up Pavel. You know he doesn't have a way to get here."

Dad nodded and said we'd come early as we shut the door and left for home. It appeared all Grandma's plans were in order. As Dad started the car and pulled out of the driveway, he looked at me and smiled, "Maggie, we are going to have a great

Thanksgiving."

Thursday morning, we entered Grandma's house to the delicious smell of turkey and dressing that had been roasting for two hours. Grandma was up early to get things ready because she liked to dine at noon sharp. Her table, which I usually set, was already set for four with a white tablecloth and a horn of plenty filled with gourds as a centerpiece and tall, slim silver candle sticks with orange candles on each side. In the refrigerator were two fresh pumpkin pies and cream, bought from Mrs. Tollefson and ready to whip. She even had the potatoes peeled and ready to cook.

For the first time in my life, I saw Grandma down in the dumps and not herself. She did not even try to smile, and she fidgeted and worked constantly as I sat there wondering how to help because everything was done. She must have been up all night.

Dad read the daily newspaper, *The Minneapolis Tribune*, as he waited for the time to pick up Pavel. He and Grandma made small talk. Dad stated his opinion about Pavel's situation, "I'm surprised his family hasn't come to see him. Maybe they could help find out what's wrong."

"They aren't very concerned. I think they gave up on him long ago." Then she added, "I think it's his heart. He sounds congested, wheezes when he breathes, and has no energy."

"Well, he doesn't exactly take care of himself. All that drinking's finally taken a toll," Dad added.

"So?" Grandma retorted, offended that her son would say such a thing about her friend who may be dying.

Dad retreated from the conversation. It was obvious that this was not the time to discuss her friend's weaknesses. They both were silent for a while.

"Time to go pick him up," Grandma said. "I told him to be ready at eleven."

Dad put on his black four-buckle overshoes, his brown heavy overcoat, white scarf, and brown hat and quietly left the house for Pavel's tar paper shack on the other side of the railroad tracks. Grandma sat down to have a cup of coffee and wait for them to return. I grabbed one of the Norwegian cookies and began to munch on it. Grandma didn't say anything. It was more like the saddest day in our lives instead of Thanksgiving.

Dad returned close to noon, but Pavel wasn't with him. He was grim and had lost his bounce as he came into the kitchen, where everything was ready for Thanksgiving dinner. He looked at Grandma and quietly said, "Ma, Pavel is gone! He was found frozen to death this morning outside by the steps of his shack."

There were tears forming in Dad's eyes, and he was sad, sad for never understanding Pavel. Sad because Pavel never went back home to California and died without his family. Sad because Pavel's family just didn't seem to care where he was as long as he wasn't their problem. Sad because Grandma would mourn deeply for her childhood friend and miss him.

We all knew that once someone was dead and gone, there was little one could do to help him. The community had treated Pavel as some kind of joke while he was alive, and now it was too late. It seemed his life had been wasted. Thanksgiving dinner today had become a time to mourn instead of celebrating.

Grandma turned to Dad and said, as if her heart were broken, "I knew this was coming, and didn't know what to do about it. I feel so bad." She began quietly to weep as my dad put his arms around his mother and held her. And no one said much of anything for a long time.

Finally, she said, "I'll talk to Pastor Wood from my old church in the country after I contact Pavel's brother and sisters. If they don't mind, maybe we can have the funeral out there and lay him to rest in the cemetery by the church. I think it would be good if he stayed here in Minnesota."

With the death of a man considered the town's derelict, our Thanksgiving festivities ceased. There were more import-ant duties that needed our attention. Dad and I stayed with Grandma as she called Pavel's oldest sister, Mrs. Juliana Lewis. Yes, she would contact her younger sister, Mrs. Beatrice White, and her younger brother, Mr. Ivan Ivanovich. Yes, it was acceptable to have a funeral in the small country church seven miles out of town. Yes, they would be here within a week, but they'd drive because Ivan was afraid of flying. And then she requested Grandma to do her a favor.

Her request changed the whole focus on Pavel's death for a few days. Mrs. Lewis said, "Our family just sent him one thousand dollars to pay for fuel to heat his house, buy food and warm clothes, and have something left over for the holidays. Would you please check Pavel's belongings and home for the money that he probably received yesterday?"

Grandma called Sheriff Palmer before she called Pastor Wood. Grandma kept repeating as we went to Pavel's shack, "I always knew that his family sending him money would do him more harm than good someday, but I didn't know that it probably would kill him. God, please have the money be there. Please!"

The sheriff and his deputies were already there, but the money was not. The stove was out, the place was ice cold and they shivered as they searched through Pavel's few belongings. There was no money anywhere. All anyone knew was that the day before he was at the beer joint in town and he staggered home after dark. No one knew what happened after that. When there was nowhere left to look, we left, and the sheriff locked up his place.

Not long after everyone returned from their holiday celebrations, the news of Paul Ivanovich's death spread like wildfire. Everyone seemed to know that he had frozen to death outside of his shack and that he had a thousand dollars that was missing. The people from the beer joint said he had left about 5 PM the day before and he was walking well. Examination of his body showed that there had been no struggle. He didn't even have a bump on his head from hitting the icy ground. When the sheriff first arrived to investigate, his house was unlocked.

Grandma asked me to go with her when she went to meet with Pastor Theodore Wood. Happy to see us, even with a houseful of company on Thanksgiving Day, he cordially welcomed us into his home.   He was a gentle, kind preacher that was more love than hell, fire, and brimstone.

Everyone in a small community, a town of less than four hundred people, knew each other so Pastor Wood knew of Pavel and Grandma's friendship. He was saddened by Pavel's tragic death, and kindly told Grandma, "I will be honored and delighted to be pastor for his funeral. And, of course, the funeral may be in our church next week on Thursday, giving the Ivanovich family time to drive from California."

Bright and early the next morning, Pastor Wood answered the door of the parsonage to find Mrs. Gertrude Amundson, president of the church's women's group. She was angry and adamant, "You absolutely cannot have a funeral for an unrepentant town drunk in my church! Our church!" she ordered. "Many others feel the same way, and if you continue pursuing this funeral, there will be trouble." She ended her tirade by firmly stating, "In fact, most feel as I do."

"Mrs. Amundson," Pastor Wood declared. "I have made a promise to God and to others, and everything will be on schedule. Besides, only God can judge anyone."

Mrs. Amundson gave Pastor Wood an angry glare as she spun around on her heels and stomped off to her car. On her way, she hollered back, "Well, you haven't heard the last of this."

Next she drove into town to Grandma's house. They had gone to the same church for years, but she raised such a fuss that Grandma asked her to leave.

"Gertie," she said. "I hate to do this, but you will have to leave now. This conversation is going nowhere, and there are many things being said that can hurt us for life. We want to be friends after this, don't we?"

Shocked that someone stood up to her, she spun on her heels again and immediately left. She said nothing on the way out, speechless maybe for the first time in her life.

"Well, I guess she won't be at the funeral, "Grandma said. Turning to me she added, "Don't worry about Mrs. Amundson, Margaret. She has never liked me since I became your grandpa's young bride. She thought she was going to marry him, and I came back with him to Norden and ruined all her plans."

For the first time in my life, I felt I knew who the person was who caused Grandma so much heartache and spread so many lies. Mary Elizabeth was right all along. There was someone who was jealous of my grandma. It was Mrs. Amundson. I doubted Grandpa would have ever wanted her. Why she thought he would I would never understand.

I was affected deeply by what was taking place and had emotions I had never known before. I felt at times I hated Mrs. Amundson, and I hated that I felt that way. I felt she was ugly, plain and simple, inside and out. She was self- righteous, fat, cruel, judgmental, inconsiderate, nosey, a busybody in the first degree, and mean as sin. To think my grandpa could have married her made me sick. It was a good thing my grandma, who was completely the opposite, came along.

I had learned firsthand that one of the bad things about a small community was that everybody knew what everybody else was doing and thought they had a right to have their noses in everybody else's business. The week passed by slowly with discussions of Pavel's worth all over town. "It is too bad that people don't have anything better to do," Grandma often said that week. "Maybe, just maybe, they should get a life."

The day of Pavel's funeral, a shiny black Cadillac Eldorado Brougham with black and white leather interior arrived in town looking for Grandma's house. In it were Pavel's three siblings, Mr. Ivan Ivanovich, Mrs. Beatrice White, and Mrs. Juliana Lewis. All of them were of stocky build and well-dressed in black. Mr. Ivanovich had a black, pin striped suit, black topcoat, and a black felt hat. Mrs. White and Mrs. Lewis had black shoes, black dresses, and black hats with feathers. On top of their black clothes, each of his sisters wore a mink coat. It certainly looked strange to see three people in town all dressed up in latest fashion, and they stood out when they stopped at Anderson's café for lunch and directions to my Grandma's. It reminded me of when David Jennewein drove into town. "Only these three are a little bit odd," I decided.

Mr. Anderson later told Grandma that the people in his café were awe-stricken with the Cadillac they drove and the clothes they wore. It was as if they were adorned from head to toe in money. No one had ever thought that Pavel had a family that wealthy.

It had been years since Grandma had seen them. She always said that Pavel was the only tall, slender member of the family, and it was obvious he was. As he became slenderer and frailer, the others became fatter and more affluent.

Just stopping for directions to the church, Pavel's family didn't spend much time at Grandma's house. It was there that they informed her they were leaving right after the service because they had to return to their jobs and families in California and probably would never return. I could tell that Grandma did not like their attitude, but she said nothing.

Not many came to say goodbye to Pavel besides his family, Grandma, Dad, and me. We all sang "The Old Rugged Cross" and "Shall We Gather at the River" before Pastor Wood began his sermon on judging others. Grandma was relieved that the family didn't know why that topic was chosen for the sermon that day.

Grandma could be proud she remained faithful to her friend till the end. His sudden death and funeral, along with the fight for the dignity of a man, was a journey for all of us. It was as though it was a fight for his right to be in this world and also in God's.

In the spring, when the ground was no longer frozen, he would be buried in the cemetery by the little white church with its high steeple. Before his family left, they asked Grandma to see that it was done properly and thanked her for taking good care of their brother.

"Of course I will," she told them. Then she added sadly, "I'll miss him," as she walked them to their car to return home.

Disagreements and fights regarding the worth of people bothered me. They bothered Grandma even more, however, because she stood nose to nose, not backing down from "Gertie" as she called her. She refused to succumb to Mrs. Amundson's ranting over Pavel being the town drunk and undeserving of a church funeral.

Pastor Wood began to look for another church immediately and planned to move the beginning of summer. He said he couldn't stay because of the hard feelings. "New blood here would be good," he said.

It did not take till spring to solve the problem and stop the negative gossip. Right before Christmas something happened that would shut up the devil himself. To begin with, it was just an ordinary day, but it ended a day to remember because of the lesson in life it taught the community, even if some probably never would admit it. Grandma received a letter from the Church Mission Society that read:

> *Dear Mrs. Olson,*
> *The day before Thanksgiving this year, we received a package and a letter from your friend, Mr. Paul Ivanovich. He informed us that we were to send you any letters of thank you and any reply. Because of his high regard for you and our extreme thankfulness for his kindness, we are letting you know that we received his package, and we thank him.*
> *Please forward this letter to him.*
> *Tell him that his $850.00 arrived safely, and we have designated this money, according to his request, that it would be used to help the poor and homeless have a better Christmas.*
> *Thank you again. And God bless you.*
>
> *Sincerely,*
>
> *Pastor Jonathan Wells*
> *Church Missionary Society*

The mystery of the lost money was solved. Grandma promptly notified Sheriff Palmer about the letter, and he suspended his search. Then she notified Pavel's family. After that, she carefully and lovingly packed the last patchwork quilt she made to keep him warm during the winter season and sent it to the Church Mission Society for a homeless person.

The news spread quickly across the community until everyone knew of Pavel's generous gift to the poor. Every time the story was repeated, he grew in stature.

One day I asked Grandma, "Will Mrs. Amundson ever apologize?"

"Gertie Amundson?" she asked. "She should, but she is too proud and self-righteous. I doubt she ever will."

Then she became very quiet, deep in thought for a while. She said, "I wonder if Pavel knew he would die that day. I bet he did because that was the very day he sent the money away. Had a bad heart for a long time. And he didn't die frozen to death from drinking as they all wanted to believe."

"That's sad, Grandma," I added. "I wish he had told us just how sick he was."

"Maggie, it is sad. But look at the lesson this town has learned because of him. The person they judged all these years was probably a good person, and they didn't even know it."

I remembered the time when I went with Grandma to see Pavel. I thought about the good-byes of which I had been a part. I thought of how I had heard Pavel and Grandma say *"Do svidaniya"* or *"Poka!"* to each other. Or the times he called her *"Katya."* When spring came and Pavel was buried, it would be their last *"Do svidaniya."* It would be their last good-bye.

It would take me years to fully understand the statement about life that came with Pavel's death and his gift to the poor. All I knew was that I was glad I wasn't Mrs. Amundson. She should eat her words, but knowing her, she probably wouldn't and just ignore Pavel's last-minute act of kindness.

And as far as Grandma was concerned, it was like a light lit up in my mind. Just because Grandma didn't agree with some-one like Mrs. Amundson, it didn't mean she was crazy. Maybe the real crazy person was Mrs. Amundson. I felt bad that I thought she was the meanest person I had ever met in my life.

The greatest lesson I learned when Pavel died is that people can never really figure out life and make judgments that last forever. Once we think we have all the answers and know everything, life changes and we have to begin learning all over again. We couldn't put life in a box and keep it there. It was impossible.

CHRISTMAS VISITOR

Parts of school days after Thanksgiving were spent preparing and decorating for Christmas. Each schoolroom had a real spruce tree decorated with glass balls, a set of lights, garland, tinsel, and a star at the top. The gymnasium had three huge, decorated spruce trees. The entrance to the school had a large nativity scene letting everyone know the "real" meaning of Christmas. Band and choir practice with the elementary students for the Christmas concert was in full swing.

It snowed a little every other day. Each day it snowed, the weather was warmer, but everyone was too busy to take advantage of any outdoor activities. Grandma asked me if I would spend the weekend with her to help plan our Christmas and prepare for the visit from Dad's lady friend. We wouldn't be spending Christmas Eve with the Andersons this year.

Our town went into December still talking about Pavel's sudden death and his gift of money to the church. Grandma said she was happy it was over and tried to focus on Christmas, just three weeks away. "He's gone to a better place and won't have to struggle anymore," she repeated to those who brought him up.

We spent Saturday morning of the first weekend rolling out sugar cookies and then cutting them into trees, bells, wreaths, stars, and angels. Grandma baked them until they were exactly right and let them cool. Then we frosted them with white frosting and made them look festive with sprinkles of red and green sugar. Last, we tasted them. If they melted in our mouths, we knew they were good.

Morning flew by as we baked and talked. "I wonder...if the mysterious Miss Ava is anything like the movie star Ava Gardner. Dark hair, voluptuous, gorgeous, and beautiful?" I said.

"I don't see your dad choosing someone like that!"

Grandma replied. "Just because they both have the same name, Ava, doesn't mean anything. Besides I thought he said she was a blonde."

"Well, what do you think she's like?"

"I'm sure she's very nice...just like your mother," she answered and changed the subject. "How about you and I going to Johnsons' General Store and buying Christmas gifts?"

"Okay," I quickly said. "I'm up for that." I loved buying Christmas gifts for my family and friends.

I wanted to tell Grandma that I was concerned about my future and that I was worried about my dad's lady friend. That I was concerned because my friends already knew what they wanted to do when they graduated from high school, and I didn't. That it was almost Christmas, and I was getting lost in all that was happening around me.

I wanted to tell Grandma that Mary Elizabeth had plans to go to Alabama after graduation and become a champion of civil rights. Not only that, but Bridget planned to go to Juilliard School of Music and study to become a concert violinist.

In the past six weeks both of them had made a name for themselves in a positive way at school. One at the Halloween talent contest. The other at the free throw tournament. I felt as if I was being left behind by a talented musician and a skilled athlete.

It wasn't like Grandma to shut down a worthwhile conversation. Talk of going shopping ended our discussion. Did she bring it up on purpose just to change the subject? Was she having second thoughts about Dad's lady friend herself? I had to let it go. We didn't have time to waste today, but someday I needed to have this talk. "The sooner the better," I thought.

Mr. Johnson's general store was somewhat cluttered but delightful this time of the year. The ceiling was decorated in green, red, and white paper streamers with paper bells and wreaths where the streamers crossed each other, and the whole store was full of Christmas merchandise. There were colorful glass balls and bells, multi-colored tree lights, silver tinsel, silver and gold garland, white and red felt tree skirts, Christmas cards of all kinds, Christmas color books with snowmen and Santa, and Christmas magazines full of recipes, even ones to make chocolate fudge and taffy. There were all kinds of Christmas paper with wreaths and bells on it and ribbon of every color to make bows for wrapping extraordinary and beautiful gifts.

There were assortments of hard Christmas candy and cream-filled chocolates, ready to buy and put in Christmas stockings, in containers that stood on the counter. There were stacks of boxes of Brach's chocolate covered cherries and bins of peanuts, Brazil nuts, almonds, and other nuts.

Bolts of new fabric, some with Christmas designs, were in the dry goods section of the store. Several colors of velvet and corduroy fabric, new patterns, buttons, thread, lace, rick rack, and ribbon were displayed for the ladies who made Christmas outfits for their children and themselves. Shoes to buy for the whole family were located at the back of the store. And there were games and toys and dolls for children's gifts.

The store had bags of flour and sugar, chocolate chips, and other baking supplies, such as spices of all kinds. Wooden barrels of lutefisk and herring stood among the different kinds of fresh meat, summer sausages, bacon, and hams.

We took it all in, at least as much as we could, as we walked around the whole store. When we were done, Grandma needed a few extra things for cooking and went to buy groceries. I went to buy gifts, and I knew what my first purchase would be.

In the toiletry section of the store, I bought Mary Elizabeth and Bridget a perfect gift. For each of them I chose a special gift box of Evening in Paris talcum powder and cologne in cobalt blue glass containers. It was very popular so I knew my friends would like their gifts. They would smell good besides.

For Grandma, I chose a box of three dainty handkerchiefs with tiny flowers embroidered in pink with green leaves. I knew Grandma would like them. For my home room teacher, Mr. White, and my Sunday school teacher, Mrs. Wynd, I bought a box of Brach's chocolate covered cherries. They were yummy and especially popular this time of the year. For Dad, I needed something special. Mr. Johnson had just received several brand-new ties, and I picked a red silk one to go with Dad's white shirt and new gray suit. It was just like those I had just seen Gregory Peck and Rock Hudson wearing in a movie magazine. By this time Grandma was done buying groceries and had come to join me. I turned to her and asked, "What should I buy Miss Franzen?"

"I know just what you should get her, and if you don't have enough money, I'll put in the rest."

She led me to the toiletry counter and pointed out a Mother of Pearl, gold-embellished comb and brush set that was lying in a gold-colored box lined in white satin. It was beautiful. "I think she'll like that," Grandma approvingly said as I bought Miss Franzen's gift.

"I think she'll love it!" I said. In fact, I thought it would really impress her.

After buying Christmas gifts for everyone, we spent the rest of the day decorating Grandma's house. We would leave the Christmas tree until it was closer to Christmas. But when we put up her tree, it would have colorful glass ornaments, silver garland, bubble lights, and silver tinsel. At the top would be a large angel with white wings and a white dress that lit up and stood straight and tall as though it was watching out for everyone, guests and all.

It was evident that every holiday was a big celebration in our family, especially Christmas. As we planned and decorated for this important holiday, we continued talking. "If Miss Franzen is blonde, Grandma, maybe she looks like Doris Day. Sweet...innocent...wholesome... nice...and beautiful." I liked that idea because I liked Doris Day and remembered how she looked in the movie *By the Light of the Silvery Moon* trying on her mother's wedding dress when she planned to marry Gordon McCrae. In my mind I still could still hear them singing, "If You Were the Only Girl in the World."

"It doesn't matter what she looks like, Maggie, just that she's good to you and your dad."

The weekend over, I was back in school Monday morning beginning a week filled with activities. Besides basketball games and schoolwork, Thursday night was the big holiday concert when the whole town congregated in the school auditorium for the Christmas program.

For the program, Bridget, Mary Elizabeth, and I had new Christmas dresses, theirs sewn by their mothers and mine by my grandmother. Our dresses were identical velvet with short sleeves and a square neck. They were fitted at the waist with full, circle skirts. My dress was red, Mary Elizabeth's was green, and Bridget's was blue. We wanted high heels, but all of us wore black patent leather flats. Grandma said, "You girls are too young for high heels."

We performed to a full house. First the elementary school put on their program. Then the high school choir and band put on theirs. People said they'd never heard "Carol of the Bells" and "Sleigh Ride" performed so well. Once the program was over, there were only two weeks left until Christmas vacation.

A week had passed since Grandma and I had gone Christmas shopping. It was Saturday again and Santa Claus Days in town. There were cartoons at the American Legion for school kids. Santa Claus handed out bags of candy, which always included a delicious apple, to everyone when they left to go home as he wished them a Merry Christmas. Of course, Mary Elizabeth and I went to see Santa.

When the cartoons were over, I walked to Grandma's to wait for Dad. As I entered her kitchen, she was talking on the phone with Pastor Wood. The church group was going caroling, and Pastor Wood needed more singers. He wanted me to come with Mary Elizabeth and Bridget?

Grandma said it would be all right and would let my dad know so I called Mary Elizabeth, who would meet me at the church. Bridget had already gone home and was unable to come.

Caroling was a yearly event for the youth group, who would visit and sing for the older members of our church and community. Wherever we went, we were given something festive and special to eat like homemade fudge, Christmas cookies, cider, or fresh rolls. After we sang two or three songs, we moved on to the next house. In town we often walked, but in the country, we rode in cars. When we finished caroling, we returned to the church for barbeque on buns, chips, and hot cocoa.

All of us wanted to go to the Hansons' place in the country at least once. Three elderly bachelor brothers and their elderly sister lived in a small, three-room house without electricity. They seldom went to town, except for supplies, and rarely had visitors. Mary Elizabeth and I had never been there, but this was the night we would meet them, and we wanted to be there fifteen minutes to eight.

One of the brothers answered the door and let us into their dark, cluttered living room, where all four of them sat around the table near a small, round wood stove that was giving off wood smell and heat. Mary Elizabeth looked horrified and moved closer to me until her eyes adjusted to the dim light from a kerosene lamp.

"Merry Christmas!" they said almost simultaneously.

"Merry Christmas!" we answered.

We began to sing "Joy to the World," followed by "Oh Little Town of Bethlehem." They listened respectfully and attentively, sometimes smiling and nodding, enjoying the attention of a handful of young people.

Shortly before eight we began "Silent Night." Just as we started the second verse, all the clocks in their house rang in the hour. The grandfather clocks chimed, the cuckoo clocks cuckooed, and any other clocks in the house began to chime.

When the clocks finished chiming and we finished singing "Silent Night," we sang "We Wish You a Merry Christmas" as we walked out the door to leave. They said "Thanks" and "Merry Christmas."

On the way back to the car, I looked at Mary Elizabeth and asked, "How in the world do they ever sleep with all those clocks?"

"Beats me," she answered.

I would never understand people like them. How could they live like that? Never going anywhere. Living so isolated. Not wanting a nicer home with a bathroom and electricity. None of them moved on. Never married... Never this... Never that... Never... Never... I would never figure them out. I was glad I didn't have to.

Christmas vacation began the weekend before Christmas Eve and would continue until the first week in January. Grandma already had her white tablecloth, best china and crystal, sterling silver, and white napkins all set on her table, prepared for her guests. The table was set for four; Dad, Miss Ava Franzen, Grandma, and me. Our Christmas Eve dinner menu included: roast pork, mashed potatoes, slivered almonds on green beans, marinated carrots, gravy, all kinds of pickles and relishes, homemade whole wheat rolls with butter, and Baked Alaska for dessert. Grandma also planned to serve Folgers Coffee or Welsh tea. I would have milk. As we did every year, we would all go out to Grandma's country church for the Christmas Eve service and return to her place afterward. Miss Franzen would spend the night at Grandma's. The next morning Dad and I would return to open Christmas gifts.

Christmas Eve morning, Dad and I met the passenger train on its way north to Winnipeg from Minneapolis. Anxious and apprehensive, we waited as the passengers stepped on the street one by one. Miss Franzen was last, and when she stepped off the train, my dad's eyes lit up in utter joy. She was more like Doris Day than Ava Gardner. Her soft blonde curls, under her off white wool beret, caressed her face, and she was slim and elegant and beautiful in her long, off-white wool coat. Miss Franzen wore black gloves and black boots with high heels, and she carried a black leather bag. Her deep blue eyes sparkled as she saw Dad and was as pleased to see him as he was to see her.

The moment I fully realized that my father was in love was when he embraced and kissed Miss Franzen. He held her so tight and kissed her so long that I knew he forgot I was even there as I stood waiting.

Finally, Dad remembered and introduced me. "This is my friend, Ava Franzen," he said. "This is my daughter Margaret."

"Glad to meet you," we both said.

Dad and Miss Franzen kept talking, but I was quiet as we drove to Grandma's. "She's beautiful!" I thought. "She's not old, either. Must be way younger than Dad. If she's as nice as she is beautiful, I can see why he fell for her."

The introductions began all over again at Grandma's the minute we entered her front door. Grandma seemed pleased with our guest.

"Please make yourself at home," Grandma graciously said after showing Miss Franzen her room.

"Thank you."

"We'll eat dinner at seven."

Once Miss Franzen was settled, Dad and she left so he could show her our farm for the first time. "We'll be back before seven," he assured Grandma as he shut the door. Barely out the door, he kissed her again.

It was more than obvious how much Dad cared for Miss Franzen and how happy they were. I didn't want to have a stepmother take my mother's place, but how could I deprive Dad of happiness?

Grandma and I busied ourselves with dinner. And, as promised, Dad and Miss Franzen returned just before seven. Dinner was ready, so we went right to the dining room. After we were seated, Dad said he had an announcement to make.

"Margaret, Mom," he said. "I have asked Ava to be my wife, and she has said yes. We are having a Valentine's Day wedding."

Just like that the big announcement was made. I hope no one saw my jaw drop or heard my gasp. Dad for sure was getting married. And on Valentine's Day at that.

Miss Franzen smiled and stretched out her left hand flashing an enormous diamond on her ring finger. "I have never been this happy," she said.

We ate our dinner in celebration of their engagement. Miss

Franzen said she was a graduate of the University of Minnesota and an English teacher. She was from southern Minnesota, and friends introduced my dad and her the first time Dad went to farming classes at the University. They had corresponded ever since and had fallen in love.

"I love Hal and can't wait to be his wife. I am looking forward to knowing both of you."

The engagement was official, and I was quiet thinking about their marriage as we drove to the little country church. "If I find Yanni before the service begins, may I sit with him?" I asked. It was all right with Dad.

I had a gift for Yanni, *The Yearling,* by Marjorie Kinnan Rawlings. I thought he would like a head start on the book since it was read and taught in eighth grade English class, and, I was sure he would like the book because it was about a boy almost our age and his pet fawn.

That night I needed a friend, and Yanni knew it. During the sermon about the gift of Jesus at Christmas, Yanni discreetly took my hand and held it for as long as the rest of the service lasted.

The church bell was ringing on Christmas Day as we left for home. People were smiling, shaking hands, and wishing each other "Merry Christmas." I waved to Yanni as I got into our car.

The next morning, we met at Grandma's to open gifts. Grandma loved her embroidered handkerchiefs. Dad loved his flashy red tie. Miss Franzen, my future stepmother, loved her dresser set and said, "This is the loveliest dresser set I have ever seen. Thank you, Margaret. Or may I call you Maggie?"

I nodded and answered, "You may!"

That is how I met Miss Ava Franzen. The day after New Year's Day, she would leave for Minneapolis on the train, only to return at the beginning of February for good.

JEREMIAH

While I was busy meeting Miss Franzen, Bridget also had Christmas company. It was her brother Jeremiah Jennewein, David's younger brother and business partner, who was home for Christmas to check on the progress of their parents' new home.

Like David, Jeremiah left home at sixteen when I was only four years old. However, he came home several times over the years, more times than David, so I knew who he was.

Although not as businesslike, reserved, or direct as David, Jeremiah was equally handsome with curly brown hair and sparkling brown eyes. Much friendlier than his brother, his infectious personality made him extremely likeable, and he appealed to others quickly.

"Jeremiah is easier going than David," Bridget said.

It showed in his casual dress. He didn't wear the latest Ivy League clothes and accessories. He preferred a short, brown wool jacket, brown leather boots, and brown wool dress pants with a sports shirt.

Jeremiah was so laid back, I thought, "Maybe being second in the family wasn't as difficult as being first and forging a way into life and business."

"Where have you been hiding those handsome brothers of yours?" I asked Bridget when they visited us at Grandma's during Christmas vacation.

She knew well that they were not only heart throbs but great catches, and she smiled. Those Jennewein men now made most girls in Norden wish they were older.

We both knew that the young women had lost out when some people felt the Jenneweins were not good enough and they quit school at sixteen, leaving home. According to Bridget, there would never be any romance of her brothers with Norden girls because of that. "The boys say that they already had their chance," she said.

"I can see their point," I said. "I can appreciate their sense of humor, too," I added, almost seeing the twinkle in their eyes when they said the Norden girls had lost their chances.

"Jeremiah says our house will be ready in March, but we won't be able to move until the snow leaves the woods."

"I guess we'll just have to wait."

"Once we can move, both David and Jeremiah are coming to help us."

"Then we'll get to see them again soon. I can hardly wait to see them again and for you to live in town."

Mrs. Jennewein looked forward to living in town. She was tired of being isolated in the woods and so far from everything. "It was too hard for all my children to get to school," she told Grandma. "Bridget will be our family's first Norden High graduate."

"I'm so glad you're moving!" Grandma exclaimed.

"My boys have done well," Mrs. Jennewein added. "Ricky, my youngest son, is in college out east now. He received his high school diploma there."

"Good for him. I always liked Ricky. What about the girls?"

"Carolyn, my oldest daughter, is working in an office in Boston. After she left home, she lived with a family in New York. They helped her graduate from high school, go to business school, and find a good job. Lois, our middle daughter, has not done as well. She still doesn't have a high school diploma and waits tables."

"Do you think she will ever try to graduate, Eva?" Grandma asked. "Sometimes children who are in the middle of a family get lost for a while. It seems as though it is hard for them to find their identity."

"I don't know. She still is angry and bitter like the day she left home. Just like Carolyn, she lived with a family out east, cooked and cleaned for them, and babysat their children until she was eighteen and could go out on her own. Blames Charles and me for all her problems and thinks she's entitled to an education and the good things in life without working for them. Lois thinks everything was handed to Bridget and can't see how much work she has done and the sacrifices she has made to get this far in school and with the violin. I tell Bridget not to pay attention to her. That Lois made her choices. Could have continued going to school here, but she didn't want to put up with the other students. And she could have learned the violin, but she chose not to. I hate to say this, but I think she just likes to complain and make excuses for herself. You have to give something to get something back. That's the way life works. Everything was her choice, and now she blames everyone else."

Grandma was listening attentively to Mrs. Jennewein and letting her talk. When she was done sharing, Grandma said, "Let's hope and pray she gets over it."

After the Jenneweins went home, Grandma and I sat talking about all that had happened the past two months. The Jenneweins' first place at the talent contest. Dad's up and coming marriage to Miss Franzen in February. Pavel's funeral. Meeting the Jennewein boys. The town finally learning of their success. Mary Elizabeth's free throw championship. The Jenneweins' new home. Lois Jennewein's bitterness.

I had witnessed good things happening to my friends despite adversity. Life was only becoming better even if Miss Ava Franzen was part of it. She would bring good things to our lives. At least I hoped she would. There was a lot to look forward to in the new year.

I knew my dad would be happy. That made me happy.

January Thaw

It was already time to return to school. Christmas vacation was over, Miss Franzen had returned to Minneapolis, Jeremiah Jennewein had returned to New York, all the decorations were taken down and put away for next year, and we had about five weeks to get ready for a wedding.

January was cold, but with little snow, making travel in our part of the world easier than last year when we had above normal snowfall. I didn't mind the cold because as seventh graders, who spent last January playing outdoors during milder, warmer days with lots of snowfall, we were too busy with school activities to have time to play.

We still had our homework, band practice, and choir. Mr. Wynd had us singing and playing and practicing for superior ratings at district and state competitions. There still were basketball games and our varsity team to cheer on to the district tournaments. I had something to do every day.

Dad and Grandma were planning the Valentine's Day wedding in Grandma's little country church. Pastor Wood already said he'd marry them. "I'll be honored to marry Ava and you," he said to Dad.

They planned a dance and reception for what seemed like the whole town at Winding River Country Club that included a meatball and gravy dinner and a three- tiered wedding cake with white frosting and red frosting roses. Miss Franzen would be wearing a long, white velvet wedding dress, and the bridesmaids dresses would also be long, but in red velvet. Grandma was going to sew my dress because I was junior bridesmaid. Miss Franzen's friend from Minneapolis would have hers sewn there. Yanni's dad would be best man. The men would wear dark gray suits with white shirts and red ties like the one I gave Dad for Christmas.

The night before I returned to school, Dad and I sat in our living room talking about the wedding and what it would mean to us. "Maggie," he tenderly said. "I love Ava, but I want you to know that I don't love your mother less. I am lonely and have this chance to be with someone else. I need you to be happy for me."

I chose to be honest. "She's beautiful and nice, Dad, but I don't know if I can ever let her take Mother's place."

"She doesn't want to, but please give her the chance to be part of your life. I think she'll be good for you. I think it will be good for you to have another woman around besides your grandma."

When Mrs. Gertrude Amundson heard about the wedding, she stormed over to Grandma's house. "What do you mean, Katherine, that your son is having a wedding dance? Don't you know that dancing and everything that goes with it is of the devil? And Pastor Wood! I suppose he's marrying them in the church, despite the dance, when he shouldn't be!"

"Is this really any of your business, Gertrude? Don't you think you are overstepping boundaries again?" Grandma asked back, her voice becoming louder and firmer as she stood facing Gertrude with her hands on her hips and continued. "Listen! Would you please get out of our lives and mind your own business!"

It must have almost killed Grandma to say that. She had literally ordered Mrs. Amundson out of her home.

I felt that Mrs. Amundson deserved what Grandma told her. For some reason she believed she was the moral conscience of the church, the town, the state, the country, and the whole wide world. Besides she still was angry with Grandma over Pavel's funeral and, I guess, her marriage to my grandpa. Now she had something else to be mad about because she felt dancing was a sin. Slamming the door behind her, she turned around and left the kitchen in a huff.

It was because of people like Mrs. Amundson that we couldn't have school dances or proms. I wondered what she would think if she knew that Bridget, Mary Elizabeth, and I danced every day after school watching "American Bandstand." Woe to us if she ever found out. She'd have us in hell for sure.

After she left, I glanced up at Grandma's sadness and thought I was lucky I was born and raised here. Grandma still wasn't understood and accepted because her ideas were different, foreign according to Norden people. I wondered if she would ever be accepted. "Oh, don't pay any attention to that," she always said. "It takes a generation to be accepted when moving into a small town." What she meant was, "Maybe I'm still not accepted, but your dad and you are."

Grandma was always standing up for a good cause when no one else would or even cared. People misunderstood and sometimes disliked her because she did. But did I want her any different? No! I couldn't see her any other way. I loved and admired her for the values and way of life she brought to this community, the same values that she taught me.

Seeing what Grandma went through, I finally somewhat understood Allison Berg and Miss Ava Franzen. Both of them came into the community, just like Grandma did, with a different value system from ours.

I promised myself that when we went back to school in January, I would be nicer to Allison Berg and I would be good to Miss Franzen when she returned at the beginning of February. This was a giant step in personal growth for me, and it brought me peace.

Right before Christmas I had found Allison Berg crying in the locker room, but she refused to tell me why. I assumed it was partly because she had been friendless from the day she came. This made part of how Allison felt my fault, and it bothered me. In my own little way I was proud and judgmental like Mrs. Amundson. The thought of being like her horrified me and made me shiver.

Giving up some of my pride, I suggested to Bridget and Mary Elizabeth that we begin to include Allison in some of the things we did. A new friendship started when we invited her to join us at lunch in the school cafeteria every day.

"It isn't that we are bad people, as Mrs. Amundson would like us to believe," Grandma said. "It's just that most people feel threatened when someone moves in and begins to change things. They feel someone will take their place or take something of theirs, especially their feeling of importance. It is like they feel if the new people are given an inch, they'll take a mile."

Grandma was right and was one of the most forgiving people I knew. The main reason I didn't like Allison Berg was I felt threatened. I felt she would take Yanni from me. In fact, it was the one and only reason. But had she taken his friendship away from me? No! He was still my friend.

Would Mrs. Amundson ever see herself as she really was? It was my wish for Grandma that she would. Perhaps it was my wish for Mrs. Amundson even more. I wished she would know the joy of accepting Grandma as her friend someday. For me, I was tired of fighting and wanted peace.

VALENTINE WEDDING

It was the first week of February, and wedding preparations were in full swing. It appeared it would be the fanciest and finest party that Norden had ever seen, and Dad and his bride-to-be were footing the whole bill. Everywhere you went, school, ball games, and church, friends, relatives, and neighbors talked about the wedding, and most planned to attend.

Miss Ava Franzen arrived on the morning passenger train from Minneapolis, and Dad and I were waiting for her. Suitcase after suitcase and box after box were unloaded, and I heard her tell Dad that more were shipped and coming later. I had never seen so many bags and suitcases belonging to one person ever. Miss Franzen smiled flirtatiously at Dad to melt him right on the spot and said, "Since I am going to live here permanently, I've had everything I own sent to my new home."

There were no questions asked. Our farm, where Dad, Eva, and I were going to live, was almost ten miles from town, and it would take too long to haul one load out there and be too risky to leave all the rest of the belongings on the street. So, we placed as many of her belongings as possible in the car, went to Grandma's to unload, and then returned to pick up some more. I think we made three trips before we finally had everything and could finally stop and carry the items she needed into the spare bedroom where Miss Ava was going to reside until the wedding on Valentine's Day.

The first thing Miss Ava unpacked was her white, velvet wedding dress with a sweetheart neckline and dainty velvet-covered buttons down the back past the fitted waistline and also on the wrists of its long sleeves that came to a point at the top of the hand. She hung it up carefully and arranged its long flowing train on the bedroom floor. Then she unpacked her double layer tulle veil. It was edged in white lace and attached to a headpiece covered with pleated white velvet and white pearls.

I had never seen a wedding dress that beautiful. It must have come from the best shop in Minneapolis. Add to the dress the bouquet, a huge cascade of red roses that Miss Ava planned to carry, and it would be elegance at its greatest.

Grandma sewed my junior bridesmaid dress with the valentine red velvet fabric Miss Franzen chose for her wedding colors. It, too, had a sweetheart neckline, was fitted at the waist, and had long sleeves that came to a point at the top of my hands. The maid of honor and I would carry white muffs, which Miss Franzen brought with her from Minneapolis.

At first, Grandma wanted me to wear my velvet Christmas dress, but it was a deeper red and wouldn't fit in Miss Franzen's wedding plans. I was happy it didn't because this dress was the prettiest dress I'd ever had.

After Miss Franzen unpacked everything she would need for the next two weeks, she came to the living room where Grandma was fitting my dress. Dad had gone to the farm with a carload of things she didn't need.

"Maggie," she said. "Since I am going to be part of your family, I think it's time to for you to call me Ava from now on, okay?"

I sighed with relief for the first time around Ava. The formality was making all of us uncomfortable. "I don't expect you to call me Mom. Just Ava," she added.

"Okay, I'll call you Ava," I said, thankful she didn't expect me to call her Mom. Maybe someday, but not now. I wasn't ready.

"We'll be glad to have you in the family," Grandma said and then turned the conversation to the Jenneweins.

Grandma said she expected the whole family to be at the wedding, all except Lois. They would all be here to pack up the Jennewein belongings for moving to their new house the first day of March. "It'll be fun to see them all again," Grandma said. "It's been a long time."

Grandma told Ava the story of the Jenneweins coming to Norden during the Great Depression and how the townspeople looked down their noses at them. "I swear some of the people could have drowned in a rainstorm because they had their noses so high when the Jenneweins came around."

She told Ava about their eldest child, David, and how he'd made his fortune in the music industry. "He's the first one of the family who quit school. Left when he was only sixteen years old. There was a teacher, a shirt-tail relative of Gertrude Amundson, who was unkind to him. Actually, I blame her for his leaving. She'd always ask him, when he was only in fourth grade, why he wasn't like the other boys in his class. He never got over the comparison and up and left, and then he comes back rich and famous. That's how much some people know."

"How awful," I thought. I had never heard that story, but I believed it after I had just witnessed Mrs. Amundson's recent behavior.

"There's good and bad in everyone," Ava answered. "I hope that teacher has second thoughts now."

"I hope so, too, Grandma." I could see handsome, kind, and gentle David as if he was standing in our living room.

"She moved from this community years ago," Grandma said. "We probably will never know."

"The secret is considering the source," Ava said. "If David had been able to deal with the bad, it wouldn't have hurt so much. As talented as he is, he probably was a very sensitive child."

"I guess he did better in New York," Grandma said. "Without his success there, there would be no new house for Charles, Eva, and Bridget."

Grandma just finished pinning the hem on my dress when Dad returned to pick up Ava. "We'll be back for supper," he smiled as they walked out the door.

The rest of the afternoon I spent looking at *Seventeen* magazines, comparing myself to the models with their cinched waistlines and full skirts over tons of crinolines, visualizing what I would look like in their outfits. "I'll be wearing a bigger bra one of these days, and then I'll really cinch in my waistline," I decided, still comparing myself to Allison Berg. The afternoon flew by because I also read some of the articles.

When the day was over, I thought I had life figured out. "You know, Grandma, I think the only way you can show people who put you down is to be successful just like David Jennewein."

"It's one way," she answered.

Yes, I thought I had the answers to life. To be successful, despite what others did or said, was the way. At least it seemed that way to me.

In school, we celebrated Valentine's Day on Friday, the day before the wedding. In seventh grade, we no longer had a Valentine's party where you gave valentines to everyone in the class. I bought valentines for Yanni, Mary Elizabeth, Bridget, Allison, Dad, Grandma, and Ava. In fact, I had them bought and addressed the first day they came out in Johnson's store. Before everyone left school, we gave them our valentine cards and wishes. Yanni handed me an envelope right before he got on his bus. "Here, Maggie," he said "as he shyly placed the card in my hand and left. "Happy Valentine's Day."

I decided to wait to open it until after I got to Grandma's. On the front of the valentine was a huge heart with an arrow right through it. On the inside it read:

When I stop to remember special friends,
I start by remembering you.
Just wanted you to know
That there is someone in your world
Who really likes you.
HAPPY VALENTINE'S DAY!
HOPE YOUR VALENTINE'S DAY IS
AS NICE AS YOU ARE.
Love, John Tollefson

"Wow!" I thought. "It's just like the song "Secret Love" by

Doris Day. It was once secret, but now it was shouted from the pages of a valentine card. I believed Yanni really liked me, and he told me so today. I read the verse again thinking how he called himself John. And I kept staring at the word, "love."

While I was reading my valentine from Yanni, I felt a flood of emotions. Yanni had acknowledged his affections. Tomorrow was Dad's and Ava's wedding day. Ole Tollefson, Yanni's dad, was best man, and their family would all be at the wedding. Soon I would see Yanni again.

Dad arrived to pick Grandma and me up and interrupted me. "Hurry up, Maggie! We have to get to the church for rehearsal. Ava and everyone else are there waiting for us."

"Here, Dad," I said as I handed him his valentine. "I don't know what I would do without you."

Dad smiled when he read the verse and where I signed, *"Love to the greatest dad in the world, Maggie".*

"Thanks, Maggie," Dad answered. "I don't know what I'd do without you either." Then he hugged me. "I love you so much."

The little church was humming with activity when we arrived. Red and white bows were in place on the reserved pews. A guest book was already set up on a table that had a white tablecloth with red confetti. The white carpet was in the back of the church rolled up and ready to go for tomorrow night. A petite brunette soloist named Lucille, one of Ava's friends from Minneapolis, was practicing "I Love You Truly" with the organist at the front of the church, and the Jenneweins were playing violins. I thought that she had a pleasant soprano singing voice, easy to listen to, and of course, the Jenneweins were almost professionals.

Miss Maria Benson, another of Ava's Minneapolis friends, was maid of honor. She was slender, medium height and had blonde hair and blue eyes. Ava's cousin Mr. Milton Franzen was groomsman. He was tall, dark, unlike Ava, athletic, and well-built like Yanni. Best man, Mr. Ole Tollefson, came early and was eager to practice and go to the groom's dinner at Andersons' restaurant. With everyone there, Pastor Wood started the rehearsal.

Dinner in town was nothing fancy. Everyone ordered what they wanted from the menu. The conversation was pleasant, but once the meal was over, all said their "Good nights," and went home. They all must have been as tired as I was.

Exhausted when we reached the farm, Dad and I hurried to get ready for bed so we would have a good night's sleep before the big day. My mind wouldn't stop thinking about the wedding, Dad, Ava, Yanni, Mary Elizabeth, Yanni, Valentine's Day, Yanni, school…I wondered if Dad went to sleep right away or if he also was thinking. I thought of my mother and what she would think about this wedding. Would she mind that her true love was in love again? Would she be happy? I lay in bed knowing that life would be different from now on. I no longer would have my father to myself. In the early morning he would be taking me to Grandma's where I would have my hair fixed and dress in my red velvet gown before his wedding. I hoped he was getting some sleep. It was a long time before I did.

Morning came, and the weather was cold and clear. The temperature had dropped to twenty below zero during the night, and everyone expected that it would be cold again. When I got up, Dad was on the phone talking to the church's janitor, asking him to stoke up the furnace. "We don't want our guests to freeze," he said.

Both of us were quiet when we ate breakfast, toast and Cream of Wheat with sugar and cream. Dad was still unsure of my feelings because he brought up a conversation we had before. "Be happy for me, Maggie," he looked at me and said. "It is lonely without someone to love. Someday you will know that."

I loved my dad so much. "I'll be happy for you and Ava," I answered. "I like her. She's a nice lady."

And so began Dad's valentine wedding day. I rushed out of the car at Grandma's so he could leave and not see the bride. "Bad luck to see the bride before the wedding on the wedding day," he told me as I shut the door. I knew I wouldn't see him until the ceremony at the church.

The little white country church, with its high steeple and lights glowing through the windows, greeted us as we arrived that evening. There were cars already parked everywhere. We could hear the pleasant hum of voices of people already in the church as we walked up to check the church sanctuary.

I gasped, it was so lovely. It was decorated in white and red roses and candlelight. "Ava sure did a great job," I told Grandma.

Ava, Maria, and I would wait in the church basement until it was time for the wedding to begin. Maria and I put our hands in our white muffs and waited. It was my cue to begin walking down the aisle right after the white carpet had been unrolled on it. I walked up to the front of the church with organist playing "True Love." I remembered it from the movie *High Society* that starred Bing Crosby and Grace Kelly. Then Maria followed. Once we were both at the altar, the organist began loudly playing "The Wedding March," and Ava, escorted by her father, walked down the aisle to meet Dad, who had never seemed happier. Mr. Franzen beamed as he gave his daughter away after Pastor Wood asked, "Who gives this woman to marry this man?"

The wedding service was beautiful. Lucille sang "I Love You Truly" and "Because You Come to Me." Pastor Wood had a short sermon on love. They exchanged vows and rings. Dad and Ava were given the blessing and everyone prayed "The Lord's Prayer." And it was over.

"You may kiss the bride," Pastor said.

After what I thought was the longest kiss ever, Pastor Wood asked Dad and Ava to face the congregation. Then he introduced them as Mr. and Mrs. Halbert Olson.

Dad smiled lovingly at Ava as he took her hand. They walked hand and hand together to the organ recessional, "I Love You Truly," to greet their guests in a receiving line.

As I walked out, I was thinking about Yanni Tollefson. *"When I marry Yanni,"* I thought, *"I want to have our wedding in this church."*

I rode with Grandma to Winding River Country Club. "You know," she said. "We all worked so hard on the wedding that is over. But a marriage lasts a lifetime."

The homemade Swedish meatball and mashed potato dinner was scrumptious, a true meat and potato farmer's meal. There were many comments on how good the meatballs were. "Just as good as the ones I make in our café," Mrs. Anderson said. The wedding cake with its creamy frosting was dessert, and it melted in my mouth making me want more. It was a perfect end to a perfect meal.

Not long after dinner, Harvey's Country Band started playing and the dance began. There were waltzes, polkas, schottisches, slow dances to country tunes, and even some rock and roll. The first time I danced with Yanni, we waltzed to "If You Were the Only Girl in the World." I thought how appropriate the song was for us as I thought of all the wonderful things I would say to Yanni, if not today, someday.

"Maggie," Yanni looked down at me and said. "Why don't you enter the school's poetry contest? You're a good writer."

"Hmm. You think I have a chance? I'll think about it."

"A good chance."

The band announced the last dance of the night. It was "Thee I Love," Pat Boone's song from the movie *Friendly Persuasion.* It was a perfect last dance for everyone, especially Dad and Ava. The words with apple trees and meadows fit right in our world, and it was as if he was asking Ava to come with him to this world because he loved her.

When the dance ended and the beautiful day ended, Dad and Ava left for their California honeymoon in their new red and white Chevrolet Impala Hardtop with *JUST MARRIED* written all over it and tin cans tied to the back bumper. I went with Grandma to spend the next three weeks with her.

It was a good day. I danced with Yanni, and Dad had a new wife.

MOVING DAY

Dad and Ava were still on their honeymoon the first days of March. According to post cards and telephone calls, California weather was perfect. They were enjoying the Pacific Ocean, and they were driving all over Southern California visiting Grandma's old friends and family. It would be another week before they would come home. "Be sure to tell the Jenneweins we're sorry we're missing their moving day."

Mr. and Mrs. Jennewein understood. Besides, they had enough help to move two houses. All of their children were home, except Lois, and Grandma, Mr. and Mrs. Anderson, Mr. and Mrs. Tollefson, Yanni, Mary Elizabeth, and I would help. David wanted it done quickly and precisely so that the family would be able to return to work as soon as possible.

That David Jennewein. He had driven to Winding River and bought expensive, new furniture for every room in the house, a set of fine china, sterling silver flatware, and crystal glasses of all kinds. "You're never going to serve a meal on mismatched dishes and utensils again, Ma. And you're never seating guests on old furniture. You're not taking any of the old stuff to your new home either." And he furnished everything.

No one had seen the inside of the new rambler, with its poured basement, that now sat on the edge of town. People drove by and saw the outside and checked on its progress, but no one, other than the builders, had been invited in. To add to the excitement of moving day, we would all see the inside for the first time.

"We'll keep all the old stuff out here in the cabin," David told his parents. "We want to keep the cabin for hunting. Don't you think that is a great idea?"

Mr. and Mrs. Jennewein thought it a good idea to keep the

cabin for hunting season. Of course there were personal items to move. The music and violins. A few favorite cooking pans Mrs. Jennewein had cooked on for years. An old typewriter, toiletries, favorite quilts and blankets, gifts they'd received over the years, clothes, and basic things they needed. But, the furniture and everything else would stay there. In that respect, moving day would go quickly and be easy.

We were astounded when we entered the beautiful, new house. It had two large bathrooms, a huge kitchen with wood cupboards, stained in soft, light brown and varnished, with a light-colored tiled countertop. There was a white electric stove, a white refrigerator, a washer and dryer, bedroom sets, a wood dining room table and chairs, and beige upholstered furniture on a beige carpet in the spacious living room. There was an office for Mr. Jennewein with an oak desk, and a music room that had a mahogany baby grand piano. And there was a large family room with an oval braided rug and a huge stone fireplace. In one corner stood a brand-new Zenith television set. There was an insulated two-car garage with a cement floor that would hold their new Chevrolet. It was also a place where Mr. Jennewein could fix things.

The bedrooms were magnificent. I especially loved Bridget's. It was painted pink, and had a blonde wooden dresser and mirror, blonde wooden headboard on the bed, blonde wooden nightstands with pink lamps with frilly white shades, and a blonde wooden chest of drawers. Her curtains were white and frilly with lace and gathered ruffles. They were *crème de la crème*, the frosting on the cake, in her extremely feminine bedroom. Bridget beamed with pride as she showed it to us, and no one could blame her. Never in her life had she owned anything as nice as this.

It seemed that David didn't forget anything needed for the new house. Not only did he have his mother's new Lennox china with the dainty blue flowers and the Fostoria goblets, sherbets, and glasses already in the cupboard, he had bought a set of plain, white ceramic dishes for everyday and filled the cupboards and refrigerator with staples such as sugar and flour and other kinds of food. He bought a white freezer, put it in the utility room, and filled it with meat, butchered at the locker plant downtown. He had arranged absolutely everything for his parents, whom he greatly respected and honored.

Mr. and Mrs. Jennewein were just as surprised as we were, and it touched them so deeply that most of the morning they wiped tears of appreciation from their eyes as they just wandered from room to room trying to take it all in, overwhelmed by what was happening in their lives. It was as though they were dreaming and soon the dream would end with them back in the woods. Their son had seen to it that they would never have to struggle again. As far as the rest of us who were there moving day, we had never seen anything like it. Ever.

That night back at Grandma's we were still talking about moving day. "I wish Dad and Ava could have been here today," I said, "They really missed something."

"They would have enjoyed it," she answered. "I am so impressed by David's generosity and love for his parents. Eva always said he was a good boy and a hard worker. Ricky and Jeremiah are good boys, too. Sure glad they could be with us today."

"Grandma, do you think not having things easy in life makes you a better person?"

"Not all the time," she answered. "Look at Lois. Hasn't gone very far in life and is bitter. Besides that, she's one of the most unhappy people I've ever met."

"Well, you want to know what I think? I think that I am glad David wasn't like the other boys in Norden."

"Me, too... But you, Young Lady, have to do your homework. And how about working on that poem for the poetry contest?"

My books were on the coffee table in Grandma's living room so I headed there to do my math and science. Once done, I took out my notebook and began writing a poem I had started right after Valentine's Day.

Writing was much easier for me than for Mary Elizabeth

or Bridget. Maybe what I was supposed to be in life was a poet or novelist of some kind. The idea of possibly becoming a great writer someday was at least the beginning of trying to figure out where my life was going.

As I thought about my poem, I thought of pink and white lady's slippers at Winding River Park. I loved it when they bloomed and stood proud and beautiful in the Minnesota sun. "Would it impress others if I wrote about them?" I asked myself. Maybe. I needed to decide because the day for submitting my poem was only two weeks away.

"What a day for the Jenneweins!" I told Grandma when I said good night to her. "They must be overjoyed tonight in their new home."

"They are humble, grateful people, Maggie. Tonight they are just more humble and grateful."

Grandma was right. The Jenneweins would never change and never hold their good fortune over anyone else's head. They would stay the same. There would never be anything haughty and selfish about them.

I could hardly wait to tell Dad and Ava about today. They had missed a special time, that's for sure.

It wouldn't be long until they would be home from their honeymoon. Maybe a week. Then what? Would I spend less time at Grandma's and more time with them? Time would tell, but with Bridget in town, I didn't want to spend all my time on the farm. Things would work out. It did for the Jennewein family. And I did hope Dad and Ava were having a great time.

POETRY FINALS

March was cold and raw. The winds blew right through our jackets, chilling us to the bone. We looked forward to the warm sunshine of spring that we always longed for this time of year.

The Jenneweins were settled in their new home and expressed to everyone how much they liked it. Dad and Ava returned from their honeymoon, and I returned to the farm to be with them.

Our basketball team made it to the district championship game where we lost by two points. That was the end of games, giving us time to practice band and choir selections for district music contests. We always worked for a superior rating from the judges, and this year was no different. Also, without basketball games, I had time to polish up my poem, which I hadn't shown to anyone. I wanted it to be a surprise.

I handed my poem in at the school office the day before the deadline. It was now going to be read and dissected by the judges, mainly the English teachers in the school. I wondered what they would think and if they would like it.

After I submitted my poem, I headed for home ec. I arrived there just in time for a lively discussion about a dessert dinner that our teacher, Miss Wilson, wanted us to have. During class we would make the dessert, decorate the room, and set the tables. Each of us was to ask a guest, preferably a boy, which would add more excitement. The eighth-grade girls would serve our guests and us our dessert. It meant getting all dressed up in formal dress in April, right after Easter. Most of us didn't mind because we would be getting new Easter dresses.

I knew who I would ask. The minute class was done, I left for our lockers to find Yanni and ask him.

"Be your guest? Of course, I will," he immediately answered without hesitation.

It was all set. Yanni was going with me. I had asked him first, and Allison Berg knew it.

Bridget and Mary Elizabeth didn't think anyone would go with them so they decided to go together. "No one will go with me," Bridget told me. "I'm not that popular with boys. Mary Elizabeth says no one would go with her either."

"Well, if you two don't dare ask anyone, how will you know?"

"Maybe we don't want to know. You have Yanni, who will go with you, and just don't understand what it's like not to be popular and have someone."

This was the first time I knew how Bridget really felt, and she was partly right. She hadn't been the most popular, but things were different now. In a few years, she'd come back just like her brothers and tell us, "Well, the Norden boys had their chances once, but not anymore."

All three of us had hurt and pain in our hearts. I knew that. Most of the time we never expressed how we felt, and yet we expected others to understand, even if everything was unspoken. "Did Bridget understand the pain I had in my heart?" I wondered. "The pain of losing my mother?"

I was hurt. It was the first time ever that Bridget had suggested a difference between us. I had never considered myself different, better than, or luckier than my friends. I thought we were all in this life together.

Mary Elizabeth? No one talked about her unusual circumstance either. And no matter what anyone said, I knew there was prejudice in our town. I learned that when she won the free throw contest at the school carnival and the star of the boys' basketball team suggested she go back down south. But it still was difficult for me to accept that nobody would go with her to the dessert dinner.

"How about taking your dads then? Miss Wilson didn't say anything about not taking a dad." I added, "You probably could take one of your brothers, Bridget." The dad idea was a good one, and it caught on. Bridget and Mary Elizabeth, plus other girls in our class, were bringing their dads to our dessert dinner, and Miss Wilson approved. They were just as excited as I was, and sometimes I wished I was bringing my dad.

We spent the rest of the week making plans. Dessert Dinner wasn't until the end of April, but we already knew what we would eat. Our class would bake apple pies, and we would have pie with vanilla ice cream. Our decorations would be light blue and yellow to look like spring. We would wear our Easter dresses and have proper etiquette we learned in class. We would look and behave like young ladies.

At the end of the week, our homeroom teacher, Mr. White, announced in math class that I was a finalist in the poetry contest. There would be a reading of our poetry in two weeks at an all-school convocation held in the gymnasium. In private he informed me, "The judges were impressed with your poem so I suggest you really practice reading it."

The next two weeks flew by. Grandma, Dad, and Ava were proud of me for becoming a finalist and wished me the best. They planned to attend the convocation and hear me read.

The Friday morning I read my poem, I wore my white blouse and poodle skirt. It was neat and fresh-looking and somehow gave me confidence. I was the youngest entry. I stood at the podium on stage speaking directly into the microphone as I read.

Every time I go to Winding River Park in the summer, I check out the beautiful lady's slippers when they are in bloom. I decided to write a poem about them.

Commencement

I used to run to the dam
To look at them,
The tiny lady's slippers growing there

For all the world to see.
How perfect they were!
Pink and white, waxen flowers,
Most fitting for a princess.
"Cinderella Glass Slippers,
I shall put you on
And dance away the night
On marbled ballroom floors,
My prince and I till dawn."
When golden sun comes up
Shining through layered, silver clouds,
Casting a rosy glow on soft, blue skies.
My sign that morning is here,
A day just waiting for a princess.

When I finished, everyone in the auditorium began to clap and cheer and whistle. My poem had impressed them. And I sat down, relieved it was over.

After all the poet finalists had finished reading, the judges met to decide the winner. Time stood still for me, and I was full of butterflies waiting for the results. It was as if I were in my own vacuum, my own little world unaware of anything else around me.

The head judge, Mr. White, announced the third-place winner, Betty Smith. Then he announced the second-place winner, Karen Jones. I held my breath. Finally, he announced, "The winner of this year's poetry contest is Margaret Olson. Maggie, will you please come up on stage to receive your fifty-dollar prize?"

As we left the auditorium, people congratulated me for being our school's best poet. "Good job, Maggie," Yanni hollered across the parking lot.

"You were wonderful! And your poem was excellent," Dad said as we climbed into the car to go back home to the farm. "I am very proud of you."

Grandma and Ava agreed. "You sure were wonderful," they said.

"Thanks. I didn't expect to win, but I'm glad I did. Glad I finally was recognized for something."

In fact, I thought I might write another poem someday soon. There is nothing like success to encourage a person. I saw this happen to Bridget. She became more confident than ever as a musician.

The poetry contest was over, and soon it would be the end of March. April would bring Easter and dessert dinner. Then there would be May, just as if we snapped a finger, with Mother's Day, Memorial Day, the school picnic, final exams, and graduation. It would bring the end of seventh grade and the end of initiation to junior high. By next fall we would be authentic junior high students.

MAY FLOWERS

May came with warm, beautiful, summer-like weather. Leaves were out, pussy willows were long gone, and fruit trees were blooming, sending heavenly sweet perfume across the countryside. Farmers were making use of the good weather diligently seeding their crops before the rains of June. They would be done earlier than other years. Everyone was expecting another perfect growing season.

Another year of school was almost over. The thought of ending seventh grade brought mixed emotions after a year of mixed blessings.

There were the blessings of Jenneweins' new home and musical talent, Dad's marriage, others learning about Mary Elizabeth's athletic ability, and the good feelings even after the disagreement over the wedding dance.

This past year was unlike the year before. It brought with it responsibility such as building our homecoming float on time, practicing so that the band would please the community and gain its favor, doing our homework more independently, making it to class on time, and scheduling everything to work together.

We made decisions about friendships, shuffling back and forth the things that were important in relationships and throwing out what wasn't. There was more independence, such as my asking Yanni to the dessert dinner instead of my dad. Sometimes we chose what was best for us individually.

Doing what was best for us individually would carry over to summer vacation. Mary Elizabeth planned to work at the café and go down south to visit. Bridget would go to New York to see her family, practice the violin, and concentrate on her music. I planned to help the Larsons by babysitting Emily now and then.

It had been over a year since they were stranded in the snowstorm and were rescued by Mr. Anderson and my dad. Emily was going on two years old, and Mrs. Larson was as Grandma said, "in the family way."

No, it wouldn't be like the blissful summer of last year, a summer of playing with friends, swimming at Winding River Park, and living our childhood dreams. Our new independence came at a price, and I felt my heart tightening with the feeling of loss. I tried to make myself feel better by thinking, "You can't remain a child and play forever."

I found Ava a mixed blessing also. I loved having another woman around our house, but she took time away that I used to spend with Dad.

It was easy to see why my dad was crazy in love with her. Elegant, feminine, and beautiful, she had brains and class. I could still see them getting into their decorated Chevrolet leaving for their honeymoon with Ava in her fitted winter white wool suit and wide brimmed winter white hat. It was almost as if an angel walked beside Dad, arm in his. She looked fragile, and Dad certainly treated her as if she would break into a million pieces when he gently opened the car door for her and helped her in, showing the world watching that he was in charge and taking care of his lovely new wife.

Before Thanksgiving, Dad sold all our livestock so that there wouldn't be any hard farm chores for Ava to do. His farming operation would only include grain, corn, and potatoes, and it had gotten so big he didn't have time for anything else such as milking cows and feeding pigs and chickens. And they certainly weren't jobs he wanted for his new wife.

By now, Ava had taken over the house and the yard, trying to make up for the years that a woman was absent. Gradually, she had painted walls, changed curtains and furniture, added femininity to everything, and made it look less of a widower's house and more of a family home.

It was in the yard that I found Ava much stronger than I thought she was when I saw her mowing the grass with the push mower. She'd smile and wink, "This is one way I can keep my girlish figure."

She also showed a talent for gardening, both vegetables and flowers. Each day she added something around the white, two-story farmhouse to enhance its beauty and the beauty of the farm. She dug and hoed around the old perennials to give them new life once the tulips had finished blooming. The hollyhocks of pink, maroon, lavender, and white were against the wall and background flowers. She planted Shasta daisies, daylilies of all colors, tall columbines that were white, pink, purple, and yellow, purple coneflowers, and some additional lavender and white irises after cleaning and thinning the old ones. She planted all kinds of annuals in her flower garden. Pink, lavender, and white tall larkspur, gold and orange marigolds, white, red, and yellow nasturtiums, orange, red, peach, yellow, and white snapdragons, zinnias of several colors, dainty little bachelor buttons of pink, lavender, purple and white, and tall, beautiful cosmos of white and deep rose. She finished with blue and pink forget-me-nots that she hoped would come back the following year. Carefully and well-thought out, she planted everything with the taller plants in the back and graduating to the smaller ones in front.

Together, Ava and I planted a vegetable garden. It had rows and rows of everything: peas, carrots, beans, red beets, radishes, rutabagas, lettuce, cucumbers, tomatoes, winter and summer squash, potatoes, cabbage, cauliflower, broccoli, and sweet corn. Among the corn rows, we planted pumpkins so we would have jack-o lanterns for Halloween and pie for Thanksgiving.

Rhubarb was at its best to pick this time of the year, and Ava made pies, jam, and sauce. She said that after the Fourth of July, we shouldn't pick rhubarb because it needed what was left to produce next year's crop. The asparagus was shooting out of the ground and soon would become one of our special vegetables. She took the greens from the wild dandelions and make salads for us. "It's quite healthy," she'd say. "And it tastes good. Something like lettuce. The flowers make very good wine, too, if we wanted to make some. Can't drink too much of it, though.

It's very strong and has a kick to it."

Sometimes it bothered me that I was helping someone take over and run my mother's house. It just seemed different, and I hoped my mother didn't mind, especially since I was beginning to like Ava. She was proving herself to be more than a pretty lady from the city.

Every year since I could remember, Dad had gone to Minnesota's fishing opener on Mother's Day weekend, but this year he had decided not to go. "I want to spend Mother's Day with Mom and Ava," he shared with me one day. "And you," he added.

On Mother's Day, Pastor Wood announced in his service that he was moving to North Dakota. "I've accepted a call there and will begin the first of June."

Everyone knew why he was moving. As the rest of the congregation expressed regret and sadness, Mrs. Amundson, the catalyst of all the turmoil, sat in front of us stoic and quiet as if nothing happened and as if she didn't care.

Grandma especially felt bad since it was after Paul Ivanovich's funeral that things got bad for Pastor Wood, and she felt responsible in some way. She confided this to us on the way to Andersons' Café for Mother's Day dinner.

"Ma, it's not your problem. It's Mrs. Amundson's problem," Dad volunteered as he tried to make her feel better.

"Suppose we'll be out hunting for another preacher soon," Grandma added as we were being seated in the café. "Hal, do you want to be on the committee to find one?"

"No thanks. I know it's important to have good people on the committee, but I have other things to do." With that he walked to the kitchen and came back with two bouquets of red roses in crystal vases. "Happy Mother's Day, Mom. And Happy Mother's Day, my darling Ava," he lovingly said as he gave a bouquet of roses to both.

Dad looked at Ava and winked. Then he announced, "Ava and I are expecting a baby sometime in late November.

"Congratulations! I am so happy for you!" Grandma said as she hugged both of them. She had always wanted more grandchildren and was truly overjoyed. "Maggie, aren't you happy that you are having a brother or a sister?"

I was happy for them, but I really didn't know if this is what I wanted or not. I lost my mother. My dad got married, and I had to share him with Ava. Now I had to share him with someone else. It would take time to sort this out, but I looked at Dad and Ava and said, "I am happy for you."

"While everyone else was finishing their fried chicken and mashed potato dinner, Mary Elizabeth and I went for a walk around the block passing the hardware store, Johnsons' General Store, the Standard station, the John Deere dealership, the post office, and several other businesses. Finally, Mary Elizabeth broke the silence, "You might like having a brother or sister, Maggie," she offered. "It gets lonely being the only one. At least have an open mind. Doesn't sound like you have a choice in this anyway."

"It is true what Mary Elizabeth said," I told myself that night as I lay in bed trying to fall asleep. I had no choice. I needed to accept this and be happy about it. I was glad that I had made Ava a Stepmother's Day card and given it to her. It mainly just said, *"To my Stepmother. Have a Happy Mother's Day."*

There were now less than three weeks until summer vacation. In early May we had our band and choir spring concert and then continued practicing for the Memorial Day program and parade. Mr. Wynd had us marching every day. The plan was to follow the flags carried by the American Legion to the graveyard where there were rows of crosses with wreaths for those who died in the military.

We practiced "Beautiful Savior," "Battle Hymn of the Republic," "The Star-Spangled Banner," and "My Country Tis of Thee" until we knew the words and notes by heart. Mr. Wynd always made sure we were ready to perform for the public.

"Make sure your uniform is pressed and clean and your shoes and gloves are spotless white," Mr. Wynd ordered. "Be here and ready to go an hour before the program so we can tune our horns." And to Joyce Jenson, who would play "Taps" after the gun salute, "Joyce—practice 'til you can play it in your sleep."

Grandma said that after World War II, the auditorium was always packed with people on Memorial Day. She never missed going to honor and remember Grandpa. This year was no different. There was a full house for the program.

As the band marched down the streets toward the cemetery, I thought of my beautiful red-haired mother, who had been gone four years now. A lump moved into my throat making it difficult to play my flute. I was glad when the only thing left was the slow beat of the drum pounding in my ears and my heart beating in my chest as we neared the cemetery.

My whole body felt chilled, and I began to shiver thinking about mother. Would I always remember her? What she looked like? How she talked? Or would I forget someone I had loved so profoundly and simply as a child? And, although my new stepmother was beginning to take her place in my life and growing on me, I still wondered how you go on without your real mother.

Dad had moved on with his life. He had his beautiful, blonde, blue-eyed Ava and a new baby coming in the fall. Yet, I knew I would always remind him of mother with my strawberry blonde hair and freckles across my nose. I was her daughter.

My thoughts went to Pavel Ivanovich, also gone from our lives. I hadn't understood how much a part of me Pavel had become. It was through him that Grandma taught me the value of friendship and to stand by someone, even if he was the ragged town derelict that no one understood. She was there for his spring burial among the oak trees in a little country cemetery where his troubles ended and where he was finally safe. That day Grandma said her final good-bye in Russian to Pavel. "*Do svidaniya, Pavel. Poka!*" she said as she threw him a kiss and then wiped tears from her eyes. Eventually he would be covered with vibrant green grass and the colorful flowers Grandma would lovingly place on his grave every year.

When the Memorial Day ceremony at the cemetery ended, different family members picked up flags and placed them on the graves of their lost loved ones who served in the U.S. military.

We walked back to the school to put away our uniforms and instruments. Our part in the day's festivities was over.

There were more activities for us in May, however. There was graduation day with our band performing "Pomp and Circumstance" as the seniors marched in. There was our school picnic at Winding River Park, usually held the day before graduation. And there were final tests to take and subjects to pass.

The weather on picnic day couldn't have been more perfect. It was sunny and seventy degrees with a gentle breeze. Dressed in Bermuda shorts, tee shirts, jackets, bobby socks, and tennis shoes, Mary Elizabeth, Bridget, and I boarded the bus, along with Yanni, that would take our seventh-grade class to the park. We made small talk all the way, and it didn't take long to get there. We would spend the day with friends, playing softball, hiking, and eating roasted wieners with catsup and mustard, pork and beans, and roasted marshmallows.

As we exited the bus, I noticed the sun highlighted Yanni's blonde hair more than usual. He had grown taller and even more muscular, no longer looking like a boy but a young man, tan already from helping his dad on the farm, and he was exceptionally handsome.

Yanni must have been also looking at me. "The red in your hair is really shining today, Maggie. It's almost glowing."

I had grown a few inches myself. And I'd matured. No longer was I the little sixth grade girl that walked with him a year ago around the whole Tollefson farm looking at the flowers, trees, and animals. For both of us there were only five more years before we graduated from high school. And I thought, "That will go fast."

Besides playing in the junior high softball tournament that we seventh graders lost, Yanni and I walked around the park talking most of the day. Now and then we'd sit on the bank of the river and watch it flow with white caps and foam in places. We waded over rocks in shallow spots, threw stones to make them skip in the water, and hiked the path along the river and into the woods.

"I want to be a doctor, Maggie," Yanni shared. "What are your plans?"

"I don't know yet. I can't decide." Yanni was always so organized he already knew what he wanted in life.

"You need to have some idea so that you take the right courses in school the next few years."

"Well, I've sort of thought about being a nurse...or a teacher. There aren't that many choices for girls." I felt good. At least I had some idea of my future now, and I'd said it out loud to Yanni. It was a big step and an important one because all my friends were focused on their futures already.

"We'll always be friends, Maggie?" It sounded like a question. Then he bent own and kissed me on the cheek.

It was my first kiss ever from a boy, and it was from Yanni. I blushed and said, "Yes, we'll always be friends."

Our school picnic marked the end of seventh grade. The next day was graduation for the senior class. The day after graduation we went back to school for our report cards and then home as eighth graders for summer vacation with its new obligations: jobs...music lessons...farm work...babysitting.

During the past year our bodies and minds developed into those of teenagers with hopes and dreams for the future. I wondered what the next five years would hold before I, too, would graduate and go on to college. These past few years had taught me that life is ever changing, and I sighed as I contemplated what might lie ahead.

Thank goodness we had five years left to be part of Norden. Then I knew I would be ready to leave home for college, new life changes, and challenges.

A DOZEN SUMMERS

Copyright 2024

Bonnie Rokke Tinnes

SUMMER OF 58

Grandma Olson was often at the farm helping Ava that summer. One day at June's end, Ava was resting on the couch with her feet raised on a pillow. I, Margaret, was at the kitchen window checking every two minutes for Mr. Larson's car and my ride to their house for another day of babysitting Emily. It was a lovely summer morning with sound coming through the screen of the open kitchen window of singing, chirping birds and a crowing rooster as they sang as a choir welcoming the beginning of a perfect warm and sunny summer day.

Inhaling deeply, I sighed and said, "The air sure smells good, Grandma." That day I was especially glad to be alive. "I just love the sounds and smells of summer," I added.

"It IS beautiful out there. Just listen to the birds agreeing with you. And, we can't forget the trusty old rooster," Grandma replied as she smiled and nodded in agreement.

There were no *ands, ifs, or buts* about it. Grandma loved the farm where she had lived her best years with her husband Albert Olson, her one and only true love, and raised my dad, Halbert, Hal as everyone called him.

Deep in thought, I hesitated for a moment and said, "I miss Mary Elizabeth and Bridget, though. It is lonely this summer and not the same with them gone. Not fun and carefree like last two summers." I looked up at Grandma. "Taking care of Emily has helped."

"Just part of growing up, I guess."

"I know, but today I've decided growing up is not fun. Not even one little bit."

"Tomorrow will be different. You'll see."

Mary Elizabeth went back to Alabama to visit family right after school let out, and Bridget left for New York to stay with her handsome brother David Jennewein and other family. I thought that perhaps she was checking out Julliard School of Music. With them gone and my living so far from town, it was quiet and uneventful.

"When we said good-bye the last day of school, Grandma, I had no idea of how long the summer would be without them."

"I know. Three months can be a long time when you care about someone and enjoy their company," Grandma agreed.

The discussion ended when Mr. Larson turned into the driveway and I ran out the door saying, "Bye, Grandma! By Ava," barely looking back.

The day had just begun, and in the living room was my once energetic and enthusiastic stepmother Ava, already worn out and exhausted, who was expecting a child in November

But the summer was hard on Ava. Each day she became more swollen with the baby she was carrying inside of her, and each day housework and gardening became more tiresome and difficult. Heat of summer's sun and humidity caused Ava to perspire more excessively going into July. We all were concerned about her health, especially her "Darling Hal" as she called Dad.

. She was good to Father, and it was obvious he was crazy about her. "She has made Dad so happy. I can see the big change in him," I thought to myself and often expressed to Grandma.

It was the weekend after July 4, when my dad told me that he had deep concerns about Ava's mental and physical health, but there was a reason for her not feeling well. "Yesterday at Ava's regular doctor's appointment, Dr. Brown said her weight gain, tiredness, and need for rest were mostly caused from having twins. Twins, Margaret! We're not having one baby, but two. I am so happy that I can't believe it!" Dad gently but excitedly told me, his one and only child and daughter.

"Twins?" I questioned to make sure she heard correctly.

"Yes, twins." Dad smiled and then added, "I need you to give up your job at the Larsons and help Ava and me at home.

"Do I have to?"

"Yes!"

"But... It's the only good thing I have going this summer till band practice starts the end of August. Frankly, Dad, I don't want to quit my job! Besides I like the money."

"I'll pay you what you make at the Larsons plus still give you your allowance."

"I still don't want to."

"Well then, it's an order. You are coming home to help." And that was that! The next day Dad drove me in our new blue Hudson to the Larsons and explained the family situation and told them I was needed at home because of Ava's health and need for rest.

"My mother will come for a week and help us so you have time to find someone to take Margaret's place," Dad assured them. He was fair-minded and tried never to leave anyone in a bad situation if he could help it.

The next week passed quickly, and when Friday came, Emily, Mr. and Mrs. Larson, and I were all teary-eyed as we said our good-byes. I cried all the way home. I knew deep inside my soul that with all the activities in the Norden community and with twin siblings coming in four months, my life would become so busy I would not have time to babysit at the Larsons again. With mixed emotions, thinking of the changes coming, today I was sad, head down, chin-on-the-chest sad.

"Grandma," I asked. "Does Dad love Ava more than he loved my mom?"

"No. Someday you will understand. He Loved your mom. Well, I guess you can. You knew your mom and dad were kindred spirits. Thought alike. Worked together. Had the same goals. It was tough on him when she passed away. Really tough. He was too young to spend the rest of his days alone, living by himself. He felt he needed a helpmate, a life partner. I'm glad he found her."

"Does Dad love Ava more than me?" I asked despite feeling that Grandma was becoming irritated with me. How dare I question her one and only son!

"No to that, too, Margaret. He loves her differently than he loves you. Some day you will understand. Children eventually leave home to find their own lives, leaving parents at home living their own lives so they don't have to depend on their children all the time. It's life. One day this will be clear to you as clear as a sunny day without a cloud in the sky. It will be bright and shiny and perfect."

"I wish I could believe that, Grandma."

"You will as time passes."

A whole month of summer had gone by, and I had not seen Yanni Tollefson. With Mary Elizabeth and Bridget gone, I missed the camaraderie of friends my own age. I missed our discussions about school and hopes and dreams for the future. I missed Yanni talking about being a doctor and going to the university.

I missed talking to Bridget about her life dreams that were even more exciting than Yanni's. She wanted to be a famous violinist, and this was something she talked about all the time. Then there was Mary Elizabeth who was bound and determined to stand up and fight for civil rights, especially for black people, not only those down south but all over the country. It amazed me that they had such lofty goals that were like God-given destinies.

"I am lucky to have such wonderful, talented friends," I often told myself.

But, here I was spending the rest of my summer helping Ava. As the summer sped on, it was more difficult for her, who spent most of the day resting in bed, to care for the house and garden. Grandma was out at the farm every day helping us. In addition to all her household duties, Ava had planted a huge garden that spring. Growing in the sunshine with regular, soft, gentle rains in the rich black soil, it was almost producing enough to feed everyone in the whole town of Norden and in its surrounding community. It was way too much even for a healthy person to handle.

"I just hate shelling peas," I emphatically stated one day. "Seems it takes a whole day of shelling to get a cup of them!"

"Tedious, for sure," Grandma calmly answered.

And we continued shelling, we talked about all the things going on in the community and the new babies coming in November. It was our way of making mundane activities exciting.

My Dad stuck his head in the kitchen and asked, "Hey Margaret, do you want to ride with me to check on the crops?"

I looked up at Grandma with please written all over my face.

"I need her help right now, Hal," Grandma said. "Got to get these peas done."

So I missed the trip around the farm and the time with my Dad. It was about an hour until he returned.

"Crops look good," Dad said. "Won't be long until we'll be harvesting wheat. Looks like wheat and the potatoes are bumper crops. With no hail, heavy rains, or anything else that can destroy them, we do okay this year."

Ava smiled at him when he said that. She had very few words these days because they took energy that she didn't presently have. It was the smile and the look of complete adoration on her face when he walked into the room that gave her away. She loved him dearly and was on his side one hundred percent. Yes, Dad made Ava happy.

Yanni must have read my mind and known how lonely I was and how I needed company. He was too young to have a driver's license so he biked over to see me one beautiful August day before harvest began. We walked around the farm and through the woods leading to the fields and the path that led to the flowing well where we planned on having a drink of cold, fresh water. We enjoyed just seeing each other and having time together.

Yanni had grown taller and even more muscular and had that summer tan from working in the fields. My heart skipped a few beats because it seemed to me he was especially handsome today.

"Are you ready for school, Yanni?" I asked. "I am waiting for band practice to begin in a couple of weeks so I can see everyone. Thanks to my trusty old flute, I am part of the school band."

"Yes, I am," he answered. "This summer has been more work than fun, and I'm ready for a break. I'm out for football again and plan to be in band, too. Football practice has already started. It's at 6 AM before it gets too hot."

Margaret changed the subject. "I think I will be a teacher, Yanni. I want to help kids, and that's a good way. I'd pondered my future a lot lately."

"Good choice! My plan still is to go to the University of Minnesota and become a doctor."

We discussed the changes taking place in my family and the many changes to come with brothers and sisters. "I think you'll like having brothers or sisters. I wish I did. You'll probably never be lonely again."

Yanni was wise for his age, and I believed he was right. I would love siblings, and I probably would never be lonely again. Giving up my number one spot in the family could be a gift. Anyway, that's how Yanni made me feel.

As time went on I saw that what Yanni said was true. I would love twins in my family. I'd bust my buttons with pride thinking and talking about them, but just could not see it now. They would become one the greatest gifts of my lifetime, a family.

Dad made it absolutely apparent it was important for me to help during the summer of 1958. Losing my mother at age nine and sharing time between the farm with my dad and in town with my grandma made me feel as if I didn't have a place in life.

He said. "You were too young then and never had a chance to realize that also was family. It will take a while, a few years, to recognize and appreciate your stepmother, Margaret. Seems like you can't feel family when everything is chaotic and someone leaves us. I know I felt like that when your mom passed."

I was sad and uneasy discussing Mom's death. "Dad, can we talk about this later?" I asked.

I knew it would take a while with Dad, Ava, and two new family members I had never met, but I also knew it was important spending the summer working with them, my family, as we forged a new life.

"Okay, Margaret," Dad replied. "We'll continue another time." And he went outside to do some chores around the yard.

On that summer day Yanni got me thinking. We were alike and we were different. His goals were way above mine. I suppose you could even say Yanni was more popular than I was in the community and school. At this time we were still just good friends with a kiss on the cheek as we parted to cement our friendship. Was there something deep in our future? I didn't know, but if there was, it was so profound I couldn't put my finger on it.

Grandma used to tell me the greatest love story she had ever heard. It was both happy and sad. Maybe that was what life was all about, one or the other.

RING AROUND THE AUGUST MOON

It was a hot, sweltering, iced-lemonade-drinking August day in Winding River, Minnesota. If you watched the passers by walking on the sidewalks downtown, it was not difficult to see the uneasiness and uncomfortableness they felt as they quickly darted in and out of shops to get relief from the sun as they pushed toward their destination one of which was to get home as soon as possible. Beads of sweat were seen on the brows of many as they wiped their faces with their handkerchiefs if they had one or shirt sleeves if they didn't. The weather with its thick humidity made breathing difficult, and it felt as if it was already raining.

In a two-story building on Main Street, Marie Smith, one of Grandma Olson's good friends, sat at her desk in an office on second floor as editor of the town newspaper, *The Winding River Chronicle*. Busy getting the weekly paper ready for the following day, she was oblivious of what was going on below her on the town's sidewalks and in the stores. She didn't know the town beggar wasn't out there begging for money as he was every other day because of the heat. Getting the paper published was the most important task of the day after her husband Bob had passed away during Christmas about seven months ago. She threw herself: body, soul, and spirit into publishing that hadn't yet replaced the loneliness.

Amy Martin, Marie's personal secretary, brought the mail to her. Digging through the daily trash mail, loan offers, and other advertisements, Marie put her hands on a hand-written, white, parchment envelope addressed personally to her. Eager to find out who sent it and what it said, Marie opened it quickly with her silver letter opener.

Dear Marie,

My class from Winding River High School are having a reunion on August 31 at Loon Lake Resort. It would be my pleasure if you would come as my guest. Sincerely, Jordon Lewis.

RSVP to the return address on the envelope.

Marie looked shocked to the point that Amy asked, "Are you okay? You look almost sick."

"I'm fine," she answered.

Jordon Lewis! It had been thirty years since Marie had heard from him. "Why now?" Why was he contacting her now? Did he know Robert had died? Was he keeping track of her and wanting to form a relationship again? Torrents of questions flooded through her confused mind.

She was no longer a fifty something woman but a seventeen-year-old girl again. Her aching, yearning heart frightened her. She thought she was over him years ago. Now it was if it was yesterday when he left Winding River never to return. Jordon Lewis, heart throb, who was tall, dark, handsome, and rich, had nonchalantly contacted her and walked right into her life as he did before, making her vulnerable again.

Amy couldn't help but notice that Marie quickly glanced into the mirror to assess herself. She was graying a little and looked matronly. There were crow's feet around her eyes and wrinkles around her mouth. She thought out loud, "If Jordon Lewis didn't want me as a seventeen year old beauty, how in the world would he want me now?"

Amy turned to Marie and asked, "Who is Jordon Lewis?"

"An old boyfriend. Please don't tell anyone about this. He wants to take me to his class reunion."

Thirty some years earlier Marie was an All-American girl, raised on a Minnesota farm. With natural blonde hair, blue eyes, and a slim, hour-glass figure, she looked like Doris Day according to the people in Nordon. With all that going for her and her outgoing personality, she was elected the school's homecoming queen.

Marie's family was poor compared to Jordon's. Her parents scratched out a living so their children would be clothed and fed, but they all had jobs fending for themselves to earn spending money for extra things they needed or wanted.

Marie took a job cleaning cabins and waiting tables at South Point Resort on Loon Lake the summer before leaving for a small Minnesota college to become a teacher. And that is how it began. A sweet, beautiful but poor country girl and a rich, handsome town boy, who was there on vacation, were together at a lake all summer.

Jordon's father owned a huge, successful construction company, and Jordon was planning on attending Yale in the fall. But that summer the two of them met in the moonlight by the lake every night after work was done and talked into morning hours. He held her in his arms and said, "I love you, Marie. I hope you will marry me one day."

Then he added promising, "Oh, I'll write to you every day and be back next summer."

And Marie loved him, her handsome, debonair, soul mate as she had never loved before. "I love you, Jordon Lewis. I'll wait for you."

It was the end of August and Jordon was leaving for the city the next morning and from there to Yale. "Meet me tonight by the dock," he said. And night came and the moon was full shining its light softly on the lake and the dock. There was a soft breeze and the scent of all kinds of wildflowers filled the sweet, night air.

That night Marie wore Jordon's favorite dress of hers, a flowing pink, soft cotton that was gathered at the waistline. After work, she hurriedly closed the lodge so she could meet him. The beautiful harvest moon seemed larger than usual with a huge ring around it and seemed to shine even more brightly on the water. The air was still, except for a soft summer breeze, and everything was quiet except for the croaking of the frogs around them. Approaching the dock, she couldn't see Jordon. "He must have been delayed," she told herself.

As Marie waited in the moonlight on the dock that night, Jordon never came. Minutes passed and then hours. She began to sob into the night because she knew in her heart the truth. He was not coming, and she would probably never see him again. He was going to Yale, and she was going to a small, Minnesota college. The two would never meet. She felt the power of society's classes send her reeling into despair and abyss.

The following May as Marie was waking up from anesthesia, she heard someone say, "You have a little boy. What are you going to name him?"

"Jordon. His name is Jordon."

Then they took him, her first-born, to hand him over to "a fine, upstanding, childless couple, who will be able to give him a good home."

"You will be able to go on with your life and plan as if nothing happened," they said.

Twice in her eighteen plus years of life she had felt this kind of loss. The first time was when Jordon walked out on her. The second was now. They were slicing off part of her heart, and it would never heal.

Marie put down the parchment invitation almost with pure rage thinking that Jordon Lewis would dare come back into her life. She wasn't ready for him, but something deep inside of her told her to answer that letter. For a moment everything inside her soul and spirit screamed, "Ignore that invitation! Ignore that invitation! Ignore it!" Then the same inner voice settled down and gently said, "Maybe it is time that Jordon Lewis knew about their son because wherever that little boy, over thirty years old now, was today, she knew he was special."

Marie answered Jordan accepting the invitation. He said he cried hearing about little Jordon. Later, they became friends and searched and found their son, a physician in Minneapolis. Somehow, things had turned out especially well for Jordon Senior. His wife could not have children, and she had recently passed away.

But because of an invitation to a class reunion, he had a friend in Marie and a son, a successful one at that.

As I reminisced about Marie and Jordon's story, I thought of Yanni and me. Yanni was leaving for a big important college. I was staying closer to home. Our positions in life also would be different. Would he leave me because his importance overpowered mine?

"Uffda," Grandma always said when I brought it up. "You and Yanni are both only fourteen. Honest to Pete!" The conversation ended like that all the time. Abruptly. Grandma refused to talk about something she thought stupid.

I wanted to ask Grandma who Pete was and what he had to do with our discussion. I wanted to ask her what "Honest to Pete" meant but didn't. I didn't dare. She had changed and seemed to have become more impatient with me. It was her way of making me move on, I think. Her way of saying, "Honest to Pete, Margaret! Grow up!"

Nope! It was obvious my coddling days were over. No way was I to grow up a rich, little brat. No way! At least I felt this was what Grandma wanted. I would become someone that was responsible, considerate, and caring.

A NEW REVEREND

It was two weeks until September with school starting the day after Labor Day. Grandma, Ava, and I were sitting at the kitchen table with its red and white checkered oilcloth and frilly white curtains having chocolate chip cookies, still warm from baking, and coffee. Well, I had milk because Grandma always said, "If you drink too much coffee, it will stunt your growth."

There was a knock at the kitchen door leading to outside, and I hurried to answer it. On the steps stood a man in his mid-forties with graying hair and a pleasant look on his face. He was medium height, and I guessed about five feet nine inches. Extending his hand, he greeted me saying, "Hello! My name is Pastor Isaiah Tollefson, your new pastor."

I shook his hand and asked, "Are you related to Yanni Tollefson?"

"No relation at all." Then he changed the subject asking, "Is your mother at home?'

"My grandma and stepmother are here. We're just having morning coffee and fresh cookies. Would you like to join us?'

"Yes," he answered as he walked confidently and quickly through the kitchen door.

"Pastor Tollefson, this is my stepmom Ava, and this is my Grandma Olson. And this is our new Pastor Tollefson. No relation to Yanni," I said as I quickly introduced all of them and reaching my arm toward Pastor making sure he was acknowledged.

"Pleased to meet you," he said. "I was driving by on the way to the church and decided to stop and make your acquaintance."

We visited for a while, chit chatting about the community, farming, school, the church, and anything else they felt important. Of course, he asked Ava how she was doing. "When is your baby due?" he asked with concern because she looked exceptionally tired.

"Babies," Ava said. "The babies are due in November sometime.

I couldn't help but think of Pastor Wood, long gone mostly because of the community's nosey busy-body Mrs. Gertrude Amundson. "She scared more people away from church, especially from taking communion because no one felt good enough, than the devil," Margaret thought. "Sure hope this time around, it goes better for Pastor Tollefson."

In just those few minutes with Pastor Tollefson, I had already sized him up. He was not as meek and gentle as Pastor Wood, and I decided that his outgoing, confident, and self-assured demeanor would be able to take on and handle Gertrude.

As Pastor got up to leave, he shook everyone's hand and extended his invitation to church. "I sure hope we see you in church on Sunday and that you will take part in activities. I have planned to make our church grow and to be full of the Spirit. God and I will need all the help we can get."

"That is for sure," I thought.

Grandma was the perfect helper, and she loved that country church. Right next to it was the graveyard where her dear, beloved husband, my grandpa, lay. It also was where my mother, her daughter-in-law, and Pavel, her Russian friend, whose full name was Paul Ivanovich, were buried. They were three of the people she loved most in the world, and one day she would be there, too. All of them were in the Olson family plot right there on the prairie among grasses with wildflowers and pine and oak trees surrounding them. It was one of her most beloved, beautiful spots on earth. There was no doubt whatsoever that she'd always be faithful to the church.

All of this brought back memories of Pavel's funeral almost a year ago and Grandma's fight to overrule Gertrude so he could be buried there. Pavel's relatives, looking extremely wealthy, odd, and different all sober and dressed in black drove their black Cadillac from California to say goodbye to Pavel, their beloved brother, as he was laid into the ground. His funeral brought about Pastor Wood's departure. Or was it the other way around? Was Pavel's coffin the final nail?

The community's poor attendance was obvious, and Pastor Wood's sermon on judging was more obvious. It now seemed like a dream what took place in one spot on the prairie

So Pastor Isaiah Tollefson was here to change all of that. We hoped.

"I really like him," Ava said.

"I like him, too," Grandma answered.

"Good luck, new pastor" I thought.

"Anyway, Margaret, there is band practice tonight, and we have to get busy and finish canning these green beans before we head for town. You can spend the night with me, "Grandma said. "Back to work!"

Grandma told Margaret many times that "God had His way that day." He had His way even if Pastor Wood left after that final intolerable "stunt," as Gertrude called it. It was the final nail.

BELLA MEANS BEAUTIFUL

Grandma drove back to town after supper and let me off by the school for band practice. I was early and sat on the steps waiting for the rest of the band members. Mary Elizabeth and Bridget weren't home yet so I didn't expect to see them. They were both coming home in a week, a week before school started. Yanni promised he was coming, and he was the next to arrive. Mr. Wynd was waiting inside the band room.

Yanni and I couldn't figure out who the tall and graceful girl was coming up the sidewalk. "She must have just moved here from the cities," Yanni turned to me and said.

"Must have."

As she got closer to the school, they heard, "Hi, Margaret and Yanni," a cheerful shout from across the school yard. Along with the cheerful "Hi," she was waving and evidently happy to see them.

Yanni and I looked at each other, eyes and mouths wide open, with surprise and utter amazement. "Bella?" we asked each other. "Bella?"

"Hi!" we shouted back overwhelmed by her total body makeover that had taken place during the summer. It was like looking at someone else who had Bella's voice.

Bella ran up to them and hugged them. "I am so happy to see you two. So happy."

I could barely concentrate on band practice after seeing Bella. The rest of the band students were as shocked as I was. Mr. Wynd was also shocked, I bet, but he didn't let on. Yanni and I were glad when band practice finally ended.

The last time they saw Bella, she was known by everyone as Big Fat Bella. She had come back from summer vacation looking like a movie star, like Natalie Wood. Both Yanni and I thought,

"If anyone deserves to be beautiful, it is Bella." No one in the whole school was bullied as much as she was. We were witnesses to that.

Bella came to their school in first grade. She walked into the classroom, disheveled, overweight, looking lost and alone. It was an indelible impression left in my mind, probably everyone else's, too. There were snickers behind her back, and no one came right out and told her, but one often heard, "That girl is homely as a mud fence and fat as a pig."

"Mom, they are mean to Bella," I would sadly say after school.

"You be nice to Bella, Margaret. Be nice. Just give life a few years, and you will see how things change and what happens to mean people. Sometimes the most unattractive children become the most beautiful adults."

"You mean like the story of the ugly duckling?"

Grandma nodded and said, "Ya, just wait until the class has its fortieth and fiftieth class reunion. Sometimes it takes that long."

I remembered the crushed sad look on Bella's face one Valentine's Day. Everyone had valentine boxes, and Bella had one huge valentine that just didn't fit in her box. She was thrilled while waiting with anticipation for the class Valentine's Day Party to open her huge valentine. "Must have cost a fortune," she told me. "Somebody cares."

Valentine's Day came and the party came, and Bella opened her valentine. She didn't cry, but her eyes clouded up and became sad when she saw the big fat pig on the card that she had waited so long to open. I felt sick in my stomach and almost cried for her. It hurt.

That day I came home from school and told my mom, "They have to stop that!"

"Stop what, Dear?"

"They have to stop putting the scale to weigh the school kids in the middle of the classroom! It's cruel, Mom. It's cruel! Now everyone in class knows how much Bella weighs."

It was cruel, and whatever possessed them to do that, I will never know. I wanted to believe that no one on earth could be that mean. I would also never believe that one day Andy would raise his hand in the middle of class and ask, "Is it true Bella means beautiful?'

And right in the middle of the classroom, teacher immediately said, "Yes, it does." I would never believe that everyone in class laughed except Bella, Yanni, and me.

Because of Bella, I hated cruelty. I would fight back. Bella refused to. There were times I would shout at them, "Shut up and leave her alone!"

I didn't sleep much that night after band practice where I saw beautiful Bella for the first time. Memories of conversations and things that happened in the past, good and bad, filled my thoughts as I tossed and turned thinking how fortunate older people were having already gone through everything and having seen the end results. "Just wait a few years," they had said.

All I said to Grandma that night was, "You should see Bella. She is beautiful."

A few years later when Bella was in college, she had finally overcome the sadness of her childhood and dared to speak about and share in an honest, more matter-of-fact way her experiences and the lessons she had learned. One semester for creative writing class she penned a short story and shared it with me.

A PIECE OF CAKE
By Bella Carter

There it was, a most delicious piece of cake, sitting in the center of the table. There it was, and it was magnified before her eyes. She could feel her salivary glands hurriedly going to work as she hungrily viewed the velvety chocolate with its soft, white icing. "Aw nuts!" she exclaimed, "It's only one piece of cake."

Sighing with contentment, she devoured the last crumb. Then slowly rising from her chair, she clumsily walked to the mirror on the wall at the opposite side of the living room. "I'm not fat," she thought. "In fact, I believe I have lost a few pounds." Then she patted her excess rolls and trudged to her bedroom, deciding that tomorrow she would really diet.

As she prepared herself for bed, the day's activities drifted through her mind. Today had been a perfect day for her. It was her birthday. Business at the grocery store was slow in April, and Mr. Johnson allowed more free time. Today, she had watched the afternoon matinee, "I Love Paris," on television. She had always wanted to go to Paris.

Tonight, she had three surprise visitors, who brought her the birthday cake. Henry Johnson, her employer, was one of them. He was likeable even if he spent the whole evening amusing himself with his own jokes. Judith Pratt, a virtuous schoolteacher, never missed Martha's birthday. All evening, Miss Pratt attempted to hold an intellectual conversation concerning Einstein's Theory of Relativity with John Davis, a scientist, who spent his winters in a deserted mountain village.

The conversation seldom concerned Martha. Once, however, Miss Pratt asked "Martha, how old are you today?"

"You know better than to ask a woman her age," Henry scolded, but then laughed.

Miss Pratt continued, "She can't be any older..."

"I'm twenty-seven," Martha abruptly interrupted.   She knew she would not be young very much longer, and it always annoyed her when it was mentioned.

"Well, it's about time you left Winthrup," John suggested. "You haven't gone anywhere since your mother died eight years ago, have you? You can't live alone in this spacious house all your life.

"I think she should find herself a husband," Henry added. Ironically everyone laughed, and the conversation went back to Einstein.

Martha had two loves, food and food. When she was young, her classmates called her fat sow and other distasteful names. "You'd make a good circus fat lady," they taunted. And she would cry.

Her dream was to leave Winthrup and return slim and beautiful. Then everyone would be astonished and say, "Martha Dobbs, how lovely you are!"

And she would look at them and say, "Thank you." Then she would look at Connie Thompson, queen of their class, who now was fat and ugly.

The day after her birthday, as she was stamping prices on soup cans, a young man entered the store. He had shopped there at least once before, but today she especially noticed him. He was whistling and almost skipping between the rows of canned goods looking for peanut butter and jelly. Today he was so happy he especially caught her attention. Plus, he was very good looking.

Martha hurriedly went to the cashier's stand, and when he came with his groceries, she rang up his bill.

"Good morning," he said.

"Good morning," she answered. The times were rare when someone, such as he, would make a special effort to speak to her.

"He would never notice me," she thought. He was pleasantly congenial and smiled at her when he left. "It was a smile on which to build a dream," she thought. As his jeep slowly traveled up the mountain road, she stood by the window and watched.

His name was Charles Coulter, and he came to the store shopping for groceries once or twice a week. Each time he was always positive. "Thank you for everything," he always said and sometimes stayed to chat awhile. Then he paid his bill, tipped his hat, smiled, and left.

No one seemed to know where he came from, but they knew he lived in a small cabin in the mountains. "Enjoying my privacy," he told the townspeople.

Martha waited for his visits. There were days when they would only discuss the weather. It was beautiful weather, and June was coming with its tourists traveling through the village to vacation and hike in the mountains. Tourists were important bringing in new excitement and conversation for everyone, including Charles and Martha. Things weren't as dull in town the weeks they were there.

One day Charles lingered at the store longer than usual. "Martha," he asked. "Have you ever been on the west side of Shallow Creek?"

"Yes. Been a few years, though. Why?"

"Have you ever been there in May or June?"

"No."

"This spring it is covered with flowers of all colors-blue, yellow, red, and pink. I have never seen anything that breathtaking. The flowers and the trees next to the creek seem like an enchanted garden kaleidoscope. Do you want to go there with me before the tourists pick all of them?"

Martha tried not to look surprised but quickly replied, "Yes. Yes, I'd love to go." She also knew the tourists and knew time was limited.

The next two months after meeting Charles flew by. Martha felt accepted and loved and forgot to nibble on snacks and had lost enough weight for Mr. Johnson to ask, "Martha, have you lost weight?'

Others noticed, too. And as time passed losing weight was

easier. Charles' friendship made everything worthwhile, and Martha felt she was not only pleasing herself but him. Someone cared, and it made a huge difference.

Another day Mr. Johnson asked, "Martha, have you ever been in love?"

"Not the romantic kind," she answered sadly.

"Your day will come."

By the middle of summer, it was easy to see the change in Martha. Different young men asked her for dates, and she would go. She dined, danced, and had a wonderful time with them. But, she still waited for Charles to come, and each time it seemed she looked younger and prettier.

She never forgot the time he came to the store wearing knee boots.

"Do you like trout?" he asked.

"Yes, have you been fishing?"

"Yes."

"I guess that was a silly question. You look like you've been fishing." They both laughed.

"Just a minute." Going to his jeep, he took something from it and brought it into the store. He set a huge bucketful of trout on the counter by Martha. "It's yours."

"What am I going to do with all that fish?" she asked.

"Share with Mr. Johnson, I guess. Maybe he could sell some. The creek is full of trout now, and I spend a lot of time fishing for recreation. Maybe you'd like to go fishing with me some day, and...maybe we can cook this trout into something delicious together."

Finally Martha got to ask Charles a question she had longed to ask for months but hadn't dared. "What do you do when you aren't fishing?"

"I'm doing research and writing a ...," he began but caught himself. That day Martha learned he was a writer. She was the only one who knew what he was doing in their part of the country.

A few weeks later Charles quit coming to the store. No one

seemed to know where he was. They said he just took off one day, bag and baggage, and didn't say good-bye. Some tourists said it was "Good riddance to him." They were the ones he'd bawled out for picking flowers by the creek.

Martha missed him so much, battling the temptation of going back to her old eating habits now that the secret love of her life was gone. In fact, she felt like Doris Day in her popular song "Secret Love." It was so much like how she felt and the crush she has on Charles, she wanted to shout from the highest hill, tell the trees, the flowers, and everyone. She was sad now that it had ended abruptly, as quickly as it began along with a reason to live, to be beautiful, to work, to do everything. "Dear God," she said. "Why is love so important?"

"Charles," she'd say. "Why wouldn't you stop to say good-bye to me?"

He must have known how she felt. Would they meet again sometime? When or where? So many questions.

But, deep down inside of her was a gift he had given her. A spark of self-worth she had never had. Charles was a gift from heaven in that respect. And deep down inside of her, she knew she could go on with her life and not crash and fall apart. She knew. And deep down inside of her was the knowledge that they would meet again, and this was not over. She believed it.

This was the story of hope that beautiful Bella Carter turned into her creative writing instructor. It was difficult to believe that that story came from her own pain, but it did. Those of us who knew her knew the truth.

SECRETS

Finally Bridget and Mary Elizabeth returned from their summer vacation. I was so excited that I begged Grandma to take me to town to see them. It was okay with Grandma because she needed to go to the General Store to buy groceries for Dad, Ava, and me.

It was nice that Bridget and her family now lived in town by the school in the house her brother David built for them. There was no more going out through the woods to their cabin. Mary Elizabeth and her parents lived upstairs above their restaurant, but the plans for the Andersons were to soon build a house in town. It made things easier for me because we could all meet in Norden.

We just hugged and giggled because we were so happy to see each other. "It's like old times and like you've never been gone," I said.

"It is!" They answered in unison.

"Sure have missed you two," I added.

We began sharing. Mary Elizabeth met her mother in Alabama. "She's a pretty, blonde, blue-eyed lady," she said looking down and almost appearing sad.

Bridget had spent time with her brothers, David and Jeremiah, and her sisters. "We have lots of uncles, aunts, and cousins in New York. I also visited them I looked Juilliard over and even had a few violin lessons.."

I couldn't talk fast enough it seemed. "I had to give up my babysitting job with the Larsons. My stepmom Ava has been on bedrest most of the summer. She's having twins and is having many difficulties. Grandma and I are taking care of the garden, yard, and house. Yes, in November I will have two siblings. Pastor Tollefson just moved into the parsonage, and he is not as meek and quiet as Pastor Wood. I like him. Yanni biked over one day to see me and spend the afternoon. We have been going to band practice. Yanni will play football again this year. And Bella is beautiful. You won't believe it! Looks like a movie star. I am so happy for her. I can't wait till you see her."

It just seemed like I couldn't stop talking until I had to take a deep breath.

"Wow, Margaret, sounds like your summer was anything but dull. Makes me wish I stayed home," Bridget said.

Her statement was quickly followed by Mary Elizabeth's, "Me, too."

As we sat on the bench in front of Anderson's Café, Pastor Tollefson walked up to us and said, "This evening we are having a picnic at Winding River Park. You don't have to bring anything because we'll have hot dogs and beans and smores. Just bring yourselves and come. We'll stay till dark, play some games in the afternoon first, and then sing songs around the bonfire in front of the swimming pool. Hope to see you there."

"We're all coming," we chimed in together.

What a beautiful day to be with my friends for the first time all summer. It was a warm, harvest type of day that gave us an afternoon swimming and visiting one another. The three of us were sitting on the beach at the east end of the swimming pool watching the bright, yellow sun go down in the west as a silver fog mist rose from the quiet pool and enhanced the charming glow of a beautiful evening.

"You want to know what I learned this summer?" She didn't wait for an answer. "I am a Jew. One hundred percent."

"Bridget, why are you so sad?" I asked. "This news should make you happy."

"I don't know for sure. Because...Because so many of us died in the war in those concentration camps. Because of the fear my dad has inside. I don't know." Bridget was bewildered and questioned everything, including humanity's cruelty. "Why?" came out of her along with a sorrowful sob coming from deep inside of her.

"What do you mean, a Jew?" I asked. And then I wondered if Grandma knew this all along. She probably did because she was a true secret keeper and knew more about people than all the rest of us put together.

Mary Elizabeth sat quietly thinking and listening to our extremely important conversation. "Please don't tell anyone," Bridget said almost begging. "I don't think it's going to be easy being a Jew in Norden."

"How in the world did you get way up here and why?" I asked.

"My Dad came here with our family to hide from Hitler. We had relatives in concentration camps that died, and he was afraid that Hitler would win the war and come here and rule the United States."

"Oh my goodness," I thought. Then I said out loud. "Bridget, I cross my heart and hope to die. I will never tell anyone but Grandma, who probably knows already. It sure explains a lot, though." I was shaken. Thinking of the fear they had and still had and that they were off by themselves, hiding far away from home, I felt sad.

Mary Elizabeth finally spoke up. "I cross my heart and hope to die, too." Then she told us that she had spent a long time during the summer with her beautiful white mother. "My mother is white, Norwegian and has blue eyes. I'm half black and half white. My adopted dad, Peter Anderson, is my mother Mary's brother. He is my uncle, and that is how I ended up in Norden, Minnesota. They are good to me and truly related. My stepmom, Marion, is good to me. For now, please cross your heart and hope to die not to tell anyone about this either. I'm not ready for it yet."

"We do, Mary Elizabeth. We do!"

I am sure Grandma already knew this. I thanked God many times she taught me not to see color. Under the circumstances, my two best friends were as different as anybody that had ever come to town. And I loved them.

"I went to see *West Side Story* this summer when I was

in New York. It was a beautiful story. There's a song in the musical," Bridget said. "It's called "Somewhere." The words go like this, 'There's a place for us. Somewhere a place for us.' In some ways we are all misfits, but I believe there is a place for us." Then she shivered as she smiled.

We were quiet until it was time to go. The fireflies were flitting about sparkling and lighting up the night. This was a good place.

GETTING TO KNOW YOU

The revelation of both my friends' backgrounds was explosive and troubling for a fourteen-year-old. I mean. I tried to put myself into their situations so that I would have more understanding and empathy. To think of a family like the Jenneweins, so desperate and afraid, they'd leave a life in New York City for almost the end of the world, it seemed, and move there to hide out in the woods from an evil dictator and government across the ocean was too much to take in, let alone comprehend.

I tried to imagine the fear they held inside that explained the uneasiness and shyness of Mr. Jennewein, a demeanor that had rubbed off on his children. It explained their distrust of people and their moving away as soon as they were old enough. I was so thankful Bridget stuck it out and became my good friend.

If it wasn't so sad, it would be almost humorous thinking of the fear they even had for these stoic, laid-back Scandinavian people in Norden, who had some of the personality traits of the Germans and other northern Europeans. They were hardworking people who often gave the shirt off their backs to help others. Close-mouthed, they would seem stand-offish, but they really weren't. "They are good people," Grandma said. "Always working hard and putting others first." Their values were noticeable because the two first things they built when they settled in this country were a church and a school, putting God and education on a pedestal.

I didn't realize it then, but as I grew older, I had learned first-hand what war did to a family, community, country, and world. It destroyed and wasted some of the most brilliant, talented young and old people in the world. War tore people apart like it did the Jenneweins.

"Thank God for the Andersons, who adopted Mary Elizabeth as their own, Grandma," I said. "She is a bombshell of energy, always moving, always studying, always excelling."

Grandma nodded in agreement.

I continued. "Despite being abandoned by her biological father and most of the time by her biological mother, it seems that there is something inside of Mary Elizabeth Anderson driving and guiding her for good that knows no boundaries. She is going to excel, be somebody, and make this world of ours a better place. I just know it."

I saw no color when I looked at my friend. She was like me, and I admired and loved her as a true sister. To think of all the sadness she had experienced in her short life was troubling also, but as I got to know and love Mary Elizabeth, she was a rock and had inner strength I had never seen in anyone else.

"Oh, Margaret, I am going to Minneapolis to visit friends for a few days. You will be staying with Ava and looking after her when I am gone. My last get-away before life gets busy for all of us."

I looked up at Grandma with dismay and surprise, "But… I only have a few days left of summer vacation, and my friends just got home. I need this time. I just can't do it. I can't!"

"There is no one else, Margaret. I am counting on you." It sounded more like an order.

True, Grandma needed a few days off. She would be busy with the end of harvest when she returned, and when the babies came, she would never get a day off until Ava was strong enough to take over.

I would spend the last days of summer with my stepmother, someone who still was a stranger to me. I wouldn't even think about bringing the subject up to Dad, and Grandma had said so. I just hoped those long seven days, a whole week, went fast.

These last two weeks before eighth grade had to be a coming-of-age crossroads in my life even if I didn't know exactly what a crossroads was. Is my time with Ava my time to really grow up and begin accepting more responsibility? The babies, her health, her vulnerability shouted out to me that she needed me. And maybe with Grandma gone, I would finally get to know my stepmother. And maybe I would learn that I needed her, too.

"OK, Grandma. I will do my best to watch over Ava and get her through the next week."

Grandma smiled, "Thanks!" Then she picked up her suitcase, went to her car and headed for Minneapolis. Ava was still in bed resting. Grandma had stopped by to say "Good-bye" to her earlier.

As the days of the week passed, Ava began to tell me her story, intriguing and enveloping, bringing me into the real her, the real person, the idealistic young woman, a teacher with hopes and dreams to change things, someone almost like me instead of someone from a different world.

I sat amazed with all kinds of emotions fluctuating throughout my mind, emotions all over the spectrum of feelings ever conceived. "Ava, these conversations are profound," I said. "Deeper than anything I had imagined in my first real adult conversation ever."

They were challenging because Ava was changing my opinion about a lot of things, especially my opinion of her. Not only was she beautiful to look at, but she was beautiful inside making me so happy that I finally realized it. I learned quickly that even Ava had overcome difficulties in her life.

THE JUDAS LIE

Ava had the saddest story, and as I listened to her slowly and precisely narrate, I thought that the evilest of sins man thought of was judging others. It was a grave sin that God warned everyone about in the Ten Commandments, actually the first one because God alone was judge and by judging, we were making ourselves God. The next evil sin, I was positive was lying, bearing false witness against your neighbor.

Ava was a beauty with her blonde hair and blue eyes, light skin, and hour-glass figure. Other than eye and hair color, she came as close to being second in looks, a body double, to movie star Ava Gardner, Mrs. Frank Sinatra at one time, as anyone who had ever lived. Men loved her, women hated her, and everyone overlooked her inner beauty and exceptional mind. She was no dumbbell, for sure. I admired her strength after I heard her story. Just maybe, however, my calling her a close double to Ava Gardner was a bit exaggerated.

"It always bothered me that no one saw me, the real person," she sadly stated as an after- thought. "I worked hard right alongside my brothers and father on the farm and dreamed daily of going to college to become a teacher. We were poor coming out of the Great Depression, and I knew that that would involve great sacrifice."

Somehow, it worked out, and Ava got the chance she'd longed for. After graduating from high school, she enrolled in a nearby teacher's college and after two years was hired by a small-town school district in Minnesota as an elementary school teacher.

"I loved teaching," she said. To influence children so early in life was a destiny of mine, and I was happy working and minding my own business, trying to be the best teacher I could possibly be until..."

Small towns could be icky, sometimes. I know as much as I liked Norden, I know it was not always a good place for outsiders. I saw it in how Grandma was treated, and I saw it in how the whole Jennewein family were treated. It took them years to fit in, and they still hadn't quite made it. If the Andersons hadn't been pillars of the community, it would have been a lot harder for Mary Elizabeth. Grandma was always progressive, loved the city, and this didn't help her much with the town's ladies. Her saving grace was her numerous interests and broad outlook on the world and its people. Grandma admired difference.

"The story of the Tower of Babel should tell it all," Grandma often said. "Everyone wanted to be alike in every way with the philosophy that if no one was different, man would be like God and have all the power on earth and universe, making it impossible for anyone or anything to touch them. "Being alike would make all jealousy disappear," they thought. Then all individual gifts of difference given to man began to disappear, and the tower was destroyed by God, mankind was scattered and spoke different languages to stop the destruction of the personal soul. It's a tough life being a judge."

Beautiful, fine, and gentle Ava was invited to the women's club luncheon at the home of Mrs. Smith, the most important woman in the town. Ava was twenty years old and trusted everyone. She had no idea what was coming on that quiet, still, no wind, misty fall Saturday. Grateful in her heart for her teaching job and being able to meet more townspeople, she made her way to the Smiths.

There were about a dozen ladies there, some Ava had met when she first came to town. They chit chatted and had coffee and cake, a welcoming gesture to their new teacher, and time flew until it was time to go home.

Ava felt it was a good day, and as she left, she thanked everyone. Then she walked through the mist to her small apartment.

The next day in church, people were whispering to each

other, covering their mouths so that they couldn't be heard or their lips couldn't be read. Ava wondered what was going on and asked one of the ladies who was at the coffee party. She told Ava she didn't know.

It troubled Ava that she didn't know what was going on, but she had to do some lesson preparation for the next day and couldn't pursue the matter any longer. The next day there was a note in her mailbox at school from Superintendent Hanson requesting she report immediately after she arrived for work to discuss an important matter with him.

"Good morning, Mr. Hanson. Your note says that you wanted to speak with me."

"Good morning, Miss Franzen," he said in a not-so-friendly way unlike last time they spoke. "It is a matter that happened Saturday at the Smiths. It seems that Mrs. Smith has a valuable ruby ring missing. It was on her dresser in her room where all the coats were placed during the coffee party. And they think you are the culprit that took it." He seemed relieved that that part was over.

"You mean that they think I am a thief," Ava said.

"Did you take it?"

"No, I never even saw it. I don't know what you're talking about."

"This is going to make it very hard for you to stay here and teach no matter what happens."

Speechless, Ava's heart sank. She was thinking he was right. She knew small towns, and if they even thought you had done something like that, you would probably never get your reputation back. Shocked and heartbroken, she left his office for her classroom wondering what to do next.

I looked at Ava and said, "That to me sounds like a set-up job. Someone wanted you out of there, but why?"

It reminded me of how people from the cities would send ads out to the country for babysitters and hired girls for the summer. It reminded me of how they would leave change like 75 cents or something in a dish on the countertop, testing the help to see if they were honest. Sometimes it would sit there all summer. You'd think they'd remove it at least after a month.

As I sat there listening to Ava, I felt nervous and anxious because of the unfairness of it all and the thought of what could happen to her after that. I couldn't believe she went through all of that at age 20. "Just not fair, Ava. Not fair at all."

Ava packed up her belongings and went home. Defeated and lost, she had to pick herself up and start over going back to the University and continuing her education there. She looked at me and asked, "Do you want to know what happened?"

"Yes!"

"Nobody told me this until I met one of the townspeople downtown Minneapolis one day when I was shopping. Right after I left, they found the ring in the room where the coats were. It had fallen to the floor and rolled under the dresser. I was proven innocent, and no one let me know."

"Why, I wonder."

"Good question. I really don't know, but what I do know is that Mrs. Smith's niece got my teaching job."

"That says a lot."

It didn't matter to them if Ava had a broken heart and felt like a failure. Sometimes I hated life and people. This was one of those times.

COMEUPPANCES

Grandma returned from a week visiting friends in Minneapolis relieving me of taking care of Ava so I could get ready for school. She said she had a great time seeing everyone and renewing friendships by sharing everything that had happened the past year. It was good to see her because everything felt normal around the house again.

I was able to be with Mary Elizabeth and Bridget the week before school started spending time walking, talking, laughing, and going to Winding River Park. There was planning to do like registering for classes like Algebra I, which was important for our college future wherever we'd go.

Of course, we had a trip to Winding River for new outfits for school. I bought a soft white wool sweater with a hood to go with a Tartan red, gray, and yellow, plaid pleated skirt, knee highs and saddle shoes. Bridget and Mary Elizabeth bought similar outfits. We were cool dressed in the latest fashion with our ponytails tied with ribbon in a bow. "We're cool!" we smiled and told each other. The shoes felt strangely uncomfortable after running barefoot around the farm all summer.

We were waiting in Mary Elizabeth's parents' café for a hamburger and fries when some townspeople came in for coffee. They began talking.

"Did you hear what happened to Harry Amundson?"

"No, what?"

"He partied at the beer joint in our neighboring town and got so drunk he started fighting with some of the people there. You know. The town where everyone goes to drink to hide it from everyone here?"

"No kidding! What happened then?"

"He ended up with a broken nose and a horrible nosebleed

and passed out. Right there on the floor of the beer joint. Gertrude, red-faced and humiliated, had to come and get him and take him to the doctor. Boy! She was really mad. Really mad."

"Is he okay?"

"Ya, but Gertrude isn't. Hardly dares show her face around town now."

Mary E., Bridget, and I looked at each other. We were shocked and couldn't believe the gossip we just heard. Mrs. Amundson, the judge and jury of everyone in the community for years just had a major problem of her own to overcome. She was the one who refused to allow Pavel a funeral in the church because "he was a drunk."

"How is she going to get out of this one," I looked at my two friends and asked. "How is she?" For a moment I felt happy and giddy and delighted that she was finally getting what was coming to her.

My ill will toward Mrs. Amundson didn't last long. Even if I had spent hours of my life mad at her and wishing her bad and avoiding having an encounter with her, I was now spending hours it seemed feeling sorry for her.

She couldn't complain or say anything. She couldn't chastise her husband to others. She was humiliated and embarrassed, brought down to earth like a deflated balloon. Crushed and broken, she'd be seen if she had to go in public, disheveled, with messy hair and red, bloodshot eyes as though she had spent day and night crying.

Is this what Jesus meant when He said what we give to others we get back, overflowing, pushed together and room for more? Or when he said not to judge others so we wouldn't be judged?

"Grandma, I think I got it!"

"What did you get?"

"You know what Jesus meant when He said we get back what we give and get it back overflowing. It's what's happening to Mrs. Amundson!"

As much as I hated Gertrude Amundson, I began to feel

sorry for her. "Grandma," I said. "Everything she stood for and used on others is gone. She has nothing left."

"Margaret, she will have to start over, confess her sins, and eventually make amends.'

"Not that easy, Grandma. Not easy."

Grandma thought and then said, "Hmm! I know," she said. "I feel sorry for her, too. I really do. Maybe for the first time in her life, she understands what she has done to others. That's tough. Really tough!"

"It's hard. Really hard for me to feel sorry for her. I'm mixed up and torn inside." I kept thinking of all the mean things she said to Grandma and all the judgments she placed on her. It was like she never had a life of her own with her nose in everyone else's.

"You've grown up, Margaret. You have matured. It is good to know that you care and are being kind to others. That's all I have to say right now. Yes, be kind and you'll be okay."

"It's sad, though," I replied. It was almost as if my thoughts were coming from a faraway land and not me. From someone else.

"You're learning compassion and are making me proud. Yes, for sure, proud."

Grandma's affirmation built my self-esteem. She smiled, and I believed her when she said, "We need to pray for them. Mr. and Mrs. Amundson are rarely seen these days after the bar fight. They don't show their faces in public. We need to pray that they heal and come out of isolation."

I thought I grimaced and Grandma saw me. I knew we had to move on in life if we wanted to be productive and wonderful. We'd go from swallowing a tough pill and gritting our teeth to a joy-filled life, but it was nothing compared to what Mrs. Amundson had to do. Her humble pie was enough to make anyone choke. Yes, she had a lot of rebuilding to do.

"I believe you, Grandma."

A slow grin spread over Grandma's face, and her face lit up.

A SPECIAL THANKSGIVING GIFT

It seemed like Ava was getting bigger by the minute. It was difficult for her to even walk around the house as she got close and waited for the birth of her twins. I was anxious, too, because Ava took every extra minute of ours. Grandma never said anything, but I know that she felt the same way and would be glad when it was over and she could go back to her own life. However, these were her grandchildren, and grandmas did everything for their grandchildren. She would never ever complain. She often told me, "Grandchildren are a blessed event. A gift from God."

School at Norden Public was in full swing. Yanni, as an eighth- grader, was the star of the football team. They did well in the playoffs when the team came in second. With football season over, began basketball practice and would be on the B team. I mean, wasn't he good at everything?

Mary Elizabeth, Bridget, and I were taking our place in band and choir. Bridget was the honor student there with her knowledge of music and violin and everything else. The rest of us were just typical eighth- graders.

"It's November," Grandma said. "And it's a perfect one."

She was right in her opinion. The trees were barren, and there were patches of snow lying around trees and buildings that told us that snow was going to come. It was Thanksgiving time, for sure.

I noticed a huge change in Grandma. She had aged, and it was obvious her hair was grayer and she had slowed down. She had placed her energy in Ava and the birth of her future grandchildren. That's where her life was now with her only son and his children. We were her future, and that is all that mattered to her. I felt bad seeing her slowing down and less active. At my age, I didn't know the downside of aging.

She changed so much that she quit making quilts after Pavel died. She also didn't need to make a Thanksgiving basket for the Jennewein family, who were living in town and had sufficient everything because of their son David from New York. They also had other friends in the community besides her. This made Grandma happy because she had always wanted them to be accepted for the talented, wonderful people she knew. She felt bad sometimes because she knew their acceptance had a lot to do with money and always reminded me that "Money talks."

Grandma decided here only concern was Ava, my stepmother, her son, and their twins Ava was carrying. They were her future and mine. Thanksgiving became a second priority for her and for everyone in the family. She had organized a turkey with dressing meal, however.

Everything stopped when Ava went into labor the day before Thanksgiving. Dad drove his beautiful wife to Winding River Falls where his babies, his sons, were born on a brisk November Day. I think everything went smoothly with babies and mother in perfect condition, so I was told.

As a Thanksgiving gift, Matthew Albert and Michael Halbert were born the day before Thanksgiving. They were identical twins, real Scandinavian boys, who were in my eyes the most beautiful babies I'd ever seen. They weren't beautiful because of how they looked but because they were here and part of our family, here in our world and were needed, loved, and appreciated. Ava had given birth to them, and they were my siblings, my little brothers, whom I immediately loved. "I have family now," I told Grandma, who smiled. Yes, I fell in love with them. They were my future. They were my little brothers.

Dad was happy, and I was happy for him. He had two sons to carry on his name, a true Thanksgiving gift. The almost-forgotten turkey tasted extremely better that Thanksgiving day in 1958.

CAMELOT

Eighth and ninth grade passed smoothly as we, Mary E., Bridget, Yanni, and I became more accustomed to high school. Mary E., Yanni, and Bridget had become exceptional students, excelling in the studies they wanted and needed to move into their future goals and dreams. Bridget was constantly studying music and pursuing her flute and piano. Mary E. was more interested in politics and changing the world. Yanni was studying making straight As in all the science and math courses to make sure nothing would keep him out of med school. All of us were in the band and chorus. Yanni was a star athlete. Football, basketball, baseball. You name it. He excelled. Working on the farm all summer helped build his stature and strength, which added to his athletic ability.

Matt and Mike were our gift that kept on giving. Now toddlers making their way on their own walking and running in the yard, inquisitive about everything, talking already. "They sure are smart," I thought to myself. It seemed that they learned and caught on to everything so quickly that it was hard for anyone to fathom their progress. I never realized before how fast things can change. Grandma said, "Enjoy every moment of those two. Soon they will be in high school, and when they graduate, those days will be gone."

I kept a journal, taking down all the notes I could about our lives, community, school days, relatives, and friends. I occasionally wrote a poem that I felt made sense but was too shy to share. My dreams of being a writer were still alive, and I chose to keep them that way.

Our sophomore year of high school was a year of change for our country, not only Northern Minnesota but our whole country, the United State of America. "You can add the whole world to that thought," Grandma often said. Big changes were coming, and we relied on a young, handsome man, who was running for president in the fall of 1960. I remember it well. I was sixteen years old, going on seventeen.

President Dwight David Eisenhower was finishing two terms as president of the United States. The summer of 1960 the Republican party chose his Vice President Richard Nixon for their candidate. The Democrats chose John Fitzgerald Kennedy.

"Well,' many people said, "we cannot have a Catholic for president in this country."

And then they said, "If we elect him, the Pope will run us."

That's the way the summer of 1960 went. Grandma had advice for me. "Be careful how you discuss politics, Margaret," she said.

"Why, Grandma?"

"Because politics is personal. It's everyone's right to believe what they think is the best. Kinder, too, and saves a lot of hard feelings."

I was happy thinking of a young president, youngest one so far, who would be the future of our great country. Yanni and I campaigned that fall of 1960 and walked door to door handing out brochures for the Democrats and JFK.

Most young people wanted young blood in the Whitehouse. We especially did. "He's for all the people," Yanni said. I believed him.

Actually, who cared about his religion. He was a Christian, and that is what mattered. Grandma agreed with Yanni. "To make you feel better, I'm for JFK," she said.

President John Fitzgerald Kennedy won the election and became President January, 1961, while all the young people in the country, it seemed, rejoiced to have his wife Jackie, their young daughter Caroline, and newborn son, John Jr. move into the Whitehouse with him. It was like Camelot, a dream and magical but also real.

Grandma said, "The televised debates showed Nixon didn't think much of farmers."

I guess that was the final blow that got JFK elected.

A BEAUTIFUL DAUGHTER

January 1961, President John F. Kennedy was inaugurated our thirty-fifth president in Washington D.C. almost two months after his son John Jr. was born. We sat by our black and white television sets and watched him take his oath of office and promise to uphold the Constitution of the United States of America. With his hand on the *Bible* and his wife Jacqueline by his side it was official.

A junior in high school now, I had become editor of our school newspaper, *The Norden School Gazette.* I was thrilled to have the job because writing was something I loved to do. The editor's job increased my interest in all news, local, state, federal and world. It also kept me busy.

There were deadlines to meet before we'd run off the paper on a mimeograph machine and staple the pages together. There was news about school sports and other extracurricular activities. There was a gossip column, as long as I could remember, that had always been in the paper. I made a point to make it as nice as possible because I was afraid of repercussions from printing gossip.

One morning an upperclassman came to me and asked, "Did you hear so and so is pg? Why don't you put that in the gossip column and ask if it is true?"

I didn't answer but walked away ignoring her and the question. I thought, "Is she trying to set me up and get me kicked out of school or run out of town by suggesting I do that?" I would never ever stoop that low. Never.

It was almost an epiphany for me. All these years, I had never faced cruelty like that. Not even with Mrs. Amundson. Here it was facing me square in the face, smacking me so hard with the truth making me sick inside. All these years, I thought the people in Norden were good, kind, and gentle people. At least most of them. I thought we all were safe here, protected from the cruelties of the outside world. I thought we could trust everyone.

I had to work after school that day to finish an editorial for the newspaper. Afterward I walked to Grandma's where my dad would pick me up. I must have looked sad when I entered her house because she looked at me and asked, "Are you okay, Margaret? You look depressed."

"I am depressed. You'd never believe what happened today."

I began telling Grandma about my day, the request that I had gotten that day, and how I couldn't comply with it. I told her how disappointed I was with the snotty girl who asked me, the school, the town, and everyone. I told her how helpless it made me feel because the cruel person was an important person in town. I told her how I just stood there and said nothing and then walked off. I told her how it ruined my day, and maybe my life. I told her, "Grandma, I will never trust anyone again!"

"First of all," Grandma said. "You made the right decision. You would have gotten into deep trouble if you did what she asked. Second, you showed that you cared about people and refused to humiliate someone. Third, maybe you needed to know that you shouldn't have been blindly trusting everyone as you have in the past. I think it was a good day for everyone. The pregnant girl will probably never know what you did, but you and I and God do. We all know you stood up for what was right."

"Thanks," I said. I felt better.

"Margaret, let me tell you a story, so they say, that happened here years ago. Years before I came so I never knew or met the people involved. It seems they disappeared. The story pops up now and then, and the community people say it isreal. It's an ugly story about greed, cruelty, hate, power, and jealousy that had severe consequences for everyone involved, especiallly two families, one good and the other one cruel and mean.

Rarely discussed by anyone, it's like a cancer in this community hiding underground trying to show its face now and then. It isn't like a dark cloud hanging above us constantly, but a hidden secret boiling and fermenting that everyone wants to keep that way. Each time it erupts like a volcano and surfaces, you think that it just happened because the countryside changes and the signs of the culture change and it is almost as it happened in modern day times and settings. Then it goes back down and ferments and boils some more.

I've heard the story two or three times since I came to Norden. And all those who were involved have disappeared and are no longer part of our world. It could have happened in the stone age, the days when the Vikings first came, the horse and buggy days, or present days. No one seemed to know what happened to any of those involved."

Then she added, "No matter what. There is a good lesson in everything that happened to everyone. Greed, jealousy, lust, hate, and dishonesty are not good attributes to possess. They get you in the end. They really do." She stopped and thought for a moment and then added, "Margaret, some will try to convince us that Norden is heaven on earth, but it isn't. Good and evil are everywhere."

Grandma's story began like this.

He could hardly stand watching her grow up. She was a slender, graceful creature, talented and intelligent, whose singing voice was more pleasing to the ear than any of the songbirds in his yard. Her long, brunette hair curled around her ivory colored face with her large, deep violet- blue eyes, brought only turned heads and raving comments as she passed. His greatest suffering came when she passed him, and he had to look away so that they didn't notice any lingering stares or looks of longing and admiration coming from him.

To make things worse, the beautiful creature, born from his greed, lust, and vengeance toward his neighbor, was growing up and being raised by the man he looked down on and hated the most, and there was nothing he could do about it. He called her a creature because she seemed too unreal to even exist.

It was as if he was being punished to his death, getting his "up and comings," by watching her, Anne Marie Reynolds become a woman and a daughter he would never be able to claim let alone touch. And the longing in his heart to hold her in his arms and tell her, "You're *my* beautiful daughter," ate at his body, mind, and soul, breaking his heart and sending him to the medicine cabinet for Rolaids regularly.

Faith, Hope, and Goodwin Young, children from his wife Ruth, were homely in comparison to Anne Marie. They had large facial features with large, crooked teeth and were husky and large-boned. None had her perfectly shaped mouth and straight white teeth. None had her grace and poise. He almost hated his own children and wished they were more like her.

Little Anne Marie squealed and giggled with delight when they called the name Lily Rose Reynolds to receive her high school diploma. "That's Sissy, Daddy. That's Sissy."

Paul Reynolds, along with his wife Caroline, sat in the front row of the packed auditorium watching their daughter, Lily, graduate. It was their daughter Lily's graduation day. She was their only child until Anne was born. At the sound of Anne's voice, music to their ears, they glanced quickly at each other and smiled, feeling the joy of their younger child taking part in this special occasion.

They also knew that almost everyone else heard her squeal, and they felt proud. They felt relief and satisfaction that they were not alone. "She'll keep us young," they told each other.

"It is what it is, Caroline," he assured his wife. "We'll make the best of it and make it a good thing."

That was their decision, all three of them. Paul, Caroline, and Lily's. And it was the right decision at the time.

Levi Young was born rich. His grandparents Elle and Andrew were early twentieth century immigrants to America, and they chose the flat, valley land where they heard there was great farming on which to settle. They came with wealth in the first place, and this allowed them to add more land to their original homestead. By the time Levi came along, he was set up in community high society and his own importance, although the community looked longingly up to him, not because of his morals but because of his money and position. They wished they were Levi Young.

The day he married Ruth Black, daughter of another wealthy farmer from a neighboring community, the town celebrated with them. She was the perfect mate for him because money attracts money. The two families joining only made them more important and powerful. "We have it made now," Levi told Ruth. "Nothing will touch us ever."

An enormous, three-story, white Victorian-style home with red shutters and a second-story balcony and a huge front porch with tall white pillars, was built on the family farm when their ancestors settled there. It was the chosen home for Levi and Ruth, a perfect home to make them look important and an ideal place to raise their family. It was on a park-like setting with green grass and flower gardens everywhere. Some were in the front yard and some in the back. A stone-laid sidewalk led right up to the front porch steps. And on the porch was brand new patio furniture and a white porch swing.

After their wedding ceremony in the church just a few miles down the road, everyone went to the farm for a garden reception. There people mingled with each other enjoying that for once they got to see the Young farmhouse and yard. There they had pink champagne with their outdoor barbequed beef dinner with all the trimmings and wedding cake.

Paul Reynolds, on the other hand, scratched in the dirt on his original one hundred and sixty acres to make a living. Without an extra cent to spend on anything but necessities for his family, he tried hard to be satisfied with what God had given him. "We're happy. Aren't we, Caroline?" he'd ask wanting so much to please his wife, who helped him in the fields and with the chores, begging for her gentle words of approval.

"We're happy," she assured him. "And we're lucky. We have

Lily Rose. God has been good to us. I just hope that someday we can afford a bigger room for her."

They had always wanted more children, a houseful, in fact, but it never happened. "God must only want us to have one child," they said.

Paul and Caroline pinched pennies and saved as much as they could and eventually had just enough saved for a down payment on a farm they were looking at. It was adjacent to their land, and they wanted it desperately. The day he learned the news in town, he rushed into the kitchen of their small, four-room, one story home and sadly informed Caroline, "I don't think we will get that land. They say Levi Young wants to buy it. You know we can't compete with that."

"We'll go to the bank and ask them if they'll give us a loan so you can offer them more money. Better yet, we'll go to the bank in the next town where Levi doesn't have influence," Caroline suggested.

The fact that Paul Reynolds was extremely afraid of Levi Young just showed how much power Levi had. It shouldn't have been that way, but Paul had lived a while and knew how loudly wealth spoke in this world. In small communities where rich, important people were supposed to stay rich and important and lesser, poor people were supposed to remain lesser and poor, it took insight and plans to overcome the status quo. It took downright maneuvering around thoughts and ideas to figure out ways to beat out someone of higher position. But, Caroline had the answer, "Go to a neighboring town and ask for a loan that will pay more than what Levi Young will pay."

It seemed like a greedy man, especially a land-greedy man, had no moral ground on which to stand. He would do anything and hurt anyone to get what he wanted. He'd lie, connive, hurt women and children, cheat, and kiss up to anyone to get that next chance to increase his property and another step up his ladder. He was a quiet watchman of his neighbor's pursuits and downfalls, his neighbor's gains and losses, and his neighbor's financial status. He watched closely as a cat watched his prey ready to pounce when the time was right to take over what he wanted and what shouldn't ever be his. And when he pounced at the opportune time, it was unexpected and threw his victim off course for the time he needed to take over. He didn't expect to be shown up or taken down by anyone, and Levi Young knew everyone knew it.

When it was announced that Paul Reynolds bought the farm he wanted, he was stunned. Bruised ego, Levi couldn't stand the thought of someone beating him out of something he wanted for so long.

The land soon was the property of Paul Reynolds, and it was productive land that would eventually provide a living that gave them a better life. The problem was that it made Levi Young seethe with anger and bitterness. And as his hatred grew, so did his bitterness, and they were directed right at Paul and Caroline Reynolds.

Levi would have killed Paul Reynolds if he could, but the words spewing out of his mouth to neighbors and friends were enough. He killed him with his mouth, isolating him from some who used to be his friends, and he swore from the bottom of his cold, angry heart to get even. "I'll fix him," he thought. "When it is the right time, I'll fix him."

Paul and Caroline Young waited years to have a child. Caroline especially yearned for a child wondering why God was punishing her by leaving her childless. "He knows I will be a good mother, Paul. Why is he doing this to me?"

The longer it took for her to hold her own child in her arms, something she longed for, the stronger her longing grew, and she became more and more impatient. Caroline took it personal as if it was all her fault and her responsibility to become in the family way. "After all, everyone wants to be a mother. It's our measure of worth," she thought.

Her husband bore the sadness and shame in his beautiful wife's heart in silence. It was painful watching her suffer, crying and longing for a child. He hated that she blamed herself every day of the year, and he knew that he could be as much to blame even if she spared him as a man and his whole manhood by not saying anything. He began to feel like he wasn't enough and that he fell short in fulfilling his wife. Her need for a child had superseded everything else. Nothing else mattered.

Then, as if all their prayers had been answered at once, Caroline came to him one day after over ten years of marriage and said, "I think we're going to have a baby. Do I even dare believe it?" But it was true. They were having a child.

"Do you mind if we call her Lily Rose, Paul?" she asked right after their baby girl was born. "You remember the story in the Bible about the lilies of the field. I think she is a lily that God has taken care of all these years and given to us. And her middle name should be Rose for the Rose of Sharon."

"It's a beautiful, perfect name for our beautiful daughter. We'll call her Lily Rose."

Lily Rose was a good child and loved her parents as much as they loved her. They did everything together, and she continued to grow and thrive as a bright child, who loved music and art, all the beautiful things in life. She grew taller than her mother and was slender with long arms and legs like her father, and she spent many days helping him in the fields during planting and harvest season and in the barn with the animals all year round.

Fourteen years had passed as if they were yesterday, and Lily was preparing for her freshman year of high school. She had grown several inches the past year, and her body had begun forming curves showing the world that she was becoming a young woman. Her beautiful brown hair with its natural curl was easy to care for as it freely flowed around her unblemished face with its big blue eyes and beautifully shaped mouth framing a soft, gentle smile of perfectly straight white teeth.

Lily was a beauty, and everyone knew it, including Levi Young. He couldn't help but notice her in town, in church, and as he passed their farmyard. He couldn't stand that she was Paul Reynolds' daughter. "She's so pretty she should be my daughter," he told himself.

It's difficult to imagine evil creeping into anyone's heart, but it does when there is an opening for it to walk right in, invited or not. Levi Young had gotten everything he wanted in life except Paul Reynolds' farm. He had sworn he'd get even and had tried, but he had not succeeded. Paul Reynolds had been blessed with good crops and had already paid off his mortgage so the land was his. No lying in waiting for the perfect time to take over would ever get it back to him, but Lily was a different story.

Lust! Lust for a young innocent girl began to take over his body and spirit. And it just grew more every day. No one was as good as Lily. No one was as beautiful. He wanted her. It didn't matter that she was young enough to be his child. He wanted her. And the idea that this would hurt his neighbors, Paul and Caroline, didn't even cross his mind. As far as they were concerned, the only feeling he had was hate. He still hated them.

And Paul and Caroline had no idea what was going on in Levi Young's mind. Things had settled down they thought. They'd just talked about it saying, "I'm so glad that Levi has settled down. At least we can talk to each other now." They felt sorry for Ruth, big as a house and ready to deliver their third child.

"Poor Ruth," Caroline shook her head and said, "She must feel terrible. The doctor has even put her on bed rest. Wonder how she manages with those two little girls of hers."

Faith was five years old, and Hope was four. They were a handful, peppy, rambunctious little girls, who were always getting into things, and they still needed watching. Once during the summer, they climbed a ladder and were found on the roof of their three-story house refusing to come down. Levi had to go on the roof to get them, and they all almost fell off because they ran away from him on the rooftop. Only when they were back on the ground did everyone relax and feel safe as Levi locked the ladders in the shed. "They'll never get them under lock and key," he said, angry that they put all of them in jeopardy.

There were two weeks until Christmas, and Ruth Young was frantic and needed help. Their girls were at her mother's, and she called on the phone one morning. "Would you let Lily come over for the day to help me clean the house for the holidays?"

"I will talk with Paul to see what we have planned and call you back."

"I don't know, Caroline, if we should let her go alone over there. Levi was pretty tough on us."

"I guess if you feel that way, we can be busy for the day. I can call her back and tell her that Lily can't come."

Knowing that his wife had wanted to be friends with Ruth for years and anxious for an end, once and for all, to the feud and hearing the disappointed tone in her voice, he changed his mind. "Okay, I guess going there once won't hurt anyone."

It was two miles to the Young farm, and the roads were plowed and good for travel. Although there was snow everywhere in the ditches and on the fields, the day was already becoming warmer so it felt as though another snowstorm was on its way. Paul would pick her up at the end of the day, hopefully before the storm.

When they reached Youngs, Lily got out of the car where she smiled at her dad and waved. "Thanks, Dad. See you later."

"Have a good day. I'll be back to pick you up."

"Come back to the car," he wanted to say. "I've changed my mind." But he didn't and let her go.

He thought of how he loved that girl and how he hated to leave her ever, especially here in what used to be enemy territory. He watched as she entered the house, turned the Oldsmobile around, and drove out of the yard.

Ruth Young was resting in bed when Lily walked into the house. "Wash the dishes first. I can't stand having dirty dishes around," she said. Next, there were several loads of clothes to wash and dry. The kitchen floor and bathrooms also needed scrubbing. "That should keep you busy most of the day," Ruth said. "I hope it isn't too much for you."

When lunchtime came around, Lily heated up some Campbell tomato soup and made peanut butter sandwiches for the two of them. "Levi went to town this morning and won't be home for lunch," Ruth said. "You needn't fix anything for him."

Lily sat in a chair in the bedroom and ate lunch with Ruth. They talked mostly about the weather and the baby that could come anytime. They also shared Christmas plans. "My whole family is coming here because I won't be able to go anywhere. They're all bringing food for Christmas Eve and Christmas Day. They're good cooks so we we'll have plenty of food."

When they were done eating, Ruth asked, "The mailman should have been here by now. Would you mind running to the end of the driveway and pick up the mail for me?"

Anxious to finally get out of the house for a while, Lily quickly said, "No problem," and put on her gray wool winter jacket, white stocking cap, mitts, and new high black boots, leaving the house for the quarter mile hike to the end of the driveway.

The sky was forming snow clouds quickly, and it appeared it could snow anytime. All the morning sunshine had disappeared, and there was absolutely no wind giving Lily an eerie feeling of foreboding that something bad could happen.

In no time she was at the mailbox picking up the letters and daily newspaper and putting them into the brown paper sack she had brought along when Levi Young pulled off the highway onto his driveway with his red Cadillac. He had seen Lily and stopped by the mailbox. "Wanna ride back?" he hollered over the radio blaring a woman soprano singing, "Silent Night."

As Lily got into the car, she smelled alcohol coming from his breath, and his clothes reeked of cigarette smoke. The smell turned her stomach. Levi had just come back from town, where he'd spent the whole morning in the tavern. He was slurring his words, and Lily wanted to get out of his car, but he had started it so fast she didn't have a chance. She moved closer to the door and hung on to the door handle trying to get as far away from him as possible.

"You're so beautiful," he said giving Lily a squeamish, uneasy feeling.

The quarter of a mile car ride with him seemed like eternity, like the clock had stopped. Levi drove the car right into his garage and jumped out, beating Lily out of the car, and he shut the garage door. Then he stood in her way blocking her from going out the walk-in door.

"You're beautiful," he uttered, grabbing her and trying to kiss her as she fought and struggled to get away from him.

"Stop it!" she screamed. "Please stop it!" But there was no one there to hear her.

Lily felt pain in the back of her head as it hit the concrete garage floor, and her shoulder began to hurt from being grabbed and pushed and then hitting the floor. She kicked, screamed, and fought as she grabbed a hammer that had fallen to the floor and used it.

One blow to the head is all it took. He was stunned for a moment. He let go and grabbed his head because of the pain long enough for her to get loose and run as fast as she could through the garage walk-in door, down the driveway, across the road to her dad's plowed field, covered with snow to her home.

She felt her heart beating faster and faster. She heard it pounding in her head as if it would burst her eardrums. It filled her whole head until she thought it would burst. Sometimes she felt she couldn't breathe but kept on running anyway. "I have to get home," she kept telling herself. "Need to get home."

The plowed fields were a problem, rough and hard. She'd trip repeatedly, get up again, and run some more. She felt her pants tear at the knees, and when she looked down, she saw cuts on her knees and legs from hitting the frozen rough edges of the furrows.

The snow didn't help either. It made the run home tougher and slowed her down. It wouldn't be so bad if the new snow had frozen over, but she sank down in the snow that covered her boots and had to take higher steps to dig her feet out and keep running. Not in shape enough for such a vigorous workout, she began to feel tired, but not tired enough to stop.

For a moment, she stopped to puke from the rotten cigarette, beer breath she had smelled and tasted in her mouth. She puked up the tomato soup and peanut butter sandwich. In her mind she was puking up Levi and everything he stood for. Then she ran again and continued, again stumbling in the hard, deep furrows and the deep snow. Frightened as a whipped dog, she ran with not one tiny bit of self-confidence and self-esteem left in her. She had to get home, had to get home, had to get home.

Exhausted, Lily finally reached her front door and then collapsed inside on the kitchen floor sobbing and wondering what had just happened to her and why. Hearing some noise and thinking Paul was home, her mother came out of the living room to find her precious child bloody, black and blue, and beaten. Her clothes were torn, and she had a black eye and a bleeding lip. But, most of all she was a whimpering and lying in fetal position on the cold floor.

Shocked, her mother gasped. "What on earth happened? Who did this to you?"

Shaking, Lily answered, "Lee-ee-ee-ee—vi."

Knowing that Levi Young, a dirty and perverted old man, had just hurt her delicate and fragile fourteen-year-old daughter was too much for Caroline. She wanted to cave in, but she told herself, "You need to be strong. You need to help Lily."

"I fee-ee-ee-l so dirty, Mommie," she cried out. "I fee-ee-ee-l so dirty."

"Oh, my precious, precious Lily. I'll help you get through this. We'll get through this." She got down on the floor and wrapped her arms around her daughter.

At that time, Paul came through the door. He'd come home early to go to the Youngs to pick up Lily. He took one look his wife and his daughter rocking back and forth on the floor and asked, "What has happened?"

"He hurt her."

"Who?"

"Levi, that's who."

It took a while for it all to sink in. And then Paul began eyeing his shotgun on the wall. "I'm going to kill him," he said. "I'm going to kill him!"

"You can't," Caroline said. "You can't. How would it help?"

Paul couldn't answer, but he had to agree. Their family had lost so much already. How would it help if they lost him, too? But it didn't stop the murder he felt in his heart at the moment.

The external bruises they found were nothing compared to the internal ones that came later. Lily's whole soul and spirit were wounded and destroyed. How in the world was she ever going to get over this? How were they? Paul immediately began to blame himself. "I should never have let her go. I knew better. I shouldn't have trusted them."

"What are we going to do?" Caroline asked.

"I don't know, but we have to call the sheriff."

"We'll never be able to fight the Youngs. They have the power and the money. They'll beat us somehow, Paul. You know them. Wrong or right, Lily won't be able to take living through all of this again."

Caroline took Lily to the bathroom and helped her clean up. She had black and blue marks all over her body. Her eye was black and blue and swollen from his elbow, and she had difficulty moving her arm where her shoulder hit the floor. From the force used against her, she probably had internal bleeding. Lily was a complete and total mess.

Plus her heart was broken. There was not a viler person than Levi Young. He had betrayed her, who had trusted him perpetrating the vilest of crimes on her. Her father wondered, had she not gotten away from him and had not run across the field, if they would have ever seen her again. He wondered if he would have disposed of her and any evidence of his crime.

Lily didn't say much for days other than, "He's a pig, Mommie. He's a pig."

She was not in shape to go to school and didn't want to go. It was only a few days until Christmas vacation so that really wasn't a problem. They'd already had their Christmas concert.

Caroline stayed home from church with Lily Christmas Eve. "You go, Paul," she said. "I don't feel up to it."

Paul went, and sitting right across from him were Levi and

his girls. Ruth was still home in bed. The two men said nothing to each other, but it irritated Paul that he was there acting as if nothing happened.

Paul's heart was deadened to the Christmas carols sung that day and the rest of December. "What joy is in this world?" he asked God and himself. "There's nothing left."

It was as though Lily had become a little girl. "I don't want to go to bed, Mommie. I'm scared, Mommie. I don't want to go to school anymore, Mommie."

They say if you want to get even, go after your enemy's children. After Paul bought the land away from him, Levi swore he'd fix him. He had done that. He had destroyed the whole family it seemed. Caroline was crumbling watching her daughter fall apart more every day, and Paul was becoming full of hatred watching them.

When you have been taught since the day you were born that some people don't have any value, you believe it. They become nothing to you, less than animals, and you have no remorse or responsibility for how you treat them. They are lower than low and nothing to you. This is the way Levi was. He walked around as if nothing happened to his neighbors and was oblivious to what was taking place in their house.

It was as though he had already forgotten what he had done to Lily and didn't care. It was as though it was all just a big joke, not too serious. After all, it was just doing what comes naturally. And she'd get over it. Besides, no one cared about them, and why should he.

Two days before Christmas, his son Goodwin was born. The birth was easy and normal, and Ruth recovered quickly returning home to care for her family. It was not long until they toted their son to church for his baptism into the Christian faith with the support of all the church members behind them, congratulating them at every turn for becoming parents of a son to carry on the family name. "Great job done," you often heard people say to the Youngs.

Levi ate it all up like he was savoring rare, sweet chocolates imported from France and the finest French wine. He loved the attention, craving for more and seeking it out. He bundled Goodwin up and took him with him everywhere he could so others could meet his beloved heir. He knew the boy was his future and would carry part of him on to another generation, and he loved him mostly for that reason. "I will live on now," he told his friends and neighbors.

It was different at Reynolds' home. Paul could barely carry on himself now as he watched his wife Caroline deteriorate, crying more often and showing lines of stress and worry. "What are we going to do, Paul?" she asked. "Lily needs help. We're losing more of her every day."

"I look into her eyes myself and can't find her anymore. It's as if she's gone and will never come back."

"Maybe we should take her to Dr. Hanson? He maybe can help her. It's the middle of January, Paul, and she needed to be back in school a long time ago."

He understood what his wife was saying. Lily rarely spoke anymore, and she clung to her mother, not wanting ever to leave her side. She didn't cry. She didn't laugh or smile. She didn't do anything. Lily was almost emotionless. She rarely ate and spent her time rocking back and forth in whatever chair she sat in. Then the head banging started so if she wasn't rocking, she was banging her head leaving bruises on her forehead that sometimes bled if she broke the skin.

"It's as if she has already died," he told Caroline. "We've lost her. Levi gained a son the same time we lost our daughter. He's responsible for both the birth and death."

"And, Dr. Hanson? What do you think about that idea?"

"We'll go. We'll take her to Dr. Hanson."

Time went by, and Anne Marie grew up. So did Goodwin Young.

Ever since Anne Marie was born, Paul and Caroline discouraged any friendship between Goodwin Young and her. "No," Paul told Anna Marie. "You cannot and must not be too close to him. You must never, ever date him."

"Why, Daddy," she asked. "He's nice, and he likes me."

Her dad was firm and unrelenting and would not permit it. "I don't like him," he'd say. "He's not the boy for you. You can do much better."

"Is it that silly little grudge you have against them, Daddy?" she'd ask.

"No, it isn't. And don't you ever say that again."

Anne Marie spent hours trying to figure out why her parents hated the Youngs so much. It all couldn't be because of land. Besides, Goodwin couldn't help the way his father was.

If Paul and Caroline saw Goodwin longingly look at their daughter, they'd cringe. Often they wondered when the right time was to divulge the secret that had been kept all these years. The task seemed too monumental to them, and it would affect many people so they pushed the truth down the road into the future to be dealt with another day. There also were many memories that would be dredged out of their own hearts, memories they never wanted to encounter again.

Each time they felt they should talk about it and reveal everything to Anne Marie, their throats tightened with thickness, and their breathing almost became suppressed. Every time they felt her sparkle and exuberance when she talked about Goodwin, they shivered, hearts pounding in their chests with fear.

It was the way they lived day by day, trying to protect Anne Marie from the knowledge of the attack and death of Lily right after graduation from high school. Her mother, their first and only born child, never overcame what happened to her.

Sometimes they thought they should have told her from the beginning, but the community didn't need to know who her real father was. It was too shameful for so many people, including Levi's wife and children, and now it was too late. And deep inside their hearts, they feared that if Lily knew, they would lose her, too, for keeping the secret from her.

It ate at them until they wished Goodwin Young would go away forever. Why did he have to be born the same time she was? Why did they have to end up in the same class and the same classroom in the same school?

They worried about her and preached, "Save yourself until you are married. You're too good for anything else." They were lucky that she listened even if it sounded old-fashioned.

It was a quiet, sunny, and warm fall day when Anne Marie drove into their yard with Goodwin. They had come from college especially to talk to her parents.

When they walked into their kitchen together, Caroline gasped, and her heart pounded. She immediately became nervous and began making quick, almost frantic, movements around the kitchen fidgeting constantly, as she asked them to sit down at the table. She busied herself making coffee and shook so much she spilled the water as she poured it into the pot.

Anne Marie walked across the kitchen to her and gave her a hug before she sat down beside Goodwin. "We've come to talk to Dad and you. Where is he?"

Just as she spoke those words, Paul entered the kitchen from the living room where he had been reading the daily newspaper. Once he saw them together, his face turned white, and he felt sick. "Keep calm, Paul. You need calm and clear thinking now," he thought.

"What can we do for you?" he asked Goodwin.

"Mr. Reynolds, Anne Marie and I love each other and want to get married. I've come to ask permission from you for her hand in marriage."

The time had come. Not quietly or subtly. It had thrown itself in their faces unexpectantly, and now, regardless of the pain it would cause, they must be told the truth.

"I have always discouraged a romantic relationship, even a friendship, between you, and it has not been easy. There is a reason. I will tell you why, but you need to know it was kept from you to protect a lot of people. Today this will change forever."

"What on earth are you talking about, Dad? You're not making any sense and are scaring us."

Paul looked right at Goodwin, "You cannot and must not marry each other. You are blood brother and sister."

Anne Marie and Goodwin gasped. They looked at him as if they didn't understand or even believe a word he said.

"Dad, what in are you saying? What do you mean we're blood brother and sister?"

Caroline knew Anne Marie was hurt and moved closer to her so that she could embrace her if it became necessary. Paul continued. "You are our granddaughter. Lily Rose's daughter. Levi Young is your father."

"My dad is Anne Marie's father? How in the world did that happen?" Goodwin asked in unbelief.

"Yes, he is."

"Lily Rose wasn't my sister, but my mother?"

"Yes, she was."

"How did it happen, Dad?"

Goodwin shrank down in his chair, bracing for what was coming next, but he had no idea of the cruelty of the violent act. Neither did Anne Marie.

"She was only fourteen years old. Levi never liked us. We were nothing to him because he had all the power and money."

"So what else is new, Dad?"

"Ruth was about to deliver you, Goodwin, and she was bedridden. She called us for help to get ready for Christmas and wanted Lily Rose. We let her go just to help. Figured it would help the relationship between families.

"Levi came home at noon drunk, attacked Lily Rose in your garage. When she finally got away from him, she ran three miles cross country over our plowed field covered with snow. She was broken, beaten up inside and out, and carrying a child. She never recovered."

Anne Marie began to cry as he was telling her what happened that December day as though her heart was broken. Caroline wrapped her arms around her daughter and began comforting her. "It's okay," she said. "It's okay. We'll make it." She knew there would be many more questions, but right now, she said,

"It's okay."

"You'd better go now, Goodwin. Nobody is as sorry as I am that this ever happened." He was thinking of Lily Rose.

Stunned, Goodwin got up from his chair and walked out of the house.

Goodwin raced to his car, almost stumbling on his feet he was in such a hurry. He spun the wheels and took off down the road oblivious to any speed limit to his father's house. To him it felt like the wheels weren't turning fast enough, but once he turned on his father's driveway, all you could see was dust from the gravel flying everywhere all the way to the beautiful, white three-story house he used to call home sitting on the lush green lawn with a red, brick sidewalk.

His mother was in the kitchen cooking dinner when he pushed open the door and tore into the kitchen, "Where's Father?" he demanded.

Goodwin's gray and ashen face covered with scorn and hatred scared her, and she was unaware of what had taken place. "Where's Father," he demanded more loudly.

"He's in the garage working on a flat tire," she answered. Then she added, "What on earth is wrong, Goodwin? You're scaring me."

He was out the door and had slammed it before she finished. He hurriedly crossed the front porch and descended the steps two or three at a time. The length of the sidewalk and the yard was short because of his big strides.

When he got to the garage, he flung open the walk-in door and saw his father still working on the flat tire. Hearing the noise of the walk-in door slamming, he looked up and saw Goodwin walking toward him. Goodwin's eyes flashed scornfully, and his face was covered with pure, unadulterated hatred that revealed he was on a mission.

Levi just knew. He knew the moment he looked at Levi that he knew the family secret that was buried for over twenty years. Goodwin knew what he had done.

"So this is where you did it? This is where you stole their

daughter. And now you have stolen my wife, the only woman I have ever loved. I hate you, and I wish I could kill you."

Levi stood there afraid and speechless. He had never seen Goodwin drunk, and he'd never seen him angry. "I never want to see you as long as I live. You are NOT my father," he gritted his teeth with his fist clenched and an inch away from his father's face.

Then Goodwin turned away and walked outside where he slid to the ground. His screams and sobs were so loud that his mother could hear them in the house, unlike the screams of Lily that day when no one could hear her, and she came out to see what was going on.

As Ruth witnessed her beloved son broken into a million little pieces, she demanded answers from Levi. The answers coming from the community came faster, however, than any from Levi.

Goodwin left the day he learned the truth. His beloved Anne Marie was his half-sister, off limits to him. That was the reason Paul Reynolds refused to allow her to date him all through school. It was not that Paul hated him.

"I'll go to Goodwin and ask for forgiveness," Levi told himself. "Even if his dreams and aspirations are shattered and his heart and love slaughtered and butchered, he'll forgive me. I'm his father, and we are family."

Truth had exploded like a volcano penetrating through all the deceit and lies until it stood naked in the sunlight destroying everyone as he had destroyed young and delicate Lily Rose. But, he had not only destroyed her, but he had also destroyed everyone he had ever loved. He prayed for numbness and lack of emotion, but it didn't come. He had to feel the pain of what he had lost. And Grandma ended her story with these words, "Levi learned too late that money can't buy happiness."

I felt sick to my stomach. It was a horrible, gut-wrenching story, and I felt worn out and speechless. To think any of this happened in our peaceful, small, beautiful community shocked me to silence. Finally, I asked, "Grandma, is it true?"

"As I said, the story began long before I got here. If it isn't true, it teaches a good lesson. I never knew any of the people in the story. No one tells the story anymore, and it has changed over the years. Brought up to date as if it just happened. I guess in that way you can call it propaganda."

"This story is sad."

"Yes, but we all need to know there are consequences for our actions, good and bad. Sometimes bad ones break through and destroy lives. I am glad you stood up for the unfortunate girl in school today. Thank you. I am proud of you."

HIGH SCHOOL GRADUATION

Finally, we were at our high school graduation. It came quickly because we all were making future plans from the day we began ninth grade. It was a no brainer for me to go to the nearest state college to become an English teacher. Bridget had her plans and had already applied to work with David, her brother, in New York. She wanted to be a musician, especially studying violin. Mary Elizabeth was making plans to go South and concentrate on Civil Rights. I really worried about Mary E., though. The tensions in our country were to the point of becoming dangerous with riots and demonstrations and everything else involved for equality.

Yanni Tollefson also had big plans that he hadn't announced yet. Yanni and I went to the movie "Bye Bye Birdie" one Saturday night. It was at least a thirty-mile drive from my house to Winding River, our closest movie theater. As we chatted on the way home, Yanni suddenly sounded serious as he changed the subject and said, "Margaret, I have enlisted in the United States Air Force, and I will be leaving the week after we graduate."

"What?" I think he heard the surprise and the concern and the loss and everything important in my voice.

"I just feel we are going to be in a war soon, and I want my military service to be over with before that happens."

"Yanni, what about medical school?"

"I am still going to be a doctor, no matter what." He hesitated before he continued, "Margaret, this is my chance to get my military service over with so I can concentrate on becoming a doctor. Please, please, please understand this decision. I will take college courses when I am in the Air Force."

"What am I going to do without you, Yanni? You are my

best friend."

"We will write to each other. I'll be home now and then, and when the Air Force allows, I will be at the University of Minnesota in med school."

"Oh," I said. What else could I have said. It was set in stone and nothing was going to change it. We spent part of our senior year of high school knowing Yanni would be leaving a week after graduation. And I prayed every night for God to preserve and protect us.

Yanni was captain of the football team, and they won all the games. Yanni was captain of the basketball team, and they won all the games and almost won the tournament to compete at state level. Yanni was our most academic classmate, and he was Valedictorian. Bridget was Salutatorian. Mary E. and I were in the top ten honor students. Bella, our beautiful friend, was home coming queen. I was so proud of her. It just seemed like everything was working out for everyone.

Graduation day came at the end of May 1963. Our class chose "I made it. So can you." for our class motto. Yanni's speech was centered around that topic. All our parents, dear neighbors, family, and friends were there to see us get our diplomas. In fact, the gymnasium was packed with loved ones. Mine were Grandma, Dad, Ava, and little brothers, Matt and Mike.

Our band played "Pomp and Circumstance" as we marched in and climbed the stairs to the stage. I can't remember who the speaker was. He was a professor from somewhere. To me, Yanni was the main speaker, and when he spoke I listened.

As he began his speech, the crowd became quiet as we listened.

He thanked everyone: his parents, his family, his friends, his teachers, his classmates, and, most of all, God for bringing us to this day. "Although it is a sad day, it is a happy day, a time to be joyful, because we are here accomplishing so many things our immigrant ancestors wanted us to do. We have gone through a depression, wars, and many other heartaches to be here. We are grateful.

In one week, I will be leaving Norden because I have enlisted in the U.S. Air Force to serve my country. I will be taking college courses there until I finish my years of service. Then I plan to come back to Minneapolis and attend med school at the University of Minnesota. I will miss Norden and our beautiful farming community, but I will never leave you.

So today, as a grateful student, I want to remind you of our class motto, 'I did it. So can you.'"

The crowd clapped and cheered and whistled when Yanni finished his speech. My heart burst with pride. Yes, he was good at almost everything, and he made use of every bit of talent and intellect he had. That was Yanni.

There was another side to the story. I was sad. In a week Yanni was leaving. Hopefully, not for war. We wouldn't be seeing him for a while. His dad had money and could afford to send him to college and med school, but Yanni was a patriot and an admirable one. I didn't know exactly what I felt. Was it grief? Was it just plain loss? Was it loneliness? Perhaps some of each. I knew that this graduation celebration was special, but the future was unknown and one without the complete guidance of those who had taken care of us for years.

It was what it was, and nothing on the face of the earth could change it. "Buck up, Margaret," Grandma said. "That's life and you'll get through it. We all did."

Everyone predicted Yanni and I would marry someday, but that day, a week after graduation day, we saw him off on the train to leave for the Air Force, it seemed like that would never happen.

That day I had tears in my eyes as we hugged. "I love you, Yanni Tollefson," I whispered.

"I love you, too, Margaret," he answered. He had tears in his eyes, too. "I will see you soon," he said and then turned and walked away to enter the train. "Bye," he said and waved to everyone.

FALL, 1963

The summer after graduation from Norden High, I spent at home with family. I helped on the farm and especially helped Ava, who was much stronger than she had ever been, always busy with her garden and her flowers. Cooking and cleaning and being a typical farmer's wife and mother. Matt and Mike were five years old and could do different errands for her and chores for Dad. When I wasn't helping Ava, I was in town helping Grandma.

Grandma had changed a lot. She was more fragile and was unable to keep up with everything. Our roles were changing too quickly for me, and when I thought of leaving home for college, I felt bad having to leave her. In fact, it bothered me a lot. After all she had raised me since I was nine years old when Mom died. She was my mother and grandma combined.

I noticed that she was developing more wrinkles in her face and her hair becoming steadily almost all gray. Not salt and pepper but completely gray. Most of all, I noticed she wasn't as enthusiastic and spunky as she used to be. Her age was taking a toll on her every day. I was glad that she had Dad, Ava, and the boys to rely on and thankful I knew they'd take care of her. I planned that summer to spend as much time with Grandma as I could.

"Are you feeling okay?" I'd often ask her. We thought with her forgetting things more than usual and a slight weakness in her left arm she had had a slight stroke. We knew we were right when her doctor in Winding River diagnosed her stroke.

My prayer every day was, "Lord, please keep all of us safe, including Yanni, and please don't let anything happen to Grandma when I am away at college."

I had begun to feel the load of responsibility that came

with growing up and thought of how good it was to be young without them. However, life doesn't stop for anyone, and this was part of life. Plain and simple, my most important task and priority now was to get my teaching degree.

"I'm feeling great!" she always answered. "Please don't worry about me now. You have enough worries with Yanni and military and college in the fall."

Yanni was done with basic training the middle of the summer and came home on leave. "Gosh, you look good," I told him. "Military life must be good to you."

"I don't mind it," he said. "The only problem I have is missing you and everyone else." Dad, now that I am gone, has a hired man to help on the farm. It's working well for both of them."

Yanni's leave flew by and seemed too short. I wished he had more time at home, but once again we said "Good-bye" at the train station hoping we'd see each other again soon.

"Please stay safe, Yanni," I said.

"You, too. I will see you soon."

I could hardly wait for two years to pass so he could be back in Minnesota and at the university. The only trouble is that when you are in love, waiting was like eternity.

In 1961 our President John F. Kennedy faced down the Russians during the Bay of Pigs invasion and won that conflict. Because of his stand against them, everyone, it seemed, thought he was the greatest president. However, Russia was always a threat, especially with Premier Nikita Khrushchev at the head of their country. He had promised to bury us, the United States. That was a worry of mine with Yanni in the Air Force. I was thankful things had settled down somewhat. Very thankful.

The last week in August, Dad, Ava, Matt, Mike, and Grandma all piled up in our car with me as we drove a hundred miles away to the state college nearby. I had said good-bye to Bridget and Mary Elizabeth right after graduation when they left for their future, Bridget in New York and Mary E. down South, USA. I said good-bye to Yanni when he was home on leave.

Once we got to the dorm where I would spend my freshman year, everyone helped me unload the car and haul my things up to the third floor, where I would live. We met my roommate Andrea, a wonderful girl from a neighboring town. I didn't know her before but immediately liked her. "This will be a good year," I thought.

Final hugs and byes were tough on all of us, and I felt sad watching them all drive away that day. "This is it," I told myself. "This is REALLY it."

I wrote to Yanni that first evening. "I'm here, Yanni. I think I will like it. Miss you and love you. Will write a long letter this weekend."

Our room was small but cozy. We each had a twin bed and a place with a desk to study. The food in the cafeteria was good. Much made from scratch. Classes were ok and were classes we needed to take before settling into a college major. I liked my professors.

I didn't like the weather. The whole freshman week was chilly and rainy, sometimes pouring down rain. Lucky for us there were tunnels between the buildings, so we didn't have to run outside and get wet. "We're lucky to have these tunnels," I told my roommate Andrea. "It will come in handy in January when temp is forty below zero and the wind is blowing."

We settled in, and the fall sped by. There was homecoming and a dance, winter formal, and many other activities we could attend. Of course, there was a band and choir and several theater productions, all of which interested me. Along with classes, there was no time to be bored.

A THANKSGIVING OF MOURNING

Thanksgiving was coming quickly, and we were anxious to get home to our families. The Northern Minnesota fall was pleasant and not too cold so that didn't hinder us from anything. We'd come and go to class like pros already. It was November 22, 1963, and Thanksgiving was on November 28.

As I walked through the lounge of our dormitory building, a college professor came running in and shouting, "Turn on television. **SOMEONE HAS SHOT PRESIDENT KENNEDY**."

There he was riding in a parade in Dallas, Texas, sitting with his wife Jackie in an open convertible, and shot. For a moment we didn't know if he had died, but it didn't take long to learn that he had.

"Who would do such a thing?" those around me were asking. It was like a dark, evil cloud was hanging over us and the rest of our country. We had lost our young president and our Camelot was gone forever. You could hear sobs and gasps all over campus, and there were tears, lots of tears.

It was difficult for us because we still had classes before we could go home, and classes continued that day, even if the flags were half-mast in honor of his death. I needed to talk to someone and called Grandma.

Thank goodness, she was home. "Grandma, we are sad here. What are we going to do? Do you think we will ever get over this?"

"It will be hard, Margaret, but we WILL get through this. We are tough Norwegian Americans. In fact, most Americans are tough enough to get through this time. I'll be honest. It will make a huge difference in our country and take a while to get over an assassination of our leader, especially one so well-liked."

"But, it feels as if all the young people in the world are cheated. It is like something evil stooped down and snuffed him right out of our lives. We thought he really understood us."

"We'll talk more when you get home next week. You go to class and do what you need to do. It will be ok. We'll be there next Wednesday to pick you up for Thanksgiving weekend."

Somehow, we made it, but it wasn't easy. We thought about how hope was gone now and how we could make things better. We talked about how brave he was standing up against the Russians. refusing to back down during the Cuban crisis. We talked about how Premier Nikita Khrushchev threatened us by saying, "We will bury you." We talked about Jackie having to fly in the airplane back to Washington DC with Vice President Lyndon Baynes Johnson and how he was sworn in as president on that plane trip.

Because of television, we watched Jackie walk behind the carriage carrying President Kennedy that day. We watched his children by her side at times. We watched little John Jr. salute his dad as the carriage went by him. It really hurt to see this, but we also watched our government continue despite a tragedy. It carried on. It had to. Thanks to the brilliant men who formed our government and its constitution, it was all in black and white and continued.

"I wonder if our country will ever get over this tragedy, Grandma," I kept saying.

She assured me it would.

I wrote to Yanni to let him know I was worried about him, especially with war looming and our president gone. He had many years left in the Air Force. "Stay safe," I said. "I love you."

I returned to school after Thanksgiving more serious about life than ever before. I finished my freshman year the next spring, one-fourth of my way to becoming a teacher.

President Johnson finished President Kennedy's term and won in a landslide the next election. He escalated the Viet Nam War, they said, and he wasn't well-liked because of it. It was President Nixon who brought the troops home. By the time

Yanni came back home to finish medical school at the University of Minnesota, he didn't have to worry about Viet Nam. He never saw war then, but he would be in reserves for a few years.

GRAY HAIR AND WRINKLES
AND FIRST JOBS

The state college I attended was not far away from home. Sometimes on weekends, I'd get on the Greyhound bus and travel north to Winding River where Dad usually met me to drive me home to Norden and the farm. Sometimes I'd find a ride with another student going home and pay them a dollar for gas. It all worked well, and I always had a ride home.

I loved to go home and visit and made a priority of visiting Grandma to check on her and also my two little brothers, growing up too fast and becoming tall and strong. They truly were Dad and Ava's pride and joy. Mine, too.

It was a strange feeling going to school and visiting my former teachers and seeing the students. "It's strange how out of place I feel in a place where I spent all those years. I don't belong there anymore," I'd comment to my family.

I was glad I went to the school one day I was home on break. As I was walking down the hall, I heard someone say, "Hello, Miss Olson." I recognized the deep, strong voice of our Superintendent Mr. Paulson. "How are you?" he asked. "Is college good to you?"

"Just great!" I said. "I'll be done this Spring."

He smiled and then started walking away. He stopped and turned around and looked at me. "I've been thinking," he said. "Would you ever consider coming here to teach English next year? We'd sure like to have you on board at Norden High School."

"I've never thought about teaching in my old school, but maybe I should."

"Great! Stop in and see me." Then he left for his office.

"Wow!" I thought. "I have a teaching job right here in my

hometown and can stay until Yanni returns. Not a bad plan at all."

Grandma was anxious to see me and was waiting for me that day because she knew I planned to come for a visit." "How's my favorite college kid?" the first thing she asked when she saw me.

"I have exciting news!"

"You do?"

"Mr. Paulson offered me a teaching job when I graduate."

"Perfect! Perfect! Thank you, God!" she exclaimed rejoicing in the news that warmed her heart. "I have missed you and am so glad you will be around here." She meant it.

"I have missed you, Grandma."

Grandma looked much older and very tired. She had more gray hair and more wrinkles. Her skin was pale and sallow. I thought she was more bent over and fragile, not surprising after all the hard work in her life. Most of all she was shakier. The saddest thing about leaving for a while and coming back was it was easier to notice the changes in the environment, and changes in people that are more subtle when you don't see them every day. The changes were hugely obvious today, and I felt sad.

"Grandma," I said. "When we're done with lunch, I'm going back to Mr. Paulson and tell him I want that job."

Grandma smiled. And I knew that in a short time, she'd be there clapping for me when I received my college diploma as an English teacher.

GRANDMA

It is so hard for a child to comprehend the warfare between good and evil. We want to believe and live in goodness, a good, safe world where people are kind to you and things work out. Catastrophe is not part of our dreams, and loss I not allowed to exist, even visit us. Then tragedy comes, jumps right into our face, and takes over our good life. We either fall to pieces or learn from it and go on. Learning is so piercing, cuts right into our heart and soul, leaving us floundering to figure out and understand what life is and how it hurts. The pain burns inside of us and eats at us, and we question God, our whole world, and our purpose and even our existence. That is what I felt when my beautiful red-haired mother was taken from us when I was nine years old.

Yes, Grandma was there to help us by taking over and giving us a safe environment in which to mourn and heal and become. "Thank you, God, for Grandma," I would pray. Yet, I was hoping that one day the pain would disappear, go away in the darkest night, and never return. It never happened like that. I had accomplished much in my life, even returning to teach in my hometown, but the burning pain of loss did not easily disappear.

Life lessons are not easy to learn, and as I grew older, one little thought at the time would come to mind and heart until I was faced with the truth about life. It was a constant sorrow. Sorrow to healing. Sorrow to healing. But I never learned why. Why God took my mother and why she had to leave us. Here I was fighting to heal my broken heart.

I knew Grandma didn't have the life of Riley moving to Norden with her husband, my grandpa, Albert Olson. She was an outsider, born and raised differently from everyone here. Different from the women in the community, she was never really accepted as one of them. Grandma had been places and seen things they never had seen or would not ever see. I never really knew how hard it was for her and how she endured the skepticism and criticism and judgment of the local people all those years. Much of it was jealousy, plain, hard-core, mean jealousy that wasn't going to allow her to succeed in anything.

She told me one day, "It was tough, Margaret. I wondered if I would ever be part of this place before they drove me crazy." She told me of the times she and her ideas were rejected and of how many times she was rudely and inconsiderately left out by the important, local people. She added, "I don't think any of them had a life of their own, so they had to mind my business and get into mine. I don't know who they wanted Albert to marry, but it wasn't me. They acted as if they had dibs on him, you know. As if he belonged to them, not me. It was a questionable ownership thing. Personally, I don't know any woman around whom he would have ever wanted. He had a flair for life, and a love for life as I did. I finally had to think it was their problem, not mine, and go on. Maybe, just maybe, money had a lot to do with it. I have told you many times that money talks. And land."

"Why is land so important to people? "

First, there is just so much of it to go around. You can't create land. Some will sell their souls to get more land. Second, it stands for money and power. They made my life miserable at times. It's true. True. Your grandpa was a number one catch for a husband because they all thought he was wealthy. They all knew that when he had a wife, he had an heir so they'd never get one acre of his land. Hopes dashed, they decided to make me pay as an outcast until I decided not to take their greed and jealousy to heart and went on with my own life. I decided to quit trying to fit in and be accepted.

She told me her story one day, and it broke my heart. "I'm sorry, Grandma. So sorry. I love you and am so sad you had to live through all of that." I was thinking of her arch enemy and greatest critic, Gertrude Amundson, who was taken down countless notches when her husband got drunk and made a fool of himself in a nearby town. It was unusual for Grandma to admit weakness and crushing hurts in her life. She was usually a strong person, I thought and believed.

To the irritation of this community, my family helped us through the depression days. They had money and were not going to let one of their own go down. Hmm. Probably made them hate us more than ever. We survived."

Grandma continued telling me that she and Grandpa lived through the depression days and dealt with evil, money-hungry and land-greedy bankers and neighbors just waiting for people to lose everything so they could get it for nothing. I had never thought about it before, but the crooks in the television movies and melodramas were real in this world and their taking advantage of the down-and-out was engraved in stone and in-your-face real. Evil had been around for a long time.

"Are you tired, Grandma?" I asked.

"I am, Margaret. Very tired."

"That makes me sad. Your story of hard times makes me sad, too."

"I know, but I am getting older. I guess tired is part of it."

I felt sad. I had watched Grandma go downhill slowly year after year. Her son, my dad, made things go with Ava, his wife, and the twins, and they were successful. I was on my own. Grandma had carried on for years as the pillar in our little family, and she was tired.

"Grandma, you will have an honored place in my wedding," I told her. I didn't want to let her know that at times I didn't think she'd make it that far. "Thank you for all you've done and being there for Dad and me. We made it because of you."

"I love you, Margaret."

"I love you, too, Grandma."

We were taking care of Grandma now. She had aged years the past few months and needed our help. I checked on her every day and tried to help her as much as possible giving her a special honored place and a true matriarch of our family. That gave her dignity, not only because it was true but because she deserved it. Grandma Olson had brought us through the tough times in life and preserved our family. She was wonderful, a beautiful firecracker, and sparkplug filled with creativity and energy.

But the lines on her face told us life had taken its toll. Her hair was grayer now, and she had slowed down, her energy diminished. I hated to think of it and the time I would have to see life without her. Just hoped that she'd be here for my wedding. Just prayed.

FIREWORKS

We graduated with high, lofty goals to be the best teachers in the world and to give honor to our little college in Northern Minnesota. It was the summer of 1967, and I was home on the farm helping my stepmother Ava and enjoying Mike and Matt.

Ava had a huge garden as usual, and I helped her with it, learning to freeze and can food like a professional. I read books and worked on lesson plans preparing for my seventh, eighth, and ninth- grade English students. I accepted the role as speech and drama coach, which meant I would be going to speech contests and directing plays. I loved that so it fit right in with my job skills and personality.

Because our country's Viet Nam situation was heating up, Yanni was held an extra month before the Air Force let him come home. Because he'd be here right before July 4, we planned a picnic in his honor. I was thrilled knowing it wasn't long until I would be able to see him.

Yanni returned to Norden by train from Minneapolis, the same train that had taken him back and forth several times in the past four years. His parents and I were there to meet him in the middle of Main Street, where it dropped him off. He stepped big as life off the train with his duffle bag and a few belongings. Tall and handsome and muscular as ever. The most beautiful person I'd ever seen. I had missed him and could hardly stand waiting in line to hug him after he hugged his parents. When he turned toward me, I jumped into his arms and hugged him and kissed him and hugged him some more.

"Thank God you are home," I said sobbing with joy. "I love you, Yanni Tollefson. I love you so much."

"I love you, Margaret, as much. So glad to be home."

Then Yanni, soon to be Dr. John Tollefson, got down on one

knee, took a box out of his pocket, and asked, "Will you marry me, Margaret Olson from Norden, Minnesota?" He proposed right in the middle of Main Street by the railroad tracks in front of his proud, doting, loving parents.

"Yes! Yes! Yes! I will marry you!

Yanni placed a beautiful diamond ring on my finger. We were officially engaged. We shouted to the world, **"We are getting married!"**

1968

Sometimes you cry because you are in physical pain, and it hurts so bad. Sometimes you cry because you lost someone or something cherished, and it hurts so bad because you are grieving. Then sometimes you cry because the world is in a mess and falling apart, and you feel hopeless and can't do anything about it.

In April,1968 when Martin Luther King Jr. was assassinated in Memphis organizing a civil rights march, I cried. I knew it would bring problems to all of us, but selfishly I thought of Mary Elizabeth. I assumed she was there, and I hadn't heard from her for a while. I worried about my dear biracial friend's mental and physical health, her welfare in everything, and she wasn't here safe with us but pursuing the dream of her life.

"Please, God, protect and take care of her," I'd pray several times a day. And I cried some more.

It frustrated me because I felt we young people, the younger generation, were the target and were taking the brunt of what the world did to destroy itself. I even felt a target, the punishment for being young and having hopes and dreams that were now being crushed into dust in the wind.

The year 1968 was horrendous and like cancer in our country. "What's the purpose in anything?" we asked each other. Young people were rioting everywhere for civil rights or against the war. We'd already been beaten down by President Kennedy's assassination in 1963, and we still had not overcome that tragedy.

Now Martin Luther King Jr. was gone from us. June came. Robert Kennedy was assassinated in Los Angeles when he was running for president and joined his brother in the grave.

Grandma sorrowfully mourned and even asked, "How

much more can this country take?" Mrs. Optimistic Hopeful had just asked those foreboding questions. "How much more can we take?"

"Can we recover?" I asked. It worried me being so young and planning a wedding and eventually a family.

"Americans are resilient," she answered.

Yanni was at the University becoming a doctor. I was teaching in Norden, but even if so far we were safe, I worried about our future. Would it be safe to have a family? Yet, I knew that all through the history of the world, people had married and had children, war and upheaval or not.

I stayed in town with Grandma during the week of Robert Kennedy's funeral. I didn't realize how much everything was affecting me until one night, I woke up in a daze after dreaming about the future of the world. Grandma woke up and found me wandering around the house.

"What on earth are you doing, Margaret?" she asked.

"I'm going to light a candle," I mumbled.

"A candle?" she asked.

"Yes," I said. "You know, for Bobby Kennedy!" I exclaimed and was then awakened into reality.

"Margaret, you aren't even Catholic," Grandma said.

"I know, Grandma, but I am so sad, so worried, so broken-hearted," and I sobbed, sobbed as much as I did when I was on the farm and a child when the mother of my pet lamb died the night of a wet, spring snowstorm.

Yes, 1968 affected everyone. Everything that took place did. It sucked hope and faith right out of you. The Civil Rights Movement, the Viet Nam War, the demonstrations in Chicago during the Democrat National Convention in August when our Minnesota Hubert Humphrey was chosen to run for president along with his running mate for vice president, Edmund Muskie against Richard Nixon and Spiro Agnew, the Republican ticket.

I personally knew young people who were paid fifteen dollars an hour to demonstrate in Chicago at the convention. That was a lot of money, and it was sad that it all was bought and paid for.

Richard Nixon and Spiro Agnew won the presidential election and were sworn in in 1969. They won again in 1972. Early in their second term, Vice President Agnew had to resign because he accepted gifts he shouldn't have. President Nixon appointed Republican leader of the House of Representatives, Gerald Ford, to replace him. Later in his second term of office, President Nixon was forced to resign in 1974 because of Watergate, and Vice President Gerald Ford became President. He pardoned President Nixon. One good thing that President Nixon did was bring the troops home from Viet Nam. For this he will always be remembered.

I'd often tell Yanni. "Wow! Our days were tragic and chaotic, weren't they." It was not a question but a declarative statement.

Yanni agreed, "They sure were, but we made it."

And what did everyone do? We kept on keeping on. We kept on living. Farmers farmed. Teachers taught. Preachers preached. Doctors and nurses took care of patients. Businesses sold and produced products. Children went to school. Carpenters built. We continued. So did our country.

And the cows continued to produce milk. The chickens continued to lay eggs. The crops grew and were harvested. The dogs barked and even chased cars. The cats purred. The flowers in the ditches still bloomed. The world continued.

In 1968 Dion sang Dick Holler's, "Abraham, Martin, and John," a tribute to our friends who sacrificed too much to make a better world. It brought tears to people's eyes and still does. The low-hanging cloud over us finally lifted and things became better when 1968 became history.

DAVID JENNEWEIN

Graduation from college with my English teaching degree was a dream come true. My old hometown Norden hired me to teach junior high English and take charge of the drama department by directing their plays and other dramatic productions. I was excited to be at home for a while and spend some time with Grandma, Dad, Ava, Mike, and Matt, who were ten years old already and growing up fast. My two little brothers would be leaving the nest in another eight or ten years. I felt warm and cozy when I thought of how I loved those two surprising gifts to our family. Yes, being home for a while till Yanni came home from the Air Force would be a special gift for me.

Besides all of that, May and June were lovely in our Norden countryside. Everything was fresh and green and growing and smelling good. Fruit trees blossomed, wildflowers started to grow and bloom like the wild roses around the corner of our woods. It was warm but cool enough to enjoy every day that seemed to always have a gentle, warm breeze blowing through our yard.

Ava and I were sitting in the kitchen chatting about my coming home from school and having a job right away. Grandma was in town hopefully sleeping in because she seemed to need more rest these days. I looked at Ava and said, "I love it here."

"I do, too," she replied. "I am sure glad your dad found me. He is a good husband and father."

"Ava, I'm glad he found you and that you are part of our family. I wouldn't give you, Mike, or Matt up for the world. We are a real family."

Ava smiled. I could tell that she felt good about what I said, and I was sure it was a relief for her to know that. In fact, we had learned to love and respect each other years ago. I needed her, and she needed me.

"How do you think Grandma is doing?" I asked.

"I think she has slowed down a lot, but I feel she's okay."

"I am glad I will have a chance to live here for a while and watch over her," I added. 'I will be able to overlook some of her bossiness now that I am older. She can be overbearing, that's for sure."

"True," Ava agreed. "But she is as good as gold. By the way, Katherine did call me this morning. She said David Jennewein was in town visiting his parents and he wanted to come out here to get some fresh country air."

Over the years, David Jennewein had come to Norden often to visit his parents. It wasn't a surprise that he would be here. I thought I knew him well, but I learned that day I didn't know him at all.

"Wow, Ava, I haven't seen him for a long time." Then I added, "Ever since Bridget left Norden after high school for Julliard and New York, we have kept in touch, thank goodness. And we still are good friends."

Ava said, "Maybe we should straighten this place up a little bit before he gets here. He's high in society now, and they say he's a millionaire. All his money came from his music business."

Because Dad had taken the boys with him to Winding River to buy a part for the potato cultivator, there weren't any distractions from our vacuuming, dusting, and wiping off counters and furniture. The house would be in tip top order when David came to visit.

"Ava, I will never forget the first time I met David. He came to town in his shiny new car, parked in front of the school to pick up Bridget. When he stepped out on the sidewalk, I knew I hadn't ever seen anyone as handsome as he was even in a movie magazine. And he was charming on top of everything else. Drop dead gorgeous. A real hunk. And, Ava, everyone in school thought the same as I did."

It was a short time after lunch that David, his mother, and Grandma drove into our farmyard. This time he was driving a brand-new gold Cadillac convertible, the best there was. It was a car that you'd see Elvis Presley driving, and it made me wonder if he really liked being that fancy or if he was trying to impress Norden people, those who rejected his family for so many years. He was still debonaire and handsome with graying hair at his temples, dressed in a black suit coat and pants, white shirt, and shiny, black patent-leather shoes. A perfect gentleman, he opened the doors for his mother and Grandma.

"You remember my daughter-in-law, Ava," Grandma said as she reintroduced them. "And you already know, Maggie, my granddaughter." As she gestured toward David, she said, "This is David Jennewein."

David shook Ava's hand and told her how happy he was to see her again. He nodded and smiled at me.

"Hi, Maggie," he said.

"Hi, David." I answered and smiled back. "It's good to see you again."

Everyone chit chatted for a while over a cup of coffee and fresh oatmeal cookies. David was fine, doing well in his business. The rest of the family was fine, especially Bridget, who now was soloing with her violin in the New York Philharmonic Orchestra. She'd gone there straight from Juilliard.

"Maggie, you want to go for a walk? I'd love to see the fruit trees in bloom. We don't have orchards like that in New York City. Would you mind showing them to me?"

"Sure. Come with me."

We left the others and took the path through the plum and apple trees, all in bloom. There also were some wild choke cherry trees blooming. We could smell the lilacs in our yard on the other side of the path. It was beautiful with the sun shining through the leaves on us. It made us feel warm and safe like the world was good and perfect for a moment on "a rare day in June" as the poet James Russel Lowell had written long ago.

"Maggie, this farm with its orchard is beautiful, special,

lovely, and everything good. It's just like you. I didn't realize when I was young, but I must say, you are beautiful, special, lovely, and everything good."

"You should buy one, David. An orchard, I mean. You have lots of money. Maybe all the money in the world."

Looking at me intently, he continued, "Are you still in love with Yanni Tollefson? Because, Maggie, I think I've loved you since the first time we met all those years ago. You know, the day I came to school to pick up Bridget. I would like a chance, Maggie, to show you how much I care. Do you realize that a great friendship is a good foundation from which to begin?"

David Jennewein obviously had been planning and not including me. I was unaware of his thoughts and feelings had taken me by surprise. I understood he was getting old and probably wanted a wife. But me? I was shaken, startled, and even embarrassed. He had been in Norden often enough to give me some kinds of vibes long before this.

For a moment, I was flattered, surprised, and confused all at once. I thought to myself, "Yes, I loved Yanni. Yes, I planned to marry him. And, Yes, I never dreamed that anyone else could have those kinds of feelings toward me." And while we were standing among all the apple blossoms, David Jennewein, after all these years, just said he loved me and kissed me before I knew what was happening."

I was wearing my blue jeans, plaid shirt, and tan cowgirl boots. He was in his fancy suit and black patent leather shoes. We must have been a strange-looking pair. Maybe in a different time and place, there could have been romance, but now I pulled away and said, "That should never have happened, and I am sorry it did." I looked David straight into his eyes and said, "I do love Yanni and plan to marry him."

I realized what David was offering was a life with few monetary worries. He was rich and handsome and well-established. It would be a new and wonderful life with all the comforts in the world. The best of everything. The good thing about it was I knew Yanni and I would build that kind of life together

I took off running down the path. David, a faster runner, caught up with me. He looked sad and rejected, but he said, "I'm sorry, Maggie. I shouldn't have kissed you. But I am not sorry I have loved you. It will never happen again."

I always wondered why at this late date in our lives David Jennewein came to change everything. He had multiple chances to be with me. His sister was one of my best friends. Why now? I was engaged to Yanni Tollefson. It bothered me that he tried to put doubt in my thoughts about Yanni. Why would he do this with zero chance of a relationship? Maybe things would have been different if he had said something years ago. Now? It was too late. And I must admit I was irritated and offended because of his romantic advances. Besides, he had been back and forth to Norden hundreds of times the past years visiting his parents, and he could have said something sooner.

"Dang you, David Jennewein, for trying to place doubt in my mind about everything." I told him. He said nothing.

We walked quietly back to the house where Grandma and Eva Jennewein were ready to go back to town. No one knew except David and me about a stolen kiss. I suppose we could have gone into *what ifs,* but life goes on and it just was not meant to be. Yanni and I would be happy. We had been friends forever, it seemed.

WITH THIS RING

The day was beautiful with a soft breeze moving through the trees surrounding our farmyard, all mowed and full and decorated with flowers for a wedding. There were at least a hundred chairs set up for guests and well-wishers. The chairs faced west and the grove of cottonwood, maple, and boxelder trees so that at 6 PM we could see the sun gradually descend behind the trees. There was a roll of white carpet at the front of the chairs for ushers to unroll right before our wedding party made its way up the aisle to the front of our outdoor church wedding for Yanni Tollefson and my wedding ceremony.

It was a given, almost the whole community's dream of a lifetime, to attend Halbert Olson's daughter Margaret's wedding. It would be a June 1, farmyard wedding when all the lilacs, apple trees, and plum trees were blooming. Dad and Ava planned this wedding for years, and Dad invited the whole community. It would be the party of parties, and according to Dad, "never another like it."

It was a perfect, sunny June day, and you could smell the fire pits with roasting pork, interspersed in the yard, for miles. It was a tantalizing, inviting, gracious odor that it seemed no one wanted to miss.

"To what song do you want to walk down the aisle?" Dad asked me.

Yanni and I had chosen "I Can't Help Falling in Love with You," by Elvis Presly. That seemed fitting and appropriate for us.

Neighbors helped him set up a loudspeaker system that sounded through the yard that would ensure that everyone heard everything. My dad, Halbert, did everything right. And the whole community of Norden, Minnesota would be proud.

Matt and Mike, only twelve years old, were almost six feet

tall now. Handsome, athletic boys with blue eyes like their dad, they helped wherever and whenever they could. I was proud of them, and everyone knew because of how I beamed when I talked about them.

"It's here! My wedding day is finally here!" I thought to myself as Leah, my beautician friend, fixed my reddish blonde hair into a bun on which I would put my braided silk flower crown of white baby's breath and tiny white roses and a veil, a double layer of soft tulle, attached to the back.

"So flower-child-like, Margaret," Mary E. said approvingly. "I bet if you weren't marrying Dr. John today, you'd be on your way to San Francisco with flowers in your hair." She smiled, "You're right in style these days of the Hippie movement going on.

"Well, I guess I am glad I'm here instead of San Francisco," I smiled back. "My wedding day is here," I continued. "I can hardly believe it. Can you two believe it?" I looked at Bridget and Mary Elizabeth. "Not long ago we three were trying out for cheerleader at Norden High."

"That it is," Bridget said. "And, by the way, you look lovely in your white silk organza dress lined with soft white silk fabric." It is you and perfect.

"It is what I always wanted my dress to be. All white with a boat neck, cap sleeves, fitted to the waistline with an A-line skirt softly flowing to the floor. Well, the ground today."

Ava helped me put on my wedding gown, and as I walked, it flowed gently and touched the luscious green grass. "I have to say, Margaret, your dress is elegant, rich-looking, and classy. And your flower crown veil is perfect," Ava told me.

Grandma's seamstress friend from town had sewn my dress and Mary Elizabeth and Bridget's dresses. Their dresses were soft blue silk organza A-line gowns, and each of them carried a long stem white rose. My bouquet was a dozen white roses tied with a white ribbon around the stems. "Very simple but elegant," I told myself. I agreed with Ava.

Mary Elizabeth was maid of honor. Bridget, my bridesmaid. It didn't matter who was who or what. It could easily have been the other way around. I was happy with my two best forever friends with me. One came all the way from New York. The other came all the way from down South.

"I am so happy for you, Margaret," Mary Elizabeth said.

"Me, too," Bridget added. "You and Dr. John are going to be the best couple and have a wonderful life."

"We love you," they said and meant it.

"I love all of you back," I said.

It was almost time for the ceremony. Dad came to check on me and to see how things were going. "Are you ready, Pumpkin? I guess I can call you that for the last time."

"Yes, I am more than ready." I had waited for this day forever. "I love you guys," I said lovingly and tenderly looking at Grandma, Ava so beautiful today, Matt, and Mike and Dad.

"We all love you, Margaret," Dad answered.

It was Matt and Mike who unrolled the white carpet and then escorted Grandma to her chair right up in front. Then they brought their beautiful mother down the aisle to sit right beside her.

As the bright golden-yellow sun started to go behind the trees, the beautiful flower-filled farmyard was filled with the sound of Elvis Presley singing, "I can't help falling in love with you."

Yanni in his black suit with a white shirt and black bow tie, along with his two groomsmen, was waiting for me, his bride, at the front of the arch where our pastor stood. He looked ethereally happy, beaming from the inside out, as he smiled watching Dad and me walk down the aisle. Childhood friends, then sweethearts, we were today becoming husband and wife. I was soon to be Mrs. John Tollefson, wife of Dr. John Tollefson, on the most beautiful day on earth.

We said our vows and exchanged our matching, engraved platinum wedding rings. Pastor said, "You may kiss your bride." Everyone clapped and cheered. Then the recessional began, and we walked off as newlyweds. It was Edvard Grieg's song with beautiful lyrics, "I love thee, Dear, now and for eternity."

As we passed all our guests; family, relatives, friends, and neighbors including Getrude and Harrison Amundson, I felt more blessed than ever in my life. I felt God was there with us. The summer evening's deep-blue sky with rays of gold from the sun shining through fluffy clouds made me feel like I was where I belonged. I felt safe.

For a flickering-of- a- firefly moment, I looked up at the sky and whispered, "I love and miss you, Mom. Just want you to know that I am finally home.

I somehow knew deep in my heart she knew life wasn't easy without her. I knew she knew everything turned out well. Yanni and I were happy. Grandma, Dad, Ava, Mike, and Matt were happy. The Tollefsons were happy. That is all that mattered today.

He said, "The first time I saw you,
I thought you were the most beautiful person
I'd ever seen in the world."
And, he added, "I said to myself right then,
'That's the girl I'm going to marry.'"
And she smiled gracefully
knowing that she was
really loved.